Choices

Arrival of The Fourth Generation

Coleen Liebsch

PO Box 206
Hayti, SD 57241

This is a work of fiction. Names, characters, businesses, places, events and incidents are either the products of the author's imagination or used in a fictitious manner. Any resemblance to actual persons, living or dead, or actual events is fictitious or coincidental.

This book is dedicated to my husband Tom. Without your never-ending support and unconditional love, this book simply wouldn't exist. Thank you for believing in me.

Chapter 1
January 1, 1941, Boston

The birthing ward was about half full when they wheeled Emma inside. She was confident she would avoid the horrors of childbirth she had heard so much about. Unlike most of her friends, she and her husband, Jonathon, had the means to afford the best of everything. That included the best obstetrician, Dr. Beleez. But things hadn't always been so idyllic for the young couple.

Emma thought about those days before she and her husband met Dr. Beleez. The doctor had beens nothing less than a miracle worker. He was the reason she and Jonathon had been able to conceive a child at all. And as talented as he was as an obstetrician, he was equally as handsome.

Now, preparing to give birth to her miracle child, Emma's face reddened upon seeing her attractive doctor. His dark hair had the slightest wave when a shock of it fell out of place above his left eye. And his eyes were magnificent. Emma blushed at the thought of his dark brown eyes and the way they went from gold to black in a starburst exploding out from his pupil. They reminded Emma of the House of Mirrors she and Jonathon had seen at the fair the year before.

His eyes seemed to go on forever and a part of her wanted to see what mysteries they held. He was so young, yet already so successful. Emma guessed Dr. Beleez to be about thirty-five, and despite his youth he was considered a leading expert in obstetrics. Emma sighed as she thought about her handsome doctor laying his hands on her. But she quickly pushed the thought away. It was a secret part of Emma's life and she knew a respectable wife and soon-to-be mother shouldn't think like that. Especially not about the doctor who'd been able to give her what she always wanted.

Emma and Jonathan were drawn to Dr. Beleez because of his success with couples who couldn't conceive. In the beginning they were sure his services would be out of their price range. But after meeting him, they were convinced he could give them something no other doctor could: hope. Hope not only to have a child, but that with a child, everything that had been going wrong in their lives would be better. He was right.

Dr. Beleez even showed concern for Jonathan's fledgling business. It was the doctor's connections who helped it become a success. With Jonathan no longer worrying about money and the treatments resulting in Emma's pregnancy, it had been a very good year. Surely some of her attraction to the young doctor was due to the fact that he had been like a caring savior to them. She was further endeared to the fact that he asked nothing in return for his generosity. Not even his normal office fees.

Yes, what normal young woman wouldn't have feelings for someone like him? And now, she would be the first woman in her family to deliver a child in a brand new hospital, and Dr. Beleez would be handling her delivery personally.

Emma focused on the joy of having the child as she tried to push Dr. Beleez's kaleidoscope eyes out of her mind. As the contractions started, she counted her blessings. There were many.

A masked nurse helped Emma onto a bed and began fastening straps around her wrists and ankles. Her earlier confidence faded.

The screams and moans from the other women in the ward certainly didn't sound like the pain free delivery she had been expecting. She wondered where they had taken Jonathon and wished he could be with her, but of course, that was a ridiculous idea. Husbands didn't attend the births of their children.

The nurse tucked a pillow under Emma's head and reminded her of the prayers that would help her endure what was sure to come. Emma began to recite the "Hail Mary" and "Our Father" prayers quietly to herself, stopping only to catch her breath when the contractions grew stronger.

Emma had no idea how long she agonized through the cramping and pulling inside her body. She did know two women had been taken to the operating room and a new one had been brought in to the ward to wait her turn. Finally, when the pain threatened to rip Emma's body in half, a new masked nurse told her it was time to go.

A new masked nurse pushed Emma's gurney through a short hallway into what she could only assume was an operating room. The smell of bleach was reassuring but the surgical instruments hanging against the wall were anything but. The saws, knives, and elaborate metal devices looked more like tools of torture than medicine. At least they were on the wall rather than the tray that was being wheeled alongside her bed.

Emma closed her eyes and tried to focus on her prayers as yet another masked person draped the lower half of her body. They were preparing her for delivery. She closed her eyes and tried to imagine something… anything, different.

She heard a nurse say it was time and opened her eyes just as the doctor entered the room. As much as she wanted to look at him, her view was abruptly cut off. One of the nurses pressed a plastic cup to her face and told her to breathe deeply. By the time the doctor turned his attention to Emma directly, she was beginning to see double.

"That scopolamine injection is putting her into twilight sleep. Slide that tray closer to the bottom of the bed." Dr.

Beleez barked instructions as the nurses scurried around to accommodate his demands. Emma watched what looked like two nurses walking away and into a white cloudy blur before she fell into oblivion.

The doctor worked in silence under the drape most of the time. Once Emma was under, Beleez announced he only needed one nurse to assist him. He instructed the one beside him to stay and sent the others away.

The nurse had no reason or qualifications to question the doctor, but something about him made her uncomfortable. She knew doctors had no patience for unnecessary delays and had already learned first-hand that this one did not ask for something twice. Dr. Beleez had gone from sickeningly sweet to outright scary, and she did not want a repeat lesson. She would keep her mouth shut and her hands ready.

She handed the doctor a pair of forceps and placed the scalpel on the tray of used instruments. She was looking down when a deafening sound rang out as metal crashed to the floor. Her body jumped before her brain realized what was happening. She froze in uncertainty.

"Nurse, hand me a cloth. Now! Quickly!"

Only his head was visible over the drape. Even obstructed by his mask, the nurse could see the excitement in his eyes and the section of hair that sprang loose across his forehead. But when the excitement turned to alarm, she started firing questions in an attempt to assist him.

"Doctor, what is it? Is everything alright?" The urgency was clear in her voice but not her hands. The doctor had not asked for her curiosity.

"HAND ME THE DAMNED CLOTH, WOMAN!"

The nurse scurried to do as instructed and fought to stop her hands from shaking. She had no time to think before he handed her a bloodied blanket wrapped around a stillborn child. Then he snapped at her.

"Get this out of my way. And do not unwrap it. Move! Get a clean cloth ready; there's another baby coming."

Another baby? A sadness for the unborn child with a still dead twin hit her.

She carefully placed the bloody bundle on the tray of used instruments and spread a fresh white cloth across her arms. Seconds later, the doctor lifted a baby girl by her feet and swatted her tiny behind. The loud wail signaled a successful delivery, and the nurse quickly swaddled the newborn in the soft cloth.

A new masked nurse entered the operating room, collected the baby, and immediately disappeared back out the door. The infant would be cleaned and checked into the nursery. The doctor would finish caring for the new mother while the operating room nurse sterilized the instruments for the next patient. It ran like clockwork… most of the time.

The nurse hesitated at the tray, unsure of her next step as she looked at the bloody bundle that held the dead twin. She had only been involved in the delivery of twins three times, but all six of the babies were born healthy. She decided she should follow the same process she would take with a single stillborn. That included finding out if the child was a boy or girl.

She began unwrapping the cloth as her heart filled with compassion for the child that would never be.

"I told you NOT to unwrap it!"

The doctor's outburst startled the nurse into turning toward where he sat too quickly. The precariously balanced bundle fell off the tray. She didn't even know she was still grasping the fabric until the bundle unwound to the floor like a yo-yo on a very short string.

The deceased infant made a wet slapping sound as it hit the floor and then everything seemed to happen at once. Beleez's chair rushed out from under him as he rose to his feet. The propelled chair hit the tray of unused instruments, causing them to clatter to the floor like a hundred cymbals clanging out of unison. The masked nurse stooped to pick up the infant, as if doing so might somehow stop the chaos around her.

Someone screamed.

The nurse didn't realize it was she who was screaming until the doctor slapped her face. "Listen to me!" He shook her briskly and her eyes focused again on reality. "You and I have both seen babies born with deformities and that is all this is!" He released his grip on her arms when he saw her awareness return.

"It is dead." His voice lowered a nanosecond before the door burst open and two nurses came through. He dismissed them with a flick of his hand. They left the room immediately with matching masks of confusion.

The scared nurse standing in front of Dr. Beleez expected to hear him scream at her for her ineptness. She was shocked when he smiled reassuringly instead. His behavior should have put her mind at ease. Instead it made her skin crawl.

He spoke calmly. His golden starburst eyes sparkled. His charming personality oozed like sap from a fresh-cut tree. "You and I have both seen deformities, especially in stillborn children. It's clear the fetus has been dead for quite some time. See how the umbilical cord was wrapped around its neck? If it had lived, I think we both know it would have been a sickly, deformed child. It's unlikely it would have survived any length of time anyway. These things happen. We need to remember there is a healthy baby out there. She and her mother must be our first concern."

He paused and let loose his charismatic smile. The nurse felt an odd sense of calm wash over her as he spoke. "I imagine you believe we should tell the parents they had twins, that we should inform them they had a son who died. But what good would it do? They are happy right now. Let's not ruin it with so much sadness."

"But don't we have to document the death?"

"Don't worry yourself over details. I will handle those. If anyone discovers what is none of their concern, they can come to me. I assure you, no one will." He brushed her cheek with his thumb and she smiled back at him. Utterly rapt, against her own will, in his words and his presence.

***

When Emma and Jonathon saw their daughter, tears of joy filled their eyes. The nurse smiled as the new parents said their baby's name for the first time. The name they had chosen when they dreamed of a daughter… Charlotte.

They had no reason to mourn. They would never miss what they never knew.

In the end, the doctor's decision seemed like the kindest choice. She had no reason to question the doctor's decision. Standing there, watching the happy family, the nurse had no way of knowing that while she was helping introduce new parents to their baby girl, Dr. Beleez was in his office phoning Germany.

"Our experiment has failed. We have proven survival of the fittest begins before birth, but I'm afraid neither of us are…" he paused and inhaled sharply, "intelligent enough to manipulate which twin wins." Dr. Beleez paused to listen to the person on the other end of the line and a thin smile spread across his face.

"I was hoping you would feel that way, Dr. Mengele. My new-found notoriety limits my ability to conduct tests personally, but I would be delighted to serve in an advisory capacity. I'll ship the specimen to you immediately, and I look forward to seeing the first results of your experiments. And Josef... please call me Tanas. We'll be working quite closely together. It's best if we're on a first name basis."

Chapter 2
75 Years Later, California

To say that Jordan Sullivan felt stupid and out of place in the waiting room was an understatement. She knew there were lots of reasons to have an ultrasound, but as she looked around the reception area at the other women waiting their turn, it was obvious everyone was pregnant. Everyone except her. There was no way in the world she could be pregnant; she was a virgin for crying out loud!

When Jordan missed her first period two months ago, she knew something wasn't right. Then other symptoms, tender breasts and feeling sick at the strangest times, started appearing last week. She had to admit the thought of pregnancy crossed her mind, but only in a fleeting, crazy, paranoid sort of way that she thought every virgin had at some point in her life. Most likely it was some kind of tumor, but at twenty-one the possibility of cancer seemed equally unlikely.

Just to be on the safe side, Jordan scheduled an appointment with her family doctor, Roger Shapiro. Dr. Shapiro was the 'doctor to the stars' with a state of the art medical facility, but the ultrasound wing was an area she'd never seen. It had none of the homey touches that made Dr. Shapiro's office warm and familiar.

His specialty was obstetrics, but Jordan was the one patient he continued to see beyond delivery. He and his wife Charlotte were friends of Jordan's parents, but after their murders a year earlier, the doctor and his wife became more like family.

For whatever reason, Jordan felt perfectly comfortable calling Charlotte by her first name, but never felt the same with the doctor. It wasn't that she didn't care for both of the Shapiros equally, she just always felt more comfortable referring to Dr. Shapiro formally. It may have had to do with the fact that he'd seen her in the most compromising of all possible positions in life. Occasionally she called him "Doc" but regardless of what he answered to, his wife was always Charlotte.

When Jordan listed her symptoms over the phone to the appointment nurse, she was asked about the possibility of pregnancy. Jordan assured her there was no possibility, but the nurse who checked her into the clinic asked again. Again Jordan told them it was impossible. The nurse smiled an 'I've heard that before' smile and directed Jordan to a restroom to provide her urine sample.

The nurse was waiting outside the door when Jordan came out with her clear plastic jar of pee. She felt a tinge of embarrassment at the idea that the container was going to be warm when she handed it to the lady.

Within minutes, a lab tech escorted her to an interior exam room and drew a few vials of blood. The woman labeled each little test-tube with a pre-printed sticker, and Jordan wondered how the nurse could possibly be so dexterous while wearing latex gloves.

The lab nurse packed her carrier up just as efficiently as she'd pulled items out. With barely a word spoken, she was gone again.

It was only a moment later that the intake nurse was taking her blood pressure and checking "none" for all of the pre-existing conditions she'd never had.

Going through family history brought on a wave of sadness. Jordan sighed at the reminder she would never know the health issues that may have affected her parents in old age. They never made it to old age.

Doctor Shapiro's personal nurse Jan was the last to come into the room. The first thing she asked was if there was a chance of pregnancy. Just like she'd done with everyone else, Jordan assured the nurse it was not a possibility.

Jan had her step on the scale and a digital readout reported 130 pounds. Jordan smiled and furrowed her brow. The last thing she was insecure about was her weight but it still took some effort not to complain about it being too high. She'd just weighed herself before coming in and her scale showed 125.

Before she could decide if it was worth bringing up, Jan reached up and pulled the metal slide down to the top of her head. "Five feet, four," she said aloud while writing the numbers on Jordan's chart. After more questions and more notes, the nurse excused herself and said the doctor would be with her shortly.

Jordan wished there were a magazine or something to look at as she sat twiddling a strand of long brown hair that had fallen out of her ponytail. The stream of nurses who'd been so attentive when she was ushered into the room were off tending to other patients. She was alone.

She noticed the mirror hanging on the wall beside the exam table and realized she hadn't even combed her hair before putting it up. As she stood to get a better view at herself, she expected the worst.

She didn't look half bad, except for the brown semi-circles under her eyes. She moved closer to the mirror to see if the darkening was just a shadow. It wasn't.

Jordan's eyes had always been her best feature. From a distance they were obviously blue but up close they were every shade of cobalt imaginable splintered into infinite facets: kaleidoscopes filled with nothing but shades of blue.

"Like a house of mirrors," her dad used to say.

The bags underneath now stood out as the dominant part, but it didn't matter. Even if she looked atrocious there wasn't anything she could do about it now. She turned away from the mirror and sat back down to wait.

A few seconds later the doctor knocked on the door.

"Hi, Doc." Jordan couldn't quite put her finger on the way he looked at her when he came into the office but he was smiling. That had to be a good sign.

As Dr. Shapiro told Jordan her pregnancy test came back positive, his odd smile made sense. It was … judgmental.

"Excuse me? That's not possible. There's been a mistake."

"There's no mistake, Jordan. The urine sample and the blood sample both test positive for HCG."

Jordan didn't know what to say. Looking at the doctor, she couldn't decide if the look on his face was disappointment in her or disbelief in what she was saying. When Dr. Shapiro started talking to her like he did when she was a kid, questioning her in different ways to see if her story stayed the same, Jordan knew he didn't believe her.

She thought back to an examination when she was four. Dr. Shapiro asked if someone else really put a lima bean up her nose. He gave her the same doubtful look then, but this time she was not lying. And this was much more serious than a lima bean up her nose.

Emotion continued to build as she realized there was no way to prove her honesty. Defensiveness and confusion showed on her face. The doctor's earlier scrutiny became irrelevant and he took both her hands into his own.

"Jordan... I'm not implying that you aren't telling me the truth, but the tests show you're pregnant." She looked down at her hands, still in the doctor's, and realized if she were in his shoes she wouldn't believe her either.

"Let me ask you this," the doctor offered. "Have you ever gotten extremely intoxicated at a party and passed out or lost time for any other reason?" Jordan's social life was as uneventful as it could possibly be. She was in the last semester of college and not only had she never been to any parties, she couldn't even think of one person she would consider a friend. If she were totally honest, the doctor and his wife were probably the closest she could come.

Dr. Shapiro may have built an empire underneath himself, but to Jordan he was the same family doctor she'd known all her life and she didn't want him to feel sorry for her.

"No. I don't go to parties, and other than sleeping, I've never lost time that I know of." A mental picture of a man from a dream she'd had, a dark haired man with a wavy shock of hair hanging loosely on his forehead, came to Jordan. The vision was so vivid she blushed at the embarrassment of having it in front of the doctor. She dismissed it quickly with a shake of her head. Not quickly enough, though. The intuitive doctor noticed.

"What is it?" he asked.

"It's stupid really, but a couple of months ago I had a very vivid dream. It was a... sex dream." Jordan thought about the details of the dream but was too embarrassed to share them with the man who brought her into the world. "I'm not a doctor but I know I couldn't get pregnant from a dream." She laughed nervously as she studied the doctor.

"Certainly not, but there is the possibility it wasn't a dream at all. Perhaps you were drugged. Perhaps someone came into your room without your knowledge and, well, took advantage of you." The doctor studied Jordan's face as she pondered his theory. "Could you describe him?"

She was too lost in her own thoughts to notice the blood run out of Roger Shapiro's face as she told him about the color and facets of the stranger's dark eyes, or when she talked about the shock of dark hair that hung down in a wave on his forehead. The doctor was still trying to compose himself when Jordan continued.

"I suppose something like that could happen but wouldn't I know? I mean, wouldn't there be some kind of sign like pain or… fluids or something?" Again she felt her face turning red.

"Generally, yes, but I would believe the likelihood of a, how should I put this, an immaculate rape before an immaculate conception. Do you remember taking anything that night? Sleeping pills? A recreational drug, perhaps?" Jordan felt how intently the doctor was watching her.

When she stared at him blankly, Dr. Shapiro smiled. "I know it's disconcerting. But if the tests are wrong, which it's unlikely they are, there could be something else going on, something more serious. I'd like to schedule you for an ultrasound so we can find out what's really going on. I'll send someone in to schedule you, okay?"

"Sure. Yeah." Jordan just sat there, dazed.

The doctor excused himself and returned a moment later with a nurse carrying a scheduling book. She flipped through a couple pages and took out her pen. "It looks like they can fit her in on Friday at ten o'clock, Doctor."

Dr. Shaprlo smiled. "Ten it is. Don't, worry Jordan. We'll get to the bottom of this."

And that's how Jordan wound up waiting for an ultrasound with a bunch of pregnant women in an office that didn't feel anywhere near as familiar as the rest of the offices in Dr. Shapiro's hospital.

She tried to concentrate on the magazine but couldn't shake the feeling she was being watched. She looked up in time to see the condescending stare of a woman dressed more for the red carpet than a doctor's appointment. Jordan self-consciously looked down at her own attire: a baseball shirt, sweatpants, and sneakers.

Everyone else looked like they were ready for a photo shoot, and Jordan had a momentary inferiority attack wondering if she should have dressed up. Too late now, she decided.

Dismissing the snooty mom-to-be's pretentiousness, Jordan wished she could see the reaction the first time the baby spit up on his oh-so-perfect cover girl mommy. Poor baby, Jordan thought.

Holy crap, there is no way I could be pregnant!

Thoughts of her wardrobe led Jordan to memories of the last shopping trip she had taken. It was with her mom, of course. Jordan would never go clothes shopping on her own. The only thing she liked about shopping was that she got to spend time with her mother, Beverly. Jordan remembered how excited her mom had gotten when she found the outfit that would look "perfectly stunning" on her "gorgeous daughter".

Jordan smiled to herself and picked up reading where she had left off.

"Jordan Sullivan?" As the appointment clerk called her name, another hospital employee was opening the door that led to the exam rooms. They ushered her into room three and she was surprised to find it almost completely dark. The only light came from equipment monitors which gave everything a strange green glow. Jordan was told to put on the gown and that someone would be right with her.

Sure, Jordan thought as the orderly closed the door behind herself. *I'm going to be sitting here in this dark room for another 20 minutes.* Suddenly she was scared.

Sitting by herself in the exam room wasn't that much different than sitting alone in her bedroom. She could be brave enough to face whatever they discovered when they looked inside her body. The false bravado reminded her of the tricks she used to summon courage when she was little.

Jordan remembered lying under her covers thinking about the monsters waiting to grab her and pull her into the dark pit of a world that existed below the very bed she slept on. But as long as she followed the rules, she would be fine.

She had no idea where she'd learned to keep tight under at least one blanket or to make sure no part of her body hung over the bed, but those were the rules that saved her on countless occasions. If not from monsters, they saved her from a childhood of sleepless nights.

She pulled the paper gown and robe a little tighter, but adjustments were pointless. She was just going to have to live with feeling exposed.

She had felt exposed in the dream that might have gotten her pregnant. She remembered lying in bed and suddenly realizing she was not alone. The room became filled with the soft light of an invisible candle, and she saw the face of the most beautiful man she had ever seen. The candlelight seemed to radiate from behind him, leaving a halo effect around his golden hair. Maybe a part of her knew it was only a dream because she wasn't afraid. The only word he spoke was her name and then he moved closer to her.

She remembered thinking she must be having a premonition about her dream man because she felt as if she had known him forever. He sat down on the edge of her bed and reached for her. As his hand touched her cheek, she wondered how anything could ever be wrong in the world again. She was filled with a love she had never known, a love that seemed so complete, nothing else in existence mattered.

Jordan stared into the stranger's eyes and was filled with the feeling of total peace. At that moment, nothing that occurred earlier in her life mattered and she didn't care if there would be anything after. Everything was perfect. Then something went bad.

The strong hand of anxiety gripped Jordan's heart even before the stranger's eyes started to change. It was as if blood was draining into and filling his eyeballs and then his eyes slammed shut.

The beautiful man's face distorted in pain as every muscle in his body crawled from the strain of an internal struggle. The man who had been sitting in front of Jordan a moment earlier was losing his battle. His features were slowly distorting into the shape of someone completely different. His soft blonde hair was replaced with dark wavy locks.

The stranger opened his eyes briefly. When his eyes met Jordan's, she saw how alike they were. His eyes were a dark brown and hers were blue but the infinite facets were the same. The sensitive curve of his face repositioned itself into a chiseled square jaw. A hint of five o'clock shadow darkened in a dimple when his perfect mouth curved into a smile.

The stranger's body shook with the final effects of the metamorphosis. The muscles in his arm stopped squirming and she saw him exhale deeply. The entire process took only seconds, but it seemed like she had been watching the grotesque display for hours while each frame played in slow motion.

Jordan started to swing her legs off the side of the bed opposite him, but before she could get her upper body in motion, one of his powerful hands grabbed her right forearm. He was brutally handsome and gave her the distinct feeling he could either kiss her passionately or snap her neck with the same lack of emotion. He chose to kiss her.

She could feel the tension in her soul urging her to pull away and run. Jordan found herself overcome with a feeling she'd never known before. A sleeping need in the pit of her abdomen woke up with a hunger.

A knock on the door brought Jordan back to the reality of the dimly lit ultra-sound room. A young technician in brightly colored scrubs introduced herself as Susan and sat down at the large machine. With a swish of her wireless mouse, the monitor came to life only to show a completely black screen.

Susan squirted some jelly on her belly. Jordan held back a snicker at the mental rhyme she had made. She realized she was more nervous than she had allowed herself to admit, and it wasn't because of the dark.

It doesn't matter how vivid it was, you can't get pregnant from a dream! Logically, there was no way she could be pregnant. It had to be cancer. The technician placed the paddle on her stomach and started moving it around.

"Can you see anything?" Jordan asked, expecting the technician to remain silent about the tumor she must be observing.

"Well, it looks like everything is developing like it should. The doctor probably already mentioned hearing multiple heartbeats, and you've definitely got a set of twins here. Would you like to know their sex?"

Jordan's mind whirled with shock and questions as the air rushed out of her lungs. The world had become a surreal place where reality and dreams traded places. It was like she had stepped out of her skin and into someone else's life. *How could I possibly be pregnant?* And then... she decided. There was nothing to worry about. Sooner or later she'd wake up and realize the whole thing had been just a dream anyway.

Ever since she was a child, Jordan had an uncanny ability to turn herself off emotionally. Her mother had teased Jordan about her "ostrich" approach to life, but her father simply appreciated getting out of the awkward teen years of a girl.

From Jordan's standpoint, any other type of approach seemed pointless. Most things work themselves out eventually. Certainly this impossibility would too.

"What's the point in worrying?" her dad would frequently ask no one in particular. Clearly she had inherited the ability to turn herself off emotionally from her father.

Now, what had the technician asked her? Sex, did she want to know the sex of the imaginary baby? Babies, she corrected herself. Then why didn't the technician say sexes? Her mind caught up to the present.

Jordan didn't know much about ultrasound technology but always thought you had to be pretty far along before you could find out anything specific like gender. She decided to play along with the dream world. "Are you able to tell this early?"

Susan seemed a little perplexed by the question but Jordan was incapable of noticing. "Well, usually we're able to tell at around four months and based on the measurements here, I'm guessing you're six months along. Right? Did you want to know what they are?"

In a fog, Jordan heard herself respond yes. She listened as Susan told her that both babies were boys and that her due date would be around February 29. "Leap year," the technician said cheerfully.

The day that shouldn't be, Jordan thought.

She shook her head to clear the cobwebs that were obviously muddling her hearing and her thinking. "Did you say twins?" Susan was nodding as she studied the monitor, and this time Jordan couldn't hold back her emotions. Hysterical laughter that had been threatening to overflow since she first walked through the door, finally won out.

The sudden laughter in the dimly lit room caught Susan off guard and the instruments on the tray in front of her rattled in response. She stared at Jordan with wide, terrified eyes, clearly wondering if she was watching a lunatic.

"I take it the doctor didn't mention the possibility of twins?" Susan had composed herself enough to turn and face Jordan but that was about it. None of her college classes had prepared her for this type of situation and she had no idea what to say next.

Jordan could tell she had completely freaked out the girl who wasn't really much older than she was. She wondered if Susan had ever scanned a lunatic before.

"You know," Jordan's voice cracked as she alternated between laughter and tears, "if the idea of twins was the only thing taking me off guard today, I could probably handle it. When I walked in here I didn't even believe I was pregnant. Now you're telling me I'm having twins… in three months?"

Susan was speechless.

As Jordan stared at the so called professional sitting in front of her with an open mouth and horrified look on her face, laughter took over again. She wanted to continue believing the whole thing was a dream. She wanted to put her head back in the sand. But as she looked at the ultrasound machine that obviously showed skeletal images of the babies inside her, it became harder and harder to withdraw.

After she had recovered enough to at least appear in control, Jordan wanted nothing more than to get out of the clinic. "I'm sorry. I'm fine now. Is there anything else we need to do?"

Susan fumbled with her machine and offered some kind of apology for being the one to deliver such shocking news. When her professional side finally won control of her mind again, Susan asked if Jordan had any questions.

Do I have any questions? Do I have any questions? I have EVERY question! There were so many things running through her mind that the whole idea of going into any of them seemed insurmountable.

I'm pregnant! The thought hit her again like a punch in the chest and another bout of hysteria threatened to erupt. It took everything she had to maintain control. One question played over and over in Jordan's mind. The simple question, to which there was no answer. *What the hell?*

Susan was busy doing something with the machine for most of Jordan's meltdown. When she turned back towards the hospital bed, it was plain to see how spooked the young woman really was. She handed the sonogram images to Jordan without a word, but Susan looked like she was bracing herself for another outburst. When there wasn't one, she quickly told

Jordan to "go ahead and get dressed". Jordan noticed Susan sigh in relief before the door closed behind her.

It was true. Jordan Sullivan, a plain looking 21 year old introvert from California was pregnant with twins and no amount of protesting her virginity was going to change it.

Jordan didn't know how long she sat in her Volkswagen looking at the sonogram pictures. She guessed it had been close to an hour. *Regardless of how real the world seems, this has to be a dream. It just has to be a dream! S*he looked down at her belly, which had been flat when she pulled her little car out of the parking lot that morning. Suddenly, it was obvious she was indeed very pregnant. For the first time in her life, she actually pinched herself to see if she was dreaming.

She felt the pinch but realized she didn't actually know if that negated the possibility of being in a dream. She didn't know anything anymore and she couldn't focus. Intelligent thought was just too far out of reach. With clarity impossible, Jordan suddenly had an overwhelming urge to lie down. All she wanted to do was escape. She figured if she could go to sleep long enough, she would wake up and find everything back to normal again. She could go back to being an unpopular college student who came and went without anyone in the world noticing.

The idea of losing herself in nothingness became the ultimate quest in life. She strained to put one foot in front of the other through the dorm hallways and into her room. She didn't bother to turn on a light or kick off her shoes before she collapsed. She slipped into blessed oblivion with her right leg still hanging over the side of the bed, in reach of the monsters lying in wait.

Chapter 3

Jordan awoke in the darkness with relief that it had all been a dream. She started to sit up and struggled with an obstruction that hadn't been there when she'd fallen asleep. Her belly was easily four times as big as it had been when she'd gone to sleep!

She flipped on the light and caught a glimpse of herself in the mirror. *It wasn't a dream.* She was definitely pregnant! She glanced at the digital clock, which read 3:02 am, and thought back through the afternoon's events. What time had she fallen asleep? Her appointment was at 10 am so she couldn't have gotten back to the dorm any later than 1. She had been asleep for fourteen hours!

She noticed the light on her answering machine was blinking and pushed play as she sat down at her desk. The message was from Dr. Shapiro and something in his voice seemed strange. For one thing, he was talking much faster than normal. Jordan smiled as she imagined the doctor racing time to get everything he wanted to say out before the beep. The doctor said he had consulted with the ultrasound technician and needed Jordan to come back in for another appointment. He was calling in a prescription for prenatal vitamins, and she could pick them up at the campus drug store. He asked whether Friday morning would work for her next appointment. Knowing she'd better write everything down, she opened the desk drawer for a piece of paper. There, inside the drawer she didn't remember opening earlier, were the sonogram pictures.

It's real.

For the first time since meeting with the doctor, Jordan allowed herself to think about the reality of her situation. She sat down on the edge of her bed, put her face in her hands, and cried. She didn't know how to be someone's mother. She'd never even babysat someone else's kid before! How could she possibly learn everything she needed to know in only three months?

A flutter started in Jordan's lower abdomen and a bulge moved from one side of her body to the other. A similar feeling was happening closer to her rib cage and her hands flew to each area that moved. It no longer mattered who their father may or may not be. What mattered was that she was their mother and they were real, live human beings.

Jordan imagined her life with babies. She didn't have any friends to speak of so she wasn't concerned about embarrassment or even explanations. She didn't even have any family outside of her surrogate relationship with the Shapiros. But still... was she ready to be a mother!

Ok... think logically. What are the options?

There was no way she would consider abortion but there was always adoption. Even as quickly as the thought entered her mind it was dismissed. As hard as it would be to raise two children on her own, she knew she could never deliver the babies only to hand them over to someone else. It wasn't like she couldn't afford it. She'd been the sole heir to her parents' estate and even the dividends were more than she needed to live comfortably for the rest of her life. What was she so afraid of?

Jordan rubbed her arms from a sudden chill and reached over to the bed for her mother's bathrobe. Wrapping herself inside it always provided the protection she needed from the world. It felt like nothing could ever hurt her inside her mother's robe.

When she pulled the tie across the front of her stomach, Jordan felt another kick from one of the twins. She spread both hands wide across her belly. She wanted to cover every inch, to feel every movement.

As she rubbed her stomach, she thought of her own mother. Wearing the robe made Jordan feel like her mom wasn't gone forever. Having babies would be a lot of work but it would also mean she wouldn't be alone anymore. She thought of how life had been with her first family of three.

Holidays were a huge event in the Sullivan household but not because of presents or crowds of people. They were special because it was just Jordan and her parents. There were no guests to entertain or clients to impress. Edgar and Beverly Sullivan removed themselves completely from the outside world to spend three days or five days or whatever they could, exclusively with their only child.

Jordan thought of their last Christmas together.

When she pulled into the circular driveway, she was met by her parents, trying to be sneaky. They were acting like someone was hot on her tail as they waved her car into the garage. She smiled when she remembered them closing the door before she even came to a stop. They had saved the traditional "securing of the premises" until she got home.

Her father always made it an adventure when they began their "hideaway holidays." She remembered crawling on her belly and shimmying herself into a standing position between the two windows in the dining room so she could push the button for the automatic blinds without being seen from the outside.

There was never anyone in particular they were hiding from, as far as she knew, it just signified the start of family time.

Thinking of her parents was something she rarely allowed herself to do. Before today, their deaths had been the biggest mystery of her life. It was hard to believe they had been gone over a year. She preferred thinking about memories from the time in life when she didn't have to make the hard choices by herself.

For as long as she could remember, her parents had taken care of everything for her. They had made all of her decisions either through direct action or persuasive advice. Either way, she never actually decided anything herself, until it came time to plan their funerals. And even that was mostly handled by strangers.

Perhaps it was because she didn't have any brothers or sisters. Ever since she could remember, her parents treated her as if she were younger than she was. She thought about her 14th birthday when they gave her a full collection of all the latest Barbie dolls. Maybe it was the fact that they knew they would never have another child that made them want to prolong her childhood. Maybe it was their conservative backgrounds. Regardless of the reasons, they were overprotective to the extreme.

They were great parents, though, and even now she felt lost without them. Most days she simply let her mind believe that her parents were still alive. It was only their busy schedules keeping her from seeing them. But here she was with the biggest news in the world and no one at all to share it with. She was completely alone because of one stupid day.

She remembered thinking how normal everything seemed as the Resident Assistant from the dorm drove her to her parents' house. By the time they reached the house, she had almost convinced herself there had been a mistake. And then she knew there wasn't. Every nook and cranny of the yard was illuminated momentarily with flashes of red and blue police lights. *How many police cars were there?* It seemed like thousands of lights coming from everywhere at once but Jordan remembered counting four patrol cars, two ambulances, and one fire truck. She remembered thinking it must be a good sign that the sirens weren't blaring. *Or maybe it was a very bad sign.*

The lights were disorienting as she stepped out of her car, and she struggled to maintain her footing. A 20-year-old Jordan stepped onto the sidewalk as terror gripped her heart. She froze mid-step.

In a flash too brief to remember later, Jordan saw exactly what had happened inside... and outside the house. She saw her parents arguing with a dark haired man she could only see from behind. The vision of it passed in less than a heartbeat, but the feelings it left behind were as vivid a year later as they were the night her parents died.

Jordan remembered the moment she entered the house. It seemed exactly as it always had. If she didn't think about the official vehicles in the driveway, she could almost convince herself there had been a mistake. Maybe it wasn't actually her parents who were dead, but instead some neighbor she barely knew. She crossed through the foyer of the house with the first hope she had felt since her RA came into her dorm room with the news.

The idealistic belief that it was all a mistake shattered quickly. From the looks of it, the glass wall that overlooked the pool area had shattered quickly too.

Jordan stood in the doorway between the foyer and the kitchen. She looked out into the backyard through a large gaping hole. All around the hole, the safety glass crackled with thousands of breaks so close together they reflected like tiny mirrors. And yet the hole itself was a perfect cutout. From where Jordan entered, it was obvious the section in the center of the safety glass had been intentionally cut away to create a cross. It wasn't proportionately correct, though. The horizontal line was too low which made the cross look like it was upside down. It wasn't the cross that would haunt her dreams, though. It was what she saw through the opening.

There was no denying it was her father hanging upside down on the back fence. His feet were crossed and his arms were stretched out as if he'd been crucified upside down. His face was bright red from the blood that completely covered him. His outstretched arms were dripping a darker red. The pooled liquid was either moving in slow motion or clotting. It formed icicles of blood that hung from his arms.

It was hard to even imagine that they were the same arms that had captured her in a thousand hugs. She wanted to go back to her childhood where none of the horror was possible.

She wanted to run into her father's arms and have him scoop her up like he always did. She wanted to pull him off that fence and save him! But the sight of the blood kept her feet frozen to the floor. She couldn't see and didn't want to know what kept his arms suspended.

When she looked away from her father's body, she noticed the barbeque pit. Something shaped like a human body was rotating slowly, secured by the large rotisserie rod. As she realized she was looking at the body of her mother, Jordan heard herself screaming and knew no more.

When the world emerged from total nothingness to a fuzzy, distorted fog, Jordan heard voices. "What the hell was she doing here?" The voice she heard was gruff but completely unfamiliar. They weren't talking to her and whoever she heard didn't realize she was waking up. "I told you to have someone explain what happened and let her know that we would be sending an officer out to talk to her. You were specifically told to keep her from coming here!"

Jordan moved her eyes around the room and remembered she was in her own home. Within a few seconds the memory of why she was there returned. As soon as they realized she was awake, a female officer moved closer to the couch where Jordan was lying.

Jordan sat up fast and swung her legs over the side of the couch. She needed to run to her parents. She needed to help them. She needed to do something! For God's sake, why was everyone standing around?

When Jordan leaned forward to stand, she felt the female officer's hands on her shoulders. She tried to maneuver her way out of the surprisingly strong hold but couldn't do it. Jordan reached up to pry the hands off her shoulders, but the officer only tightened her grip.

"Let go of me! My parents are out there, for Christ's sake! Why aren't any of you people doing anything to help them?" Jordan looked into the officer's eyes and saw pity. She also saw the officer motion with her head to someone across the room.

Within seconds another uniformed person was at her side, but this one seemed to be a paramedic or at least someone medical. Jordan turned her attention to him and grabbed his hands. Her intent was to pull him outside to help her parents, but when she looked down she saw a syringe poking out of her hand.

"Aw, geez," he said out loud. He reached for her hand that had the syringe sticking out of it.

"Don't worry, miss; it's just a mild sedative. It doesn't look like much of anything went into your hand." The paramedic looked at the female officer as he pulled the syringe out of Jordan's hand and pushed it into the medical waste container. "I'll just give you a new shot in your arm and..." He was trying a little too hard to be light hearted and was pissing her off. As he held up the new syringe, Jordan swung loose and sedative number two went flying.

Push it away, her mental voice piped in. *Ignore the feelings and eventually they will go away.* The calm settled in and Jordan regained control.

"I don't want to be drugged; I want someone to help my parents." She looked at the paramedic, then at the officer sitting next to her. "Why aren't you doing anything?" Again Jordan saw the look of pity on the female officer's face and wanted to slap it away.

Maybe it was the little bit of medication that had entered her system, or maybe it was the looks on their faces, but no matter how much she wanted someone to do something to make this go away, she slowly began to realize there was nothing that could be done. She couldn't pretend reality was wrong with so many uniformed people wandering around her house.

Jordan put her face in her hands and sobbed. The animosity towards the officers was gone and in its place was utter despair. Sobs wracked through her body as the female officer who everyone referred to as 'Officer Wilson', put her arm around Jordan's shoulder and started to rock. It felt familiar but wrong. It was too formal for a comforting hug. It was consolation from a stranger. It was probably better than nothing, but Jordan didn't care. She wanted time to rewind and take all of the horror away. As they rocked back and forth, the same thought replayed again and again in Jordan's mind. *I want my mom. I want my mom.*

After what felt like hours, the gut-wrenching sobs turned to quiet tears. The tears turned to a dull ache that started in her heart and spread to every cell in her body. Someone had given her a tissue, and as she pulled away from yet another hug she didn't remember being pulled into, she wiped her eyes and blew her nose.

"What, what happened to my parents?" Jordan asked as she wiped at her nose. She fought back the tears that threatened to return at the mere thought of the question.

"Well, that's what we're here to find out. Unfortunately, we don't have any answers for you yet." More of the pitying look, but this time Jordan's hostility over it was numbed.

"I know you feel like you need to do something, but right now we need to give the investigators some room to work. We will do everything we can for your parents." Officer Wilson looked like she was waiting for an answer to a question that wasn't asked.

"Jordan, your parents wouldn't want you here to see all of this. Do you have a family member we could call?"

Jordan tried to focus her thoughts. *Family members? Do I have any family members? Yeah, they're dead in the back yard! Where have YOU been?!* Jordan knew ranting at the officers wouldn't help her situation and she kept her hysterical thoughts to herself.

- 45 -

Neither of her parents had brothers or sisters and her grandparents all died when she was young. She had no one. Before Jordan could wrap her mind around the idea of being alone in the world, the officer started offering prompts.

"Perhaps a minister?" Jordan shook her head no and Officer Wilson continued, "Maybe a teacher, a doctor..." *The Shapiros.*

Jordan knew the number by heart and gave it to Officer Wilson who excused herself to make the call. Jordan looked around the room at all the people working. Occasionally one of them would steal a pitiful glance in her direction, but they always averted their eyes as soon as she made eye contact. It wasn't long before Officer Wilson came back.

"Dr. Shapiro is on his way here now. Is there anything you'll want to take with you from the house?" As nice as she was, Officer Wilson was simply a minor character in the background of the movie playing in Jordan's head. Her mind kept alternating between loving memories of her parents and the images from the backyard that she couldn't get out of her thoughts. *Push it away,* her mental voice ordered. *Ignore the feelings and eventually they will go away.*

Officer Wilson moved in a little closer. "I'm not sure if you heard me, Jordan, but Doctor Shapiro and his wife are on their way. They'll take you home with them tonight."

"No," Jordan answered. "I... Are you sure there's nothing you can do?... Could you maybe?..." The frantic feelings were coming back. She wanted to ask the right question or say the right thing that would turn back time and make life normal again. The realization that her parents might really be gone slammed into her chest. They couldn't really be gone and yet they were. Jordan looked down at her lap. "Where will they be taking my parents tonight?"

"Jordan," the officer draped an arm around her shoulder, "we will do everything we can for your parents. The best thing you can do for them is take care of yourself. We'll worry about everything here." It finally sank in that the Shapiros were coming to take her away.

The fuzziness of sleep or medication was replaced by the sharp fear that they would make her leave without answers. "I'm not leaving. Do you really think that being in a different place will get those images out of my head?" Jordan took a calming breath. "I want to help."

Jordan tried to tell herself that the officers meant well and were just doing their jobs, but it was getting harder and harder to pretend it would all go away. She felt a scream building in her chest. Could she scream long enough that her parents would be alive again? She knew if she let it out they would have her sedated and hospitalized before she knew what hit her. She pushed the thoughts of insanity out of her mind before anyone could notice the fault in her composure.

"Why did all of the ambulances leave? Aren't any of you even going to try to save them?" She turned to the man who was going to give her the shot. "You must be a doctor or something, right? There's no way you could help them?"

She remembered that Officer Wilson had explained how the ambulance had been there and gone, but the paramedic stayed behind in case she needed him. She thought back about how they both reassured her that there was nothing anyone could have done. She remembered that they had already answered her questions but nothing changed. There would be no undoing. The nightmare was real.

She thought back to how hard the officer had tried to get her to leave once the Shapiros arrived. She just couldn't. Not even after Dr. Shapiro explained that he had examined both of her parents and there was nothing anyone could have done. Jordan needed to hold on to the idea that somehow she could help with something.

"You mentioned someone would want to ask me questions about my parents." She turned to Officer Wilson, "What is it you want to know?"

After some whispering and gesturing, a gentleman around 50 years old came over to the couch and sat next to Jordan. He introduced himself as Inspector John Bronson and explained to her that he was in charge of crime scene investigation for the San Diego police department.

"There doesn't appear to be anything missing from the house, but the nature of the murders is... unusual." He paused and studied her face. "If this becomes too difficult for you, please let me know. We don't have to do this today." Jordan nodded her understanding.

Inspector Bronson continued, "Ms. Sullivan, in my experience things like this don't just happen randomly. It's important for you to tell us anything at all that might help us find the monster that did this. Now, we're not interested in busting anyone except a murderer, so don't hold back anything you know, even if you think it might get someone in trouble." Inspector Bronson paused for a moment before continuing, "Were your parents involved in any groups or activities that someone else might think of as occult?"

Jordan had an immediate respect for Inspector Bronson. The inspector didn't waste her time on small talk and seemed to have sized up the situation logically. As he talked about finding out who did this horrible thing, Jordan was able to lose herself in the mission of the case. It started to feel like solving it might even bring her parents back.

Jordan let her conscious mind hold onto the belief that finding the murderer would somehow undo the deed. Unfortunately, Inspector Bronson was following the wrong lead if he was imagining her parents could be involved in anything cult-like.

"My parents are very conservative. You probably already know that my dad is a movie producer so he's always been involved with some pretty bizarre people but nothing like this."

"What about drugs, Jordan? Were any of your parents' friends involved in drug use?" The inspector watched her face closely. Even in her foggy thought process she recognized his scrutiny as a search for any hint of dishonesty.

"I'm sure some of the people my dad worked with use drugs, but I don't think my parents ever did. They have a few parties a year, centered around big awards or something like that, but otherwise they're very private people." Jordan realized her error in tense and the tears threatened again. She took a deep breath and pushed them away.

"As far as enemies go, the answer is about the same. There's always somebody upset about being overlooked for a movie part and things like that, but to do something like this?" All of her efforts to keep her emotions in check failed without warning.

The memory of what someone had done to her parents was more than she could hold back. Inspector Bronson put his arm around her shoulder as her body shook with the uncontrollable sobs she had tried so hard to hold back. After several minutes she was able to compose herself enough to speak… barely.

"I'm so sorry, Inspector. I wish I had some answers for you, but I can't imagine anyone who could do something so sick."

"I know this isn't going to be much consolation, but we will find the person or persons who did this." Inspector

Bronson was more reassuring than he knew. "Would you like to have the Shapiros take you home now?"

Jordan sat quietly for a minute thinking about how totally alone she was in the world without her parents. She was grateful for Dr. Shapiro and his wife, but what would she do tomorrow or the next day? She hadn't been ready to face being a grown up yesterday, how could she be ready today?

"I suppose so," she decided reluctantly. Jordan felt more like a small child than she had in years. *I want my mom* was stuck on replay in her thoughts.

"Officer Wilson?" The inspector motioned to the female police officer to come back over. "Is there anything you'd like Officer Wilson to get from the house for you?" Jordan tried to think of what she even had in the house anymore. There were all of her school projects in the totes in the basement. There were her old band uniforms and formal dresses in her closets, but she wouldn't need them again anytime soon.

The only thing she wanted was to have her mom sit with her and rock. She wanted her mom to snuggle with her until all of the things she'd seen and heard that night went away.

"Could you get my mom's bathrobe for me please? It should be hanging on the wall in the bathroom upstairs, the one off the master bedroom." Officer Wilson went to retrieve the bathrobe, while Jordan, the Shapiros, and Inspector Bronson waited. Unfortunately, there was nothing left to say. They sat in silence for several minutes, all lost in their own thoughts.

In the days that followed the murders, Jordan spoke to Inspector Bronson frequently. In the months that followed she spoke with him occasionally. After that she stopped calling. She didn't want to hear there were no new leads.

Jordan hadn't allowed herself to remember much about that time in life and shook her head now to dismiss the memory of her parents' deaths. What an awful thing to be thinking about NOW… now that she was pregnant! The word "pregnant" was magnified beyond anything Webster could define.

She sat alone in her dorm room wearing her mother's bathrobe, just as she had done the night her parents died. But that night she had the Shapiros.

She remembered thinking how much darker it was in her dorm than it had been in Charlotte's guest room. *How many lamps did I buy for my room after staying with the Shapiros? Was it 12?*

It still wasn't enough light to illuminate the darkness that came from being completely alone. It wasn't enough to keep the monsters away.

Now… as she sat alone in her mother's robe remembering the loss of her parents, she made the most important choice of her life. She was going to keep her babies and raise them herself.

She had more than enough money for three people to live like royalty, even if she didn't sell her parents' house… her house.

The idea of getting rid of the house made her pause with an unexpected sadness. She hadn't been back to it since the murders, but she'd always thought she'd go back someday. She just always thought she'd wait until things were different.

"Well, things are about as different as they can be now, aren't they?" Jordan rubbed her hands across her belly as she spoke to her babies. She had loved growing up in the house. Why couldn't they?

Once she accepted the fact that she wasn't alone in the world any longer, she actually wanted to be home, and the house she grew up in was home.

When things turned hard, Jordan still wanted her own mother. Where would she learn how to be the mother?

Figuring it all out in her childhood home seemed, somehow, right. She had spent her entire life running through those halls. It was filled with thousands of wonderful memories and only that one horrific one. The thought of someone else living there had always been unbearable. Giving the house up seemed like it would mean losing her parents all over again. Maybe moving back into it would be like having them back.

Jordan could face that.

Chapter 4

It was Friday morning, and Jordan was waiting in Dr. Shapiro's office for her follow up visit. She was thinking about questions she should ask and jotting notes on a sheet from the doctor's note pad. She had helped herself to a sheet when she saw the pen sitting on the desk.

Jordan had written down two questions and was struggling to come up with more. *Maybe it really is true that ignorance is bliss.* Hard as she tried to come up with intelligent queries, there wasn't anything worrying her anymore.

It seemed like she had only been in his office for a couple of minutes when Dr. Shapiro came in.

"Well, that was the shortest wait in history," Jordan joked with the doctor, but he had his nose buried in the manila folder he was carrying. She wondered if it was any less politically incorrect to make fun of a doctor's shortcomings if you've known him all your life.

She was starting to think she might have offended him when he didn't respond after several seconds. He was still studying something in her chart when he sat down in the chair next to her. She recognized his expression. He was utterly absorbed in whatever it was he was reading.

"I received the results of the ultrasound, and I have to admit I was surprised to find out that…" Whatever he was about to say was immediately truncated when he looked up from the folder and saw Jordan.

"Oh, my God!" The look on his face, combined with the sudden exclamation frazzled Jordan's nervous system.

"What? Dr. Shapiro, what's the matter?" Jordan studied his face but could only read confusion.

"When you were in here last week you were the same size as you've been since you were sixteen. When did you start showing?" Relief washed over her.

Dr. Shapiro was hard to read when it came to medical stuff. He could be telling a patient her head was going to fall off and be as calm as if he were telling the patient she was fine… usually. When it came to medicine, he had always maintained a sort of professional disposition. Maybe that's why she never felt comfortable calling or even thinking of him as Roger. Usually the doctor spoke very matter-of-factly and rarely showed emotion. She wasn't sure what to think of this new dimension to the man she'd always known.

"Geez, you had me nervous there for a minute!" Jordan placed her hands on the bulge in her midsection with affection. "It's the funniest thing. Right after my ultrasound appointment I got huge! I'm not sure if there's some psychological reason like denial that kept me from showing very much before, but within a few hours, there it was: a pregnant belly! It was a good thing I was wearing sweat pants."

Jordan snickered slightly but saw that the doctor didn't share her humor. "Is there something I should be worried about?" Jordan couldn't help but smile. "Aside from the obvious things, of course."

"There's no sign of abnormality in the babies so… I guess not. But it's peculiar, to say the least." He looked down like he was mumbling more to himself than to Jordan. "There've been cases of women who discovered they were expecting late in pregnancy and even a few where the women didn't know they were pregnant until they delivered. Most all of them were large women who could hide a baby." The doctor paused for a moment as if he suddenly realized Jordan was still a part of the conversation.

She'd never seen the man flustered, and didn't know what to make of it. He noticed her scrutiny and snapped back to his normal, professional self. He cleared his throat and adjusted his glasses. "There are reasons that some women don't show until late in pregnancy so it might not mean anything at all."

He hadn't meant to let his emotions get the best of him. He also hadn't meant to jot the name "Josef Mengele" onto Jordan's chart, but he did it just the same.

There was no reason for Jordan to know that Dr. Shapiro had been thinking about one of the stories his father told him. It was about life in Germany shortly before the Second World War. Josef Mengele had already begun talk of a perfect race. In fact, in the private medical circles, to which Roger's father Hiram had belonged, everyone knew of Mengele's ideas about playing God.

Josef frequently bragged about his ability to manipulate genetics in a way that could mold and ultimately create perfect humans. One of his goals had been to perfect accelerated gestation.

Regardless of the possibilities he offered to Jordan, Roger knew her pregnancy hadn't been hidden for six months. Her babies were growing at least four times faster than a normal fetus.

But Mengele had been dead for decades and as far as Roger knew, Jordan had no idea her great-grandmother had been the victim of some of the "Angel of Death's" worst experiments.

The doctor tried to convince himself that his thoughts were preposterous. Even if there could be some residual effects from the experimentation, how strong could it be after so much time?

His fingers were shaking when he closed her file, and he hoped Jordan hadn't noticed. She had.

It was obvious the doctor was fighting to keep control of himself and she wondered what could possibly have him so riled up. She may be an unwed mother, but it wasn't like she was in high school. She was a grown woman!

She saw the doctor shake his head to dismiss the thoughts and was relieved to see him back to himself. He smiled at her and once again looked like the doctor she knew and loved.

"Most likely it's just positioning. It isn't uncommon for women with a tilted uterus to suddenly 'pop' one day. Shoot, it was a topic in one of my medical journals just last month."

A tilted uterus was actually possible, but the doctor couldn't shake the feeling that they would have seen that in the ultrasound. He began to ponder possible abnormalities that could accelerate gestation. He thought through the Trisoma Syndromes and realized he would need to do some additional research. Genetic abnormalities weren't his specialty and he didn't trust the personal spin he might put on conclusions. He was simply too close to the subject.

It really could make sense that the babies were positioned in a way that Jordan didn't show. It's less likely to happen with twins, of course, but that didn't mean it wasn't possible. Just because his father had been thrust into a test against evil didn't mean he would be.

He needed more information. His mind raced with possible anomalies that could show some kind of logical explanation. He needed to run more tests. There would be a logical explanation. There was almost always a logical explanation... almost.

"Let's go ahead and examine you. Maybe that will shed some light on this mysterious pregnancy." He smiled as he said it, but Jordan could tell there was something still worrying him.

He began by measuring her abdomen. "Hmmm," was all he said. Throughout the rest of the exam he never said an actual word but made enough noises that Jordan was becoming anxious.

"What is it? Is there something wrong with the babies?" Jordan wasn't sure she could handle any more surprises.

"Based on the position of the babies and my estimation of their size, I would guess you are very close to eight months along. These babies have already dropped. I hope you didn't have your heart set on taking Lamaze classes." She thought she saw something behind his smile.

Jordan knew she should be shocked that the doctor was telling her she would be a mother now in one month rather than the already impossible three, but for some reason, she wasn't even surprised.

When the doctor turned toward her and took off his reading glasses, Jordan was positive he was going to give her the bad news he was holding back.

"Jordan, have you thought about where you're going to live?"

She sighed openly with relief and was surprised at how attached she had become to her unborn children in such a short amount of time.

"Geez, you had me worried there for a minute! I've been living in the dorm since... everything happened with my parents, but I know I won't be able to stay there after the babies come. I was actually thinking about moving back into the house. I don't think anyone's been there since the police finished their investigation, though. It might take quite a bit to make it livable again. Why were you wondering?"

"Medically speaking, I would say you have as long as one month before the babies arrive, but a week ago I would have said you had eight. I guess what I'm telling you is that these babies could come any day. Do you really feel up to going back to the house now?" The doctor studied her face intently.

"Yes, I do, but I can't explain why. Three weeks ago I would have been perfectly happy to let the house sit, as it is, for the rest of my life. It's like the babies have given me a sense of family I haven't felt since my parents died. Not that I don't appreciate everything you and Charlotte do for me, of course. Maybe it's that I've realized it's time for me to grow up. I don't know. Either way, it's my home and I want to go back."

When Jordan finished, the doctor nodded as if to say her answer was acceptable. For the first time in her life, Jordan was irritated by someone's ownership of her. She really did appreciate his help, but it didn't give him the right to decide where she lived.

"Ok, I just wanted to make sure it wasn't because you felt like you didn't have options." At the doctor's explanation, Jordan's irritation faded to shame. She should have known him well enough to know his intentions would be kind.

"You will not, however, be doing any lifting and I certainly wouldn't want you scrubbing floors or washing windows in your condition. There's also the matter of setting up a nursery. The hospital will give you a few things like diapers and formula to get you started, but you're going to need a lot more than that. There's a moving company in town that's quite good. I'm sure they would be able to pack up and move everything in your dorm within a few hours. As far as getting the house ready, a good cleaning company should be able to have it livable within a day. If you'd like, I could ask Charlotte if she would coordinate all of that for you."

Jordan was astonished again at the doctor's generosity. She suddenly felt very guilty about her earlier irritation with him. "That would be wonderful, if you think she wouldn't mind… that is."

Jordan had never understood why the doctor had such strong personal interest in her life. She assumed it was mostly out of pity, but it was there even before her parents died. Regardless of the reason, Jordan knew how much help she needed. Everything had been happening so quickly. The idea of having Charlotte involved seemed too good to be true! It would be almost like having her mother back again… almost.

"No, I'm sure she wouldn't mind at all. Since our children left home she's been dying to feel needed again. I think this would be just the ticket. I also want to suggest you hire a nanny, at least for the first few weeks." He picked up the phone, began dialing, and continued.

"I'll give Charlotte a call right now so she can get started. I'd like everything ready for you by the end of the week." At that point Charlotte answered on the other end and Jordan listened to the doctor's half of the conversation. It wasn't long before her thoughts took her to memories of Charlotte Shapiro.

She thought about the first day they had met. Charlotte had accompanied her husband to Jordan's 5th birthday party. Jordan's parents always threw elaborate birthday parties and that year was no exception. She thought it might have been their way of trying to make her feel better about not having any friends or siblings. Little did they know, it never bothered her like it bothered them.

Jordan hadn't really paid any attention to Charlotte until it came time to break the piñata. Up until then, she was just one of the grownups at the party.

Jordan had been watching the butterflies dance around the gardens when the latest movie star's kid stepped up to take his turn to swing at the piñata. She could hear the other children yelling encouragements but didn't really care that much about what would be exploding from the papier-mâché princess. She knew the adults would make them divide it up evenly anyway. Everything always worked itself out.

The prettiest butterfly was about to land on a rose bud when Jordan felt a rush of wind and complete displacement. Suddenly she was looking at a totally different view and the other children were behind her. Mrs. Shapiro had grabbed her hand and pulled her forward... HARD!

Jordan turned indignantly to look for the butterfly that had surely been scared away. That was when she bumped her nose on a golf club that was wedged firmly inside the tree.

Apparently the movie star's child decided to give himself an edge and replaced the plastic bat the other children had been using with a nine iron. Jordan probably wouldn't even remember it if not for the commotion that ensued.

The adults scurried around and made a big deal out of the whole thing, but Charlotte's attention stayed on Jordan.

She also remembered the worse night of her life when Charlotte held her like a baby after her parents had been killed. Jordan's tears had soaked through the thick collar of her mother's bath robe, onto a silk blouse. And yet Charlotte never complained. She patiently stroked Jordan's hair and rocked her until she fell asleep.

Jordan remembered waking up in the Shapiro's house and how Charlotte had timed breakfast perfectly to the exact second she walked into the kitchen, even though Jordan hadn't come downstairs until four in the afternoon.

It was possible to handle the grief while Charlotte took care of her. It was easy to pretend it was her mother rocking her all night long. Morning was different.

Push it away, her mental voice reasoned. *Ignore the feelings and eventually they will go away.*

Her attention snapped back to the present when she heard the mounting to do list the doctor was giving his wife. Jordan started to worry that he was asking too much of her... again. When he finished the list of tasks at hand, he paused for barely a second. "I knew if anyone could work a miracle for me it would be you. One more thing, do you think you would be able to line up a nanny to help her out for a while?"

As he listened to his wife, his facial expressions gave him away. "I hadn't thought of that. I can ask her, but are you sure it's something you'd be up to doing?" Jordan sat a little straighter with the excitement of what she was sure he was going to say. *How wonderful would it be if Charlotte was willing to help with the babies... to be a grandmother to the babies?*

Almost before the doctor finished suggesting that Mrs. Shapiro would like to come and help with the babies too, Jordan enthusiastically replied, "Yes! Yes! Yes!" The doctor explained that Mrs. Shapiro would only be able to be there during the day, but she knew of several live-in nannies who came highly recommended. He communicated Jordan's response to Charlotte, but Jordan could already hear the excitement on the other end of the phone line.

Dr. Shapiro handed the phone to Jordan to allow the women the opportunity to work through the remaining details. The conversation became nothing more than background noise as Dr. Shapiro went about the business of updating Jordan's file. It was then that he noticed the name he had doodled on the page. He crossed it out with more ink than was necessary. He'd always hated the name Josef Mengele and he couldn't understand why thoughts of him were so heavy on his mind when it came to Jordan and her babies.

Millions of people had bigger reasons to hate Mengele than Roger Shapiro had, but watching his father's regret eat him alive in later years was enough.

Hiram Shapiro had seen what was happening in Germany and instead of warning people about Mengele and others who were already becoming brainwashed by the Nazi beliefs, Hiram fled with his family. He left three years before things went bad so his fortune, reputation, and family were intact when everyone else's world fell apart. His friends watched their families murdered while his family was safe.

Hiram tried to help in any way he could after the war was over, but it was never enough to sooth his guilt. When he died, the world celebrated him as a philanthropic doctor who saved countless lives. Only his family knew his personal torment.

Jordan paid no attention to the doctor who sat before her lost in thought. She was busy making plans for her future and had no interest in worrying about her past. After several minutes, she returned the phone to the doctor who said his goodbyes to his wife. Neither woman had any way of knowing the worry that was starting to build in his heart.

"Dr. Shapiro, I can't thank you enough for all your help. I really hadn't given much thought to how quickly everything needed to happen and I... I just don't know what I would do without you or your amazing wife!"

Chapter 5

Roger Shapiro walked through the front door of his house and barely had his coat off before his wife began firing questions at him. He smiled openly. He couldn't remember the last time he had seen her so excited. She was drying her hands on a towel as she rushed into the foyer to greet him. Her short grey hair was perfectly styled, as always, and her reading glasses were nestled in at the top of her head. He smiled to himself knowing full well she would be asking him where she put her glasses when they sat down to read the papers after dinner. He noticed how much younger she looked that night and knew it was excitement about the babies. He wondered if they would stop talking about babies long enough to even read the papers. His mind wandered back to the mysterious unborn children.

The doctor had been studying blood samples and ultrasound results all afternoon and couldn't find a single measurement out of line. He still couldn't shake the feeling that there was something wrong with Jordan's babies. None of the possible reasons for accelerated gestation he'd suggested actually made any sense and he was running out of guesses.

It didn't need to be his wife's problem, though. At least for the evening, he would allow himself to enjoy her enthusiasm.

"Slow down, my dear," he teased. "We have all evening to talk about Jordan and her babies. What's for dinner tonight?" He knew her well enough to know there would be no dinner until at least the bulk of her questions were satisfied, but he was enjoying the game and he wanted to forget the outside world a little longer.

"We're having pot roast, but it won't be ready for at least 45 minutes. Now, what's the rest of the story with Jordan? I'm a little surprised that you wouldn't have mentioned she was expecting before now." She cast a chastising look his way.

"Now, Charlotte," Roger said as firmly as he could, "you know I can't divulge any personal information about my patients without their express written consent."

Charlotte snatched a decorative pillow from the couch and landed a direct blow to his chest.

"Come on," she was starting to sound defeated. "Tell me what is going on with Jordan! If you don't tell me, I'm going to call her myself and ask what's up. If you think telling me yourself will delay your dinner, just wait until I get on the phone and start talking about babies."

"Ok, ok, but only because I want to eat some time tonight." The frown she aimed at him didn't go unnoticed, and he smiled at how much he loved her.

Roger explained everything he knew, but offered up only one of his suspicions… the possibility of a birth defect. He was sorry to see her facial expressions turn from open enthusiasm to deep concern, but the warning alarms blaring in his own head made him want to prepare her for the worst.

He recounted his recent visits with Jordan hoping full disclosure would limit his wife's questions. No reason to risk a burned dinner.

"Do you think she was telling you the truth about being a virgin?" Charlotte looked concerned and confused.

"I believe that she's telling the truth… as she knows it. She mentioned something about having a sex dream, though. She didn't say much about it but from the look on her face it… made an impact. It makes me wonder if something happened without her knowledge or consent." The doctor could see the concern deepen on his wife's face.

Charlotte nodded understanding, then turned her thoughts back to the matter at hand… babies!

"I only talked to her briefly, but she didn't seem upset about the idea of having a baby, much less twins," Charlotte said.

"Yes, she has definitely embraced the idea of being a mother. When I first told her the results of the pregnancy test, she reacted exactly as I would have expected. She was shocked. I don't know if it was seeing the babies in the ultrasound or having time to think, but she is excited about becoming a mother. She's excited enough to even want to move back into her house."

"I was surprised when you said that on the phone today," Charlotte confessed. "To be honest, that was the only hesitation I had. I'm not fond of the idea of spending time in that house, but I think if I make some changes it might not be so bad. It seems sort of... cursed or something, I suppose." She studied his face for the judgment that she already knew wouldn't be there.

"I wasn't expecting her to want to move back there either. I even asked her why she would consider it. She said the babies have given her a sense of family so she wants to raise them in her family home. It's hard to imagine a person wanting to live in a place where such tragic events happened."

Roger smelled the pot roast and realized how long his day had actually been. "Do you think there's a chance we'll be able to eat yet this evening?"

"I'm sorry, dear. I do get fixated on things don't I? It should be ready by now. Let's go eat." They retreated into the kitchen where they always ate when it was just the two of them.

As they walked, Roger told Charlotte for the millionth time how lucky he was to have found an angel like her to share his life. Secretly he was worrying about choices.

Chapter 6

Jordan walked to her dorm room alone with her thoughts. She couldn't believe how fortunate she was to have Dr. Shapiro and his wife on her side. She hadn't even had time to think about getting the house ready, much less setting up a nursery and moving. Now she didn't have to. Further confirmation… things do always work out alright in the end. Maybe her dad was right and patience was a virtue after all.

She had stopped for fast food on the way back from the doctor's office, but finished everything long before she turned into campus. She was already making plans to go to bed early again. Every movement seemed a thousand times harder than normal.

When she got to her room, she tossed her fast food bag, filled with only the things that weren't edible, towards the garbage can. She was too tired to care if she'd made the basket.

She turned on the television out of habit, and lay down on her bed. As the TV became nothing but background noise, she found herself lost in thought about the origination of her babies.

Jordan wanted to believe it could be her parents' way of continuing to look out for her: like they were sending her guardian angels. She just couldn't shake the feeling that it all started with her dream.

She tried to think back to exactly when she had it and suddenly she remembered. She sat straight up in her bed without even realizing she was doing it as she exclaimed out loud, "Oh, my God."

She hadn't noticed the connection before, but now in hindsight, she remembered. The dream had occurred exactly one year after her parents' deaths.

Her earlier thoughts about her parents sending the babies had been reassuring. This was not. She had no idea why she felt the apprehension, but it was definitely there. Could her babies somehow be connected to what happened to her parents? She thought about Dr. Shapiro's question about whether she had ever lost time. That was exactly what happened in the dream. One moment she was lying on her bed in the flannel pajamas she always wore, with a strange man, or men, sitting next to her. The next moment, their bodies were entwined in a passion she had never even dreamed about.

She never made a conscious choice to give in to him. In fact, she was still debating the moral implications of casual sex in a dream as she felt herself succumbing to the handsome stranger. She analyzed the situation as if she were a spectator in her own body, a voyeur to a life far more interesting than her own. *What could it hurt? It was just a dream. Wasn't it?*

Her door was locked when she woke up in the morning. She remembered that for sure, but even if an intruder could get through a locked door, how could he morph into another person like that? And it wasn't like she was looking at the same person from different angles. The two men were as opposite as they could be. Their polar differences made her feel like the rope in a tug-of-war being held over a cliff.

Could there really have been some kind of divine intervention? Jordan could still remember the peace she felt when the blonde man was by her side. But what about the dark man, was he representative of evil? While she wouldn't consider herself religious, she was certainly familiar with the story of Mary and Josef.

"Yeah right." Jordan snickered out loud. "Like God would pick me for something that important." Of course, there was that one thing she had in common with Mary... they were both virgins.

Jordan had struggled with the question of faith her entire life. To say the least, her parents were not churchgoers. She tried to think back and couldn't remember them ever even saying the word "God" in her presence. They never discussed religion so she just assumed they were atheist.

There was a time when Jordan thought she had found God. It was her first year of college when one of the "Bible thumpers" who frequented the campus caught her attention.

The stranger stood on the concrete bench in front of the bookstore and proclaimed his beliefs. Hundreds of students walked past, oblivious to his demonstration. The kind ones pretended he didn't exist. Others heckled him as they walked by. A few even spewed obscenities.

Jordan was impressed that his convictions were strong enough to keep him talking - regardless of the crowd's animosity. She sat down on the grass to listen and found herself captivated by the young man's words.

She listened for over a half hour before he finally realized someone was actually hearing his message. He jumped down off the bench, walked the 15 or 20 yards to where she was sitting, and introduced himself.

They spent the rest of the afternoon talking about God, salvation, and the power of faith. Other than her parents, Jordan couldn't really say there was anyone she truly loved. The idea of a divine being who would walk with her through anything became extremely appealing.

After attending several church services and talking with the pastor at length, she had begun the classes necessary to officially join the church. She was even scheduled for baptism. But then her parents were killed.

Jordan vaguely remembered the ride from her parents' house to the Shapiro's on the night of the murders. The only part she remembered clearly was deciding there was no way there could be a God in heaven if things like that could happen to good people like her parents.

The Shapiros could have driven her to New York and back for all she knew. Each miniscule fraction of a second was consumed by her anger. To an outside observer it would have looked like she was unconscious. In a way, she probably was. She was lost inside her own mind's argument.

In the Bible you promised to protect us from any evil! How could you allow something like that to happen? My parents were good people! They never hurt anyone. How could you let someone do that to them? How can you say you're a God of love and let stupid senseless things like that happen in the world? Where were you, God? Where were you when you were supposed to be protecting us?

Dr. Shapiro pulled his car into the brightly lit garage as Jordan was mentally professing her hatred for the God who'd betrayed her. Over time she just went back to having no religion at all.

Maybe the babies were God's way of making up for taking away the only people who had ever loved her?

She could allow herself to believe that.

Chapter 7

It had only been five days since Charlotte graciously agreed to help get her new life in order. Jordan could hardly believe that today was the day she would be leaving the dorm behind and going home. She was nervous.

She and Charlotte had gone to lunch and then shopping two days earlier. They had picked out furniture, a stroller, baby clothes, diapers, formula, bottles, and about a million other items Jordan had no idea she'd need.

She felt like royalty as she walked through Babies 'R Us pointing to items while employees hauled them off to some unknown location for packing and delivery. Jordan's family had been wealthy since she was a baby, but she was still raised to plan and budget her finances responsibly. It was fun to forget about responsibility and let herself spoil her unborn babies.

During lunch Charlotte quizzed Jordan on the types of food she liked, her favorite fragrances, and her hobbies. Things she liked to do was the shortest part of the conversation. Charlotte wouldn't allow Jordan to come along for the grocery shopping but assured her the house would be well stocked when she arrived.

As much as she enjoyed the day, Jordan was tired. Carrying around two extra people wasn't something she'd had a chance to work up to and she was exhausted. Sitting down never felt better than when she crawled into the passenger seat of Charlotte's car.

The ride to her "new" home was long enough that Jordan felt rejuvenated and ready for the next challenge. Or maybe it was nerves. The last time she'd been in the house was the night her parents died.

As they pulled into her driveway, Jordan was admiring the landscaping as if she'd never been to the place! Even in the days when her parents lived in the house, she never remembered the yard looking as nice.

The shrubbery was perfectly trimmed and surrounded by gorgeous rose bushes. Even the driveway itself appeared to be perfectly prepared for her arrival. There wasn't a single rock out of place.

Charlotte parked in front of the house, as Jordan had done all her life. Although now there would be no one to move the car around back to the garage stalls for them. That was always her dad's way of saying hello. She missed her father. She realized she should probably get used to parking in one of the stalls when she started driving again. *Enough sad thoughts!* For now, she was excited to see the rest of the house. Her car would be fine wherever she decided to park.

Charlotte opened the front door and stepped to the side to allow Jordan to go in first. The tears she had suppressed earlier welled up in her eyes. "Everything looks great …"

Charlotte's cheerful disposition never faltered. "You haven't seen anything yet. I hope things are where you'd like them to be." Charlotte made a sweeping gesture towards the foyer. Jordan led the way.

With every step she took, she felt like a kid who inherited a candy store. The vases in the foyer were filled with fresh flowers, and the hardwood floors shone with fresh wax. The sun cast brilliant rays through spotless windows, and she was surprised to notice that none of the rays contained even a single speck of dancing dust. Everything about it felt fresh, reborn. It would be the perfect place for her new start.

Charlotte was most anxious to show Jordan the nursery. As they made their way up the open staircase, Jordan thought about the thousands of times she had climbed the stairs as a child. Her excitement became mingled with a sad longing for her parents again. If only they could share this special time in her life.

When they reached the door of the nursery, Charlotte turned to face her. "Keep in mind now, we can rearrange things any way you'd like." With that she turned and opened the door.

Jordan stood with her mouth open as she tried to absorb every detail of the room. To her left, against the back wall, were two cribs standing side by side. A flowing canopy draped from the ceiling, enclosing the cribs and giving them an angelic appearance. Directly in front of her was the wall of windows that overlooked the back gardens. There were toy boxes and shelves and wall hangings perfectly placed to create a magical type of wonderland that any child would love to call home. To her right were French doors that she knew must lead into the master bedroom. The last time she'd been in the house it was a wall.

"How in the world were you able to do all of this in such a short amount of time?" Jordan crossed the room to the French doors and opened them. She had been a little anxious about the idea of moving into her parents' bedroom, but when she opened the doors, any similarities between her parents' room and the one she was about to enter were purely structural.

Jordan was speechless as she walked into the bedroom. From behind, Charlotte began to worry that the silence was a sign she had overlooked something important.

"If there's anything you'd like to change, if you'd like to bring the other furniture back in or anything..." Charlotte had been concerned from the beginning about moving Jordan's things into the master bedroom and was now deeply regretting the decision.

Jordan turned around with tears in her eyes and the two women's eyes locked. "It is absolutely perfect." She fought to keep the words from breaking up as she tried to express what she already knew there were no words for.

"I don't even know how to start to thank you. Not just for all you did but for your thoughtfulness in HOW you did it. I don't know how you knew what would be so perfect because I sure couldn't have put my finger on it, but yet you found it." Jordan wrapped her arms around Charlotte and hugged her tightly. "Thank you. Thank you so much."

Charlotte had thought of everything. The bed her parents shared had been replaced with the old canopy bed from her room.

Her bed was the place where she had always felt like a princess, but her parents' bedroom was the place she always felt safe. Merging the two together made both perfect. The best part was that she would only be a few yards away from the babies if they needed her.

Jordan wrapped Charlotte in an embrace. Tears of relief flooded their eyes as they stood holding each other. Finally, Charlotte pulled back, dabbed her eyes, and lifted Jordan's face gently.

"Let's finish this little tour so we can get some lunch in you." They walked through the rest of the house with Jordan marveling at the difference rearranging furniture made to the look and feel of the house. It still felt like home but there were enough changes that it now felt like HER home.

As they approached her father's study, Jordan thought of the countless times she had entered the room to get her father's advice. She remembered times when she would come in at night to watch him work. She couldn't imagine that this room would ever be anything but her father's study and she was afraid to see what had been changed. Jordan wished she had mentioned that to Charlotte before she'd gone to so much trouble. She prepared herself to feign enthusiasm, regardless of how it looked.

Charlotte opened the French doors and walked into the room, allowing Jordan ample space to enter. "Other than cleaning, we didn't do anything in here," Charlotte continued. "I guess it just seemed like it was meant to be a study, but again, if there's anything you would like to change, we sure can."

Jordan smiled, "I don't know whether anyone has ever told you this, but you have to be psychic! Not even psychic, you seem to know what I need and want when even I don't have any idea. I know I said this before, but it's absolutely perfect." As they walked out of the study, the look on Jordan's face changed. They had reached the last room of the tour. The only thing left was the kitchen and pool area.

She noticed when they walked past the kitchen earlier that the patio blinds were all closed. The room was almost entirely glass but the back yard was completely private so the only time the blinds were closed was during "hideaway holidays". The patio held other memories now though.

Jordan thought seriously about just pretending the backyard didn't exist anymore. As far as she was concerned, she could live her entire life without ever seeing it again. But could she really ever sleep in the house without knowing what might still be behind the blinds? No. She couldn't.

Charlotte ended the tour at the kitchen and opened the refrigerator door to pull out the lunches she had brought from home.

As much as Jordan hated the idea of going back out into the area that had haunted her dreams more nights than she could count, she knew she would rather do it with Charlotte along. She made a decision.

"Before we have lunch I'd like to go out by the pool."

Charlotte's poker face froze for the smallest amount of time, but her answer was as cheerful as ever. "We did make quite a few changes in the landscaping, but to be honest, it's not significantly different than it was... before. Are you sure you're up to going out there right now?"

"Yes, I'm sure." Jordan put on her bravest smile and grabbed hold of Charlotte's arm.

As they walked towards the double doors that led out to the pool area, Jordan's anxiety continued to mount. She tried to keep her breathing as even as possible, but she could feel her pulse speeding up. Her heart was threatening to beat itself right out of her chest and she fought the urge to run screaming through the house.

Charlotte pushed the button to open the blinds. As much as Jordan didn't want them to, the first thing her eyes searched for was the barbeque pit. It was gone!

She looked toward the back fence and although it was still there, large flowering bushes blocked the sight of it. Japanese lanterns hung elegantly from shepherd hooks throughout the yard and the chaise lounge chairs stood in perfect formation around the edge of the pool. This was not the setting from her nightmares; this was a tropical paradise, right in her own back yard! The last of her fears disappeared and she knew she was home.

Jordan spent so much time protecting herself from the bad memories that she'd filtered out too many of the good ones. The house Charlotte refurbished reminded her of the good ones. She was dabbing her eyes as Charlotte led her to an overstuffed lawn chair under the first of several giant umbrellas scattered around the pool.

Charlotte scurried into the kitchen to get their lunches but insisted Jordan remain by the pool. It was far too beautiful for Jordan to object.

After finishing their lunches, Jordan was marveling over the improvements Charlotte had made to the house. "I swear,

Charlotte, you're positively magic! How did you DO all of this?"

Charlotte took a sip of her lemonade and raised an eyebrow. "The truth is, my dear, I simply know who to go to for help." Charlotte explained the process of hiring contractors, landscapers, and cleaning crews like it were the simplest project she had ever done. Jordan knew she must have worked night and day to bring everything together.

"You know," Jordan began without looking up from her lemonade glass, "I don't think there will ever be a way for me to say exactly how much everything you've done means to me... or how much you mean to me. I guess every woman who's about to have a baby suddenly needs her mom and, well, for the first time in over a year, I feel like I have one again. I hope you don't mind my saying that, I just..."

"Oh, my dear," Charlotte interrupted, "I have never received a nicer compliment." Charlotte's face changed to worry before Jordan even realized what was happening herself.

"Jordan? Are you alright?" The tender moment was interrupted when Jordan's water broke.

Chapter 8

There had been a constant flow of people in and out of her room since Charlotte checked her into the hospital two hours earlier, so Jordan was glad to have a little solitude with her thoughts. So far labor hadn't been as bad as she'd imagined. Of course, the medication probably had a little to do with that. For some reason she wasn't the least bit nervous and thought maybe she was actually lucky to have missed out on the Lamaze classes. Having no idea what to expect meant it was easy to convince herself that her fear of delivery was for nothing. *Ignorance is bliss.*

"Oh shit!" Jordan was glad no one was in the room with her when she finally realized she hadn't even started thinking about names for the babies. She wished that she had bought one of those books that listed all the cutest choices, but of course, it hadn't occurred to her. The worry disappeared when the next contraction gripped her abdomen. She tried to do what the most recent nurse instructed and imagine herself melting into the mattress while she counted her breaths.

As the contraction began to fade, she noticed every muscle in her body had been clenching against the pain. Maybe it was going to be as bad as she had imagined after all. She was definitely going to ask for more medication when the next person came into the room.

The nurse returned when Jordan was in the middle of the next contraction and started checking the monitors. "How are you doing, honey?"

"I need more medicine or something because they're getting a lot worse now." She hadn't been timing the contractions but it seemed like they were right on top of each other.

"Dr. Shapiro will be here in a minute to check on you so I'll ask him about it. Well… speak of the devil." As if on cue, Dr. Shapiro walked into the room.

"Well, my dear, it looks like you're about to become a mother. How is everything going so far?"

"Fine, I guess, but I need more medication. This is really starting to hurt." Jordan grimaced through another contraction as Dr. Shapiro snapped his hands into a pair of latex gloves.

"Let's see how you're coming along." If she'd had a normal pregnancy, she may have had time to worry about the embarrassment of having Dr. Shapiro deliver her. As it was, she didn't care about anything except getting the babies out.

"The good news is that within a couple of hours this will all be over. The bad news is that we've missed the window for any more medication. Do you feel like you need to push yet?"

"No, but I do feel like I have to go to the bathroom."

"That's good," Dr. Shapiro explained. "That means that the first baby is pushing against your colon and should be moving into the birth canal. Don't fight the feeling to push."

He settled himself into a more comfortable position on his chair and Jordan couldn't help but think how much he looked like a catcher in a baseball game. The thought made her chuckle a little, but only for a second. It was interrupted by yet another contraction. This time she felt a strong urge to push and did.

"That's good, Jordan. Hold that push as long as you can. I can feel the top of the baby's head." After what seemed like an eternity, the contraction ended and so did her urge to push.

"That was great. A few more pushes like that and we're going to have the first baby lying in the incubator over there."

Dr. Shapiro was wrong that it would only be a few more pushes. Jordan's count was up to seventeen when the doctor announced that this was it. The baby's head was almost out. The next few moments were a little fuzzy, but she could have sworn Dr. Shapiro jumped back in his chair as she felt the baby moving out of her body.

She looked down to search his face for the severity of what was wrong with her baby, but the lights went out.

It couldn't have been more than a few seconds until the emergency generator kicked on and the room filled with the glow of fluorescent lighting. A few seconds may not seem like a long time normally, but they were the longest seconds of her life, frantically searching the dark for Dr. Shapiro's face. She was asking what was happening, but no one could hear her above their own questions.

When the lights came back on, the doctor was leaned back as far as possible, with his arms stretched out. In that instant, he looked like someone carrying a bag of toxic waste and trying hard to hold it as far away as possible. By the time anyone else looked, he was back to normal. Had she imagined it?

Dr. Shapiro laid the baby on her stomach as the nurse clamped both ends of the umbilical cord. It made a weird crunching sound as the doctor cut through it, permanently separating her body from her baby's.

She barely had a chance to look at her son before the other nurse in the room scooped him off her stomach and placed him in the incubator. She strained her neck to see what was going on as the nurse suctioned his mouth and nose and wiped his little body dry. It looked like they were being overly rough with him, but she couldn't see very well. When she heard him wailing at full volume she knew he was at least alive.

Another strong contraction reminded her she wasn't done yet.

"Ok, here we go, Jordan. Are you ready for baby number two?"

The second delivery was much easier than the first and before she knew it, both babies were lying next to each other, crying in the incubator. It probably helped that her mind was a whirling dervish from the medication, the pain, the emotions... and the questions. In the end, just one question won out.

"Can I hold them now?" Jordan forgot all about what had just happened to her body. She forgot about the unanswered questions and the terror on the doctor's face. All she wanted was to hold her babies.

The nurses were taking forever to finish whatever they were doing and Jordan's maternal instinct was going full force. Even though she trusted Dr. Shapiro completely, she needed to check them over herself.

One of the nurses placed the first baby in the cradle of her arm. He immediately nestled up to her and stopped crying. She was amazed at how much dark hair he had and at how alert he seemed. "Hello, sweetheart. I'm your mommy." The same nurse brought her second baby over and placed him in the crook of her other arm. She was stunned to see that they looked exactly the same. "Are they identical?"

"Actually, no. They're fraternal, but there are times even fraternal twins can wind up looking very similar."

Dr. Shapiro came up beside the nurse and peeked in at both babies before turning to Jordan. "We're going to need to run some blood work on them and a few other tests. It's totally standard stuff that every newborn has to go through. You need to get as much rest as you can, so I thought we'd go ahead and do them tonight if you have no objections."

Dr. Shapiro seemed hurried, like there was an emergency waiting for him in the next room. Jordan remembered jumping to the wrong conclusion about his intentions earlier and decided to just appreciate his consideration for her. She couldn't remember a time when she'd ever been more tired so rest did sound pretty good.

There really were certain tests to rule out genetic diseases that he needed to conduct, but what he saw during the delivery brought about a whole new set of questions. He wanted to check each of the babies over thoroughly, to make sure there wasn't something he had missed... some indicator. No matter how hard he tried, he couldn't erase the image that was burned into his mind.

"That actually sounds really good, Doc," Jordan decided. "Maybe I'll take a little nap while you run the tests then I'll be all refreshed when you're done. Can I have a little more time with them first, though?" Jordan barely took her eyes off her sons as she conversed with the doctor.

"Of course. You can have all the time you want." Dr. Shapiro pulled back the blanket from one of the baby's faces. "Have you decided on names for these little guys yet?"

"Yes." She raised her left arm slightly to introduce her son to the room. "This is Hudson Edgar," raising her other arm, "and this is Hayden Edgar."

Dr. Shapiro had been able to squelch his anxiety from Jordan and the nurses, but as he excused himself to "check on a few things," it hit him hard. He leaned against the wall outside Jordan's hospital door struggling to keep his delayed reaction from overwhelming him.

What is happening? He hadn't really been sleeping well lately, but there had been countless times over the years when he'd been sleep deprived and he'd never... Suddenly he needed a cigarette and a shot of something stronger than coffee.

When he reached the sanctity of his office, Roger did something he couldn't remember ever doing before. He locked his door. He sat down at his desk and reached into the very back of his top drawer. As he struggled to pull a cigarette out of the pack, he realized how shaky his hands had become. Lighting it was another struggle, but the first drag made it all worthwhile.

He was feeling a little steadier as he blew the smoke towards the open window but not enough to forget about the alcohol he had promised himself. He pulled the bottle of Jim Beam out of his bottom drawer and realized, as he brushed the dust off the top, there had been very few occasions where the job had gotten to him enough to call on his old friend Jim, and never while still on duty. His hands were still shaking as he lifted the bottle.

Leaning back in his office chair, smoking the last of his cigarette, he allowed the alcohol to work through his system. *Is there any possible way I could have seen what I think I saw?* There couldn't be. There just couldn't be and yet the memory continued to twist in his gut, securing its hold.

The delivery had been normal enough up until the first baby's head emerged. It was only a couple of seconds before the lights went out, but it was long enough to see the baby clearly. He could tell immediately that there was something seriously wrong with it. There were several veins in the baby's head that were much larger than he'd ever seen, and they were throbbing with the beat of the baby's heart. Then he saw the eyes.

He had no idea how many babies he had delivered in his lifetime, certainly in the thousands, but he had never seen one born with his eyes wide open.

If that had been the end of it, he may have been able to accept the memory, but the eyes were completely white. There wasn't a trace of an iris in either eye.

Then... as the infant emerged from his mother, the white eyes began filling with blood. They were dark as midnight by the time the jaw was out, and they squinted into a ghastly grimace. The mouth, full of ragged, pointy teeth, snarled up at the doctor.

That's when the lights went out, and if he were to be totally honest with himself, the darkness was the only thing that kept him from pulling away completely and allowing "it" to fall to the floor. When the lights came back on, he was looking at a perfectly normal newborn boy. Had he completely lost his mind?

The second baby's delivery was routine, except that the lights decided to play a trick with his mind again. When the second baby came out, the light reflected off the stirrup and made it look like light was coming up from behind the baby's head. It almost looked like a…

"Oh, Jesus!" he said aloud.

They hadn't marked the babies until after they were named. There would be no way of knowing which baby had been born first! With all of the confusion from the lights going out everyone had been so flustered. It wasn't like him to forget things like that. The nurses hadn't even put the hospital bands on until they'd been moved several times.

"Shit." The doctor shook his head as he took the last drag of his cigarette. In the long run it wouldn't really matter who was five minutes older anyway. As far as the other things were concerned, it had to have been the lights playing tricks on his eyes. Not only with the first baby but the second as well. Obviously there was something wrong with the lights or they wouldn't have gone out.

The more he thought about it, the more he remembered other situations where shadows distorted a person's appearance. *Of course, that had to have been what it was.*

He laughed out loud at the idea that a physician of his tenure could be so paranoid, especially after so many years without incident. His thoughts went to Edgar and Beverly Sullivan. *That was not related*, he assured himself. Their deaths must have spooked him more than he realized. It's not like it took supernatural influence for human beings to perform unthinkable acts.

He himself had handed both babies, who looked perfectly normal, to the nursing staff. None of the nurses saw anything whatsoever out of the ordinary. The light played tricks with his eyes. That's all it was. But even as he tossed his extinguished cigarette into the trash he reached for Jordan's file. He couldn't shake the nagging feeling that ghostly shadows were not all there was to it.

Chapter 9

As he walked through the front door, Roger couldn't remember a time when he had been happier to be home. Charlotte called a greeting from the kitchen, and he knew it would only be a matter of seconds before she started asking about the babies. He steadied himself and put on his best happy look.

Charlotte stayed at the hospital until Jordan was settled into her room, but, in her usual way, needed to do something productive to keep the wait from driving her insane.

She had reorganized the kitchen cupboards, packed up several boxes of used clothing for the local shelter, cleaned the fireplace in the doctor's study, and baked two pies. She had only called the hospital once but declined the receptionist's offer to track down the doctor for a status check. But when she heard the front door open, she folded the towel she was using to dry her hands, draped it across the oven door, and hurried out to greet her husband. She was beginning to feel as if Jordan and the babies really were family.

"So… how did everything go and how are…" Charlotte stopped mid-sentence when she looked up and saw her husband's face. "Oh, my God, what's happened?"

No matter how hard he tried, Roger Shapiro could never hide his emotions from his perceptive wife. His feelings of dread and confusion melted away from the love and admiration he felt for her. He laughed for the first time in what seemed like days.

"Everything is fine. The babies look perfectly healthy. That doesn't mean the tests won't show a developmental disease that isn't physically obvious at this stage, but so far so good." His smile was genuine as he held his wife by the shoulders and kissed her forehead. "It's just been a really long day today."

"Well, that's a relief! You had me scared half to death. You looked like you had seen a ghost. How is Jordan doing?"

"She was pretty tired, but I've yet to see a new mother who isn't. It was generous of you to give her time to rest before you meet the babies." He knew his wife well. "I peeked in right before I left and she was sound asleep. And… I had one of the nurses take about 50 pictures of the babies with your digital camera." He handed the camera to Charlotte as she grabbed both sides of his face and kissed his lips. Roger smiled. "All in all, both deliveries went very smoothly and it wound up taking about 45 minutes less than I expected, so that was good." Dr. Shapiro stretched his back and rubbed his eyes. "You'd think it was me who went through childbirth. I'm exhausted."

"Well, don't work tonight, Roger. Sit down and go through the pictures with me while we wait for dinner." Charlotte knew the answer would be no even before he started shaking his head.

"Would you like a drink?" The mints he had eaten on the way home were more than enough to hide the evidence of his earlier indulgence in the office.

"That would be wonderful. If you don't mind, I'm going to head on into the study and do a little bit of work." He saw the initial signs of her protest and raised his hand. "Don't worry; I just want to look back through some old charts. I'm not going to strain myself and I'll bet I'm still ready for bed before you are."

Knowing his tendency to dive into work headfirst and lose himself, Charlotte took that bet and won.

Roger barely noticed Charlotte enter the room and set his drink down on the desk as he rifled through boxes of old files. He pulled two files from the cabinet marked "S". The names across the top were Edgar Sullivan and Beverly Sullivan. He hadn't remembered exactly when he had met them, but based on the first entry in their charts, it had been a little over 22 years earlier.

There was a time when he didn't think he would ever forget a moment of the time he spent knowing the Sullivans. Scanning through the cover pages of the personal files he'd maintained, he realized how many details he'd forgotten.

They were one of his first celebrity families, but they weren't celebrities in the beginning. He sat back in his chair with his arms behind his head and remembered the first time they met.

The Sullivans had been trying to have a baby for about a year when they sought out his assistance. Back then there were no fertility experts, and even if there were, the Sullivans would have been in no position to afford one. Edgar was a struggling writer/producer and Beverly was a waitress at a neighborhood diner.

Even with Dr. Shapiro's limited equipment, the tests clearly showed that the infertility issue had nothing to do with Beverly. Edgar was sterile and Dr. Shapiro knew someone who wanted to help them.

Roger didn't make the referral lightly but it was the same man who'd helped him and Charlotte with their own fertility problems. When Roger saw the desperation in Beverly's eyes, he couldn't help but think of his beloved Charlotte. How much had their lives changed after their sons were born? The deal had worked out fine for them and Charlotte never even had to know. Why shouldn't he introduce the Sullivans to Tanas? But had it really worked out for them?

Roger Shapiro delivered his own children, so he knew firsthand the trial he and Charlotte had been spared. He saw the mangled corpse that should have been a second twin when his oldest son, Roger Jr., was born. The lights hadn't failed that night and he saw with his own eyes the mutilation that looked nothing short of demonic.

The fetus had been dead for several weeks so it was difficult to tell what was a deformity and what was deterioration but it was the teeth that would haunt the doctor's dreams for the rest of his life.

No one in the world ever found out the baby existed, not even Charlotte. The remains were included with the afterbirth and buried under the apple tree in the back yard. Roger Jr. turned out just fine, and the rest of their life certainly didn't seem anything short of blessed. Why wouldn't he want to share that with another couple?

As far as Roger was concerned, he knew first hand that Tanas had the ability to make dreams come true. If a haunting memory of a deformed baby was the worst torment he had to carry for the life he and Charlotte had shared over the years, it was a small price to pay.

Of course, there was always the fear that a greater bill would come due at some later date. It was that fear that tipped his opinion toward referring the Sullivans. A referral meant that his own responsibilities to Tanas would transfer to Edgar.

When Beverly came into his office only a few months later requesting a pregnancy test, Dr. Shapiro knew they had gone to Tanas. For that reason, he wasn't surprised when the Sullivan's financial success started growing along with their baby. They were all on the fast track to riches and it was all thanks to Tanas.

There were times when he felt guilty about pawning his burden off on them, but he barely knew them at that time. They were strangers. As the doctor watched Edgar's interest in the pregnancy and later the adoration for his daughter, Roger felt confident he'd made the right choice. As much as he'd always felt their arrangements were deals with the devil, it seemed like the Sullivans had come out smiling the same way he himself had.

Over the years, thoughts of Jordan's birthright became distant. It wasn't like he could ever talk to anyone about it and as far as the doctor was concerned, Edgar Sullivan was Jordan's father in every way that mattered. If any problem of birthright surfaced in years to come, the doctor had no doubt how he would handle it. He would simply say there must have been a mistake with Edgar's initial test.

Over the years the doctor thought less about the little deal he'd made so long ago. Eventually it became a part of the distant past... until recently.

As far as he knew, Jordan didn't even know Tanas existed, but how could he be sure?

The doctor jumped when Charlotte knocked lightly on the door asking if he was going to work all night or come to bed with her. He had taken just one break earlier in the evening to eat dinner. Other than that, he had spent the entire evening engrossed in a report or a memory.

He put his files away for the night and followed his wife up to bed. He fully expected to fall asleep as soon as his head hit the pillow. He was wrong. Roger Shapiro lay in bed trying to stop the trip down memory lane, but no matter what he tried, his thoughts kept wandering back to the Sullivans. He couldn't shake the feeling that Jordan's babies had more to do with Tanas than he knew. Roger thought back to the ways the Sullivans' lives changed after his referral.

Around the same time that Beverly became pregnant with Jordan, Edgar became an overnight sensation. His first blockbuster was an action film about the end of the world. It was a low-budget flick, like all of his previous works, but for some reason this one took off. The movie grossed over $500,000 and more than half of it wound up in the Sullivan's account.

Edgar's success grew exponentially, as he quickly became the most sought after name in Hollywood. Beverly left the diner, but never became the social leader the world had expected her to be. As a matter of fact, both she and Edgar became almost reclusive. They didn't belong to any religious or social groups and it seemed their only form of entertainment was the occasional cocktail party. Even those were usually focused around Jordan.

The Sullivans were always very friendly people who... who what? There was something underneath the surface that kept them from falling into any traditional stereotypes, but what was it?

As far as their parenting skills were concerned, both of the Sullivans worshiped Jordan. She was denied nothing, but wasn't a typical rich kid. Not only did they raise her without a nanny, they read to her each night at bedtime, ate dinner together, they knew the names of her teachers and classmates, and they were quick to join in any game she suggested.

The things the doctor was remembering may have been more protective than most Hollywood families but they weren't earth shattering by any means. Was there something he was forgetting, or was he looking for something that wasn't really there?

He had delivered Jordan himself, and there hadn't been anything abnormal about her birth.

Sometimes survival of the fittest happens at very early stages.

The voice in the back of his mind was so clear it was almost as if someone had spoken aloud.

Things would be clearer in the morning. He was just a spooked old man thinking about monsters under the bed. There was nothing about the Sullivans that would warrant the kind of sci-fi imaginings racing through his mind. Even if he did refer them to Tanas, it didn't mean they had to accept his deal. And even if they did, he was their doctor not their keeper.

The last thing he remembered was looking at the time on his digital alarm clock. The numbers switched to 12:00. "The bewitching hour," he murmured. A weak moan from Charlotte brought him back to reality. He kissed her cheek lightly before settling into his own pillow for sleep.

Chapter 10

Jordan woke at 9:30 am, after a good 13 hours of completely uninterrupted sleep. The bed felt nice as she stretched herself awake, but the pulling on her stitches reminded her why she was in a hospital bed. That was the instant it hit her, the babies! She had slept for 13 hours!

Babies wake up every few hours! She reached for the nurse button and pressed it harder than she would have needed. Within a matter of seconds, a smiling nurse was entering her room.

"How are the babies? I didn't wake up all night! Who took care of them? Are they ok?" Jordan was aware she was blubbering but her sense of urgency was close to frantic.

"They're doing fantastic. The other nurses and I took care of anything they needed during the night. You're going to have your hands full. Those two woke up every hour until we put them in their own bassinets. New mothers need to get as much rest as they can while they're here so we have a policy. 'Never wake a sleeping mommy.'" The nurse winked as she spoke and Jordan's fears dissipated… a little.

"Could I see them now?" Jordan barely had a chance to meet them before she'd become Rip Van Winkle.

"Absolutely! Let me take your vitals real quick, and I'll go bring those babies in to you. They are sure cuties and it's a good thing they have ankle tags. Otherwise there would be no way we could tell them apart. Normally we like to keep twins in the same bassinette, but you've got a couple of independent little guys there already. Neither of them was willing to sleep next to his brother. I have a feeling you're going to be splitting up a lot of fights in about 3 years." The nurse smiled the knowing smile of a mother who's broken up her share of sibling spats.

After the nurse finished checking her out, she helped Jordan into the bathroom. The entire process was far more painful than she had ever imagined it would be. She was grateful when she was finally able to crawl back into bed. Once she was settled into a comfortable position, the nurse went to get the babies she had barely met.

A few very long minutes later, the nurse came through the door wheeling a bassinette filled with two screaming newborns.

"I guess they still don't want to bunk together." The nurse pushed the bassinette next to Jordan's bed and both babies instantly stopped crying when they heard her voice.

"Good morning, babies." Jordan had never heard her voice sound quite like that before. She sounded like... a mother.

"How are my sweeties this morning?" She leaned over to pick up one of the twins but the nurse stopped her mid-swoop.

"Let me help you, honey. You need to remember that you just delivered two babies. You need to take it easy for a little while. Let me hand them to you." The nurse picked up the first baby and placed him in Jordan's arms.

"Hayden. What's this I hear about you not wanting to sleep with your brother?" She smiled down at his face and rubbed his cheek as he stared into her eyes.

No matter how many times she'd seen it, the nurse never tired of the way newborns and their mothers gazed at each other.

The nurse's thoughts of maternal love were interrupted. "Wait a minute, you can tell them apart without looking at their name bands?"

"I guess I can. Well, hold on, maybe I only think I can." Jordan confirmed that she was indeed holding Hayden by lifting the blanket and checking his ankle bracelet. "Yep, this is Hayden alright. Maybe that means I'm prepared to be your mother after all, huh?" She cooed the question to Hayden as she held his tiny fingers.

"Could you take Hayden for a moment while I hold Hudson?" Jordan raised her arm to the waiting nurse who carefully took the swaddled newborn from his mother. She laid him expertly in the bassinette in exchange for his brother.

As soon as the nurse placed Hudson in her arms, Jordan's eyes filled with tears. She couldn't imagine her heart being able to hold more. Then she looked into his eyes and realized it could.

"Hello, Hudson." She kissed his forehead softly and he slowly closed his eyes. He felt so warm and smelled so good. She couldn't imagine anything in the world being better than the feel of his head against her cheek. She didn't even know she remembered the song until she started singing "You are my sunshine" softly as he slept.

And then Jordan knew what would be better... holding them both. The nurse helped her arrange both babies and, after propping pillows and making slight baby adjustments, excused herself to continue on her morning rounds.

Alone with her babies for the first time, Jordan was amazed at the amount of love she already felt for them. For the first time since her parents died, her heart finally felt whole again.

Chapter 11

While Jordan was bonding with her babies, Dr. Shapiro was busy studying blood samples in the lab. He received the latest results on his desk that morning and they showed, again, that everything was normal.

He had been looking over the slides for over an hour when he finally accepted the results. Everything was perfectly fine with the twins. He allowed himself to accept the excuse that after 40 years in practice, he was bound to come across at least a few things that couldn't be explained by modern science. His forced acceptance didn't stop the tremble that had recently settled into his hands. He just needed to calm his nerves. He opened the desk drawer for the bottle that would never be dusty again.

He cleaned up his work and made his way down the hall to Jordan's room. Now that he had run every possible blood test and found nothing out of the ordinary, he wanted to see, in person, how his newest patients were doing.

"Good morning." Dr. Shapiro knocked lightly as he poked his head in Jordan's room. Regardless of his previous assurances to himself, he was relieved to find her singing and rocking the twins. "How's our little family doing today?"

"Oh, Dr. Shapiro, we're doing great. Can you believe how perfect they are?" Jordan looked down at her sons in awe. "I can't believe they're really mine." She suddenly remembered the blood tests and was curious about the results.

"Have you heard anything about the tests they did on the babies? Did everything turn out alright?"

"I actually just came from the lab and everything is perfect. You have two very healthy sons here." He pulled the blankets away from the babies' faces as he peered in at them. "The nurses were right; they are identical, aren't they?"

"I guess so, but for some reason I seem to be able to tell them apart pretty easily. I suppose it's the maternal instinct Mom always used to talk about. When do you think we'll be able to go home?"

"Now don't be so anxious, young lady. With insurance the way it is today, we barely get you checked in before you're released. Take advantage of this opportunity to rest. I can assure you you're going to need it." The doctor gave her a wink then continued, "We'll have you on your way home by tomorrow afternoon. Charlotte will be picking you up. She stopped in early this morning while you were still sleeping and let me know she already has the car seats set up in our car. Don't rush it; you really do need to get your rest."

Jordan laughed, "I don't think that's going to be a problem. I slept 13 hours last night, so I'm wide awake and feeling great. Right now I just want to get to know my babies and maybe have some breakfast. Do you people ever feed us around here?" Dr. Shapiro teased her about how hungry she must be to want hospital food then excused himself to check on other patients.

One of the nurses brought an extra bassinette in so the babies could sleep while she ate breakfast. Jordan didn't remember ever being quite so hungry and polished off every single morsel of food she'd been given.

She peeked over the edges of the bassinettes and saw both babies sleeping soundly. After carefully pushing the breakfast tray away from her bed, she pulled herself into a sitting position.

"That wasn't so bad," she said aloud. The rest of her day was filled with information and instruction on breast-feeding, diaper changes, bathing techniques, and caring for herself during her recovery. She wasn't quite prepared for the pressure washing they like to call a "sitz bath," but she survived. Besides her babies, the only bright spot was when Charlotte came in with a bouquet of balloons and two huge stuffed bears.

Jordan laughed until she thought her stitches would break at the sight of Charlotte maneuvering the bears and balloons through the door.

"Well, I guess that will give me some practice carrying those two little guys around your house, huh?" Charlotte brushed some of the hairs that had fallen out of place away from her eyes.

"Oh, I hope not… based on the number of times the bears' heads hit the doorway that might be detrimental to their health." They both laughed again and both babies woke up crying.

"Well, look at you," Charlotte cooed over the tops of both bassinettes. At the sound of her voice Hayden immediately quieted but Hudson was still trying out his lungs. She reached in and scooped him into her arms effortlessly. "Well, you're as light as a feather, young man."

Jordan watched Charlotte cradle Hudson like an expert. She was again overwhelmed with feelings of love and appreciation. She still missed her own mother, but watching Charlotte with Hudson was certainly the next best thing. Her eyes filled with tears and her heart filled with pride. For the first time in a long time she felt truly blessed.

After the babies were fed and held to the point of exhaustion, they both drifted off to their own little dream worlds. Likewise, Jordan and Charlotte were lost in their own thoughts as they looked at the twins in silence. They became aware of each other at the same moment and started laughing.

"It's amazing, isn't it?" Jordan began. "A month ago I wouldn't have thought I would ever have a family again and now. I… well… it's a miracle, Charlotte. I don't remember ever feeling so peaceful. They are truly little angels, and they are so very lucky to have a grandmother like you." Hearing Jordan's words made Charlotte's eyes fill with tears. Once again the ladies shared a teary embrace.

Charlotte was the first to pull away and wipe her eyes. "It's me who's the lucky one, my dear. Our oldest son Roger lives so far away that I hardly ever get to see my grandchildren and the youngest, Daryl, isn't any closer to marriage than the day he was born." She looked down at the sleeping babies. "Ok now, enough of this sappy stuff," Charlotte spoke softly. "We still have some planning to do before we take these babies home tomorrow.

"I put together some information about nannies. The list I compiled is individuals I would personally vouch for. I have checked their references and met with each of them personally, so I feel very comfortable recommending any of them." Charlotte's business-like summary turned personal.

"My favorite is Anna. She's been working for a very dear friend of mine the past two years."

"If she's your choice, then she's mine too," Jordan interrupted.

"If you'd like, I could ask her to drop by the hospital this afternoon so you could get acquainted a little." Charlotte was leery about making such a large decision without Jordan's input.

"You know," Jordan said, "at this point I think I have more confidence in your decisions than I do in my own anyway." She giggled a little, putting Charlotte's mind at ease. "If you wouldn't mind asking her, I'd like to have her move in now so she's ready and waiting when we get home from the hospital tomorrow. I truly do trust your judgment completely. I know I'll love her, too."

"Alright then, I will talk to her as soon as I leave here. She's going to be very excited. She loves babies!"

They said their goodbyes and on her way out, Charlotte bent to kiss each baby on the forehead.

When her lips touched Hayden's skin, she pulled back slightly at the shock of static electricity. "Oh, goodness! One day old and I've already given him a shock. Let's try that again." She kissed the same spot hoping to erase the sting that was still tingling on her upper lip.

"Get some sleep and if you need anything at all, give me a call. Otherwise I'll be back tomorrow to take you home." As Charlotte walked through the doorway, Jordan was already fading to sleep.

Chapter 12

Jordan woke at the crack of dawn, feeling like she herself had been reborn. Today was the day she would be taking her children home! She looked at the clock on the wall and saw it was barely 6 am. The nurses had told her last night she would be discharged around noon, after the doctor had made his rounds. Six hours seemed like forever to wait.

In reality, the hours flew by way too quickly. It took longer than she had expected to eat breakfast, shower, and get herself dressed. By the time she was ready, it was after 10:00. Then it was time to give the babies their baths. The nurses wanted her to bathe them herself before they left the hospital, and although it went fine, it was certainly not a small undertaking. As she was fastening the last snaps on Hudson's outfit, Dr. Shapiro came through the door.

"So, I understand you're a little anxious to get home, is that right?" As always the doctor was carrying a clipboard with a chart attached.

Jordan hardly looked up as he entered the room. "Hey, Doc, we sure are! I'll tell you though, things take a lot longer to do than they used to. This morning has flown by!"

"Well, let me take a peek at those babies to see how they're doing." Dr. Shapiro chuckled slightly to himself. Jordan had dressed the twins from head to toe in outfits she had specifically asked Charlotte to bring to the hospital. He wondered how she expected him to examine the twins when the only things showing were little pudgy faces.

It didn't really matter, though. He had peeked in on them before his rounds started at six. He knew how anxious Jordan was to go home and there was no reason to keep her waiting any longer than necessary. "How are you feeling, my dear?" the doctor asked as he lifted her wrist to take a pulse.

"Pretty good actually. I was a little sore while I was taking my shower, but overall I feel alright." Jordan was surprised at how quickly she was healing. She felt 100 times better than she had the day before.

"Then you're all ready to get out of here. Charlotte is pulling the car up to the front entrance so she should be right up. She and Anna will take your things down first and then come up for the babies. Hospital policy is that they need to be in their car seats when they leave, and you need to ride out in one of our fully-loaded wheelchairs."

Dr. Shapiro saw the look on Jordan's face and stopped. "Is something wrong?" He could tell from her expression that something hadn't set right and assumed it was because she couldn't carry her own babies out of the hospital. "Don't worry; it's just hospital policy that we take you out in a wheelchair. You'll have plenty of time to carry those babies all over town as soon as you get away from this stuffy place."

"I'm sure you're right. And don't worry, it'll be great." Jordan's disappointment actually had nothing to do with their transportation. She hadn't realized Anna would be coming along for the trip home. She had been looking forward to a homecoming with just Charlotte and the babies. Even though it had been her idea to have Anna start right away, Jordan expected their first meeting to be at the house. She supposed she would need to get used to another person being involved as soon as they got there anyway, but for some reason, she suddenly felt like an outsider in her own homecoming. She sat down on the edge of her bed and waited.

After a few brief moments of feeling sorry for herself, Charlotte burst through the door with a "Good morning, my dear! Today we take you home!"

Jordan wasn't sure if she'd expected the two women to come through the door arm-in-arm or engrossed in some inside joke or something, but she was surprised and relieved to see Charlotte alone. "Are you ready to get out of here?"

"Absolutely I am. The babies are bathed and dressed and ready for their first car ride. The doctor said that Anna would be with you." Jordan hoped the doctor hadn't noticed her disappointment and forewarned his wife to come alone.

Charlotte whipped around to face the door. "Oh, my gosh," she exclaimed. "In my excitement to get you, I must have left her behind somewhere. The poor girl insisted on carrying both car seats up here, but we were in the elevator together so she can't be far behind."

As if on cue, Anna came through the door easily managing her load of infant seats. "I'm so sorry, my dear. That was very thoughtless of me to walk so quickly when you were carrying such a burden." Charlotte was trying to help take some of the items from Anna.

"No problem, ma'am. I knew how excited you were to get up here, and I certainly didn't have any trouble finding my way. You must be Jordan." Anna had set the rest of her load on the floor and was extending her hand in a greeting. "It's nice to meet you. I've heard a great deal about you and your babies." Jordan shook Anna's hand and instantly liked her. Once again she was astounded at how her emotional worries were for nothing when Charlotte was in charge.

"I've heard wonderful things about you too, and I'm very excited to have you help raise the boys." Jordan reached out her left hand and touched the nearest bassinette. "This is Hudson." Extending her right hand, she touched the other bassinette and introduced Hayden.

Anna took a few steps closer to get a better view of the babies. "They are beautiful! I sure hope I'll be able to tell them apart." Anna reached in and lightly stroked Hayden's cheek as he lay sleeping.

"I second that," Charlotte half joked. "Fortunately, they have ankle bands with their names on them. That will get us through the first few weeks anyway. Would you mind taking Jordan's personal items and the baby gifts down to the car while I help her get the twins loaded into their car seats? The good doctor would be happy to help you. Right, dear?" She gave her husband a wink.

"Even after all these years you can tell she wears the pants in our family." Everyone knew the doctor was teasing his wife, but they also knew it was true.

The car ride was relatively uneventful. Jordan sat in the back seat of the Shapiro's car with the boys. She was busy pointing out the sights that would become much more familiar as the years passed. Anna drove and Charlotte videotaped the whole event from the front seat. Jordan couldn't imagine a more perfect way to take her sons home and again was thankful for having an angel like Charlotte in her life.

As they pulled into the circular driveway, Jordan saw the first sign announcing, "It's a boy!" She laughed out loud at the second one that read, "It's another boy!"

The front walk was lined with several different shades of blue balloons and a huge "Welcome Home!" banner that covered a good amount of the front entrance. "Oh, Charlotte, this is wonderful."

"I wish I could take some of the credit. This was entirely Anna's doing."

Jordan could see Anna's face turn slightly red and knew she wasn't comfortable with accolades. "Oh, Anna, thank you so much! I don't know how you even found time to get moved in on such short notice, much less all of this. Thank you so much for making our homecoming so perfect!"

Jordan wasn't proud of herself as she realized her tendency to jump to conclusions about people... especially lately. *Not exactly the best role model, Mom.* She would definitely try to be more accepting in the future.

Chapter 13

The days following their homecoming were a whirlwind of activities as they all adjusted to their new surroundings and activities. Charlotte came to the house by 9 am and stayed until 5 pm every week day. Jordan worried that she was asking too much of her friend, but Charlotte assured her that, with the doctor's busy schedule, it wasn't a problem at all. She wanted to spend as much time at the house as possible, at least for the first few months. After that they would play it by ear.

Anna used the time Charlotte was around to catch up on sleep or run errands, depending on the priority that day. Jordan was better at caring for the babies than any of them had expected, but Anna was the one who took most of the night feedings. All in all, the house ran like clockwork almost from the very beginning.

Jordan felt better with each day, and the boys were beginning to settle into a semblance of a schedule.

Of course, that still only meant a few hours of having their eyes open before they closed again in exhaustion, but it didn't matter what the babies were doing. All three women watched in amazement as they wiggled on a blanket, yawned, sneezed, or just lay perfectly still. Jordan didn't have a frame of reference, but both Charlotte and Anna marveled at how fortunate they were to have such good babies.

Both Charlotte and Anna joined Jordan for the babies' ten-day checkup. They were like mother hens as the nurse weighed and measured each baby. They held hands to comfort each other as the twins received their shots, and they breathed a collective sigh of relief when the doctor proclaimed the twins to be the healthiest babies he'd seen all day.

After the appointment, Jordan took the group out for a celebratory milk shake at a neighborhood diner. It wasn't often that they allowed themselves such calorie filled pleasures and they were all looking forward to the indulgence.

The three ladies had been engrossed in conversation when their waitress approached the table. Jordan hadn't noticed the familiar smirk, but her heart skipped a beat when she heard the voice from her past.

"Well, if it isn't Jordan Sullivan. These aren't your twins, are they? I hadn't even heard you were dating anyone much less married."

The voice belonged to Margo Edwards. She and Jordan had gone to high school together and, for whatever reason, Margo had always taken great joy in downgrading Jordan whenever possible.

"Margo, it's good to see you again," Jordan lied. "These are my friends, Charlotte Shapiro and Anna Pollowski, and yes, these are my sons." Jordan didn't feel the need to share her babies' names or origin with her old classmate. As much as she wanted to belittle Margo and beat her at her own game, she couldn't bring herself to do it. In truth, she never could. She rationalized it in her own mind as being the better person, but the fact was, she didn't have the guts.

Margo made a point of appearing apathetic as she peered into the stroller. "Huh. They certainly have a distinct... look about them don't they?" She had a knack for insulting someone in the worst possible way without ever actually saying anything derogatory. Jordan knew her children were beautiful but she hated the fact that Margo could still push her buttons. She tried to remind herself that Margo was just a mean person but a part of her wanted to put the snotty has-been in her place. A big part of her wanted to, just once, wipe the smirk off Margo's hateful face. Jordan decided to take the high road.

"We'd like to order three chocolate milk shakes and put those on one tab please." Jordan did her best to control the conversation, but her patience was wearing thin. She hadn't had the strength to stand up to Margo in school and perhaps it was her maternal instinct kicking in then, but at that moment, she wanted nothing more than to slap the smug look off the waitress's face.

"Big spender, huh? Anything else?" Margo may not have been the sharpest tool in the shed, but she knew when she was being blown off.

Margo had been the sweetheart of their high school and clearly wasn't happy about having to wait on an inferior like Jordan. In her glory days, Margo had been named head cheerleader as a freshman; she was voted most likely to succeed as a sophomore and then there were her pageant titles.

Margo had been the center of local gossip circles for months after she'd come back from college with her tail between her legs. Apparently, flunking out in her second semester wasn't the level of success her admirers had come to expect.

"That will be all... thanks." Jordan felt a gratifying twinge of superiority as she emphasized the server/servee relationship without actually saying it directly. Maybe she wasn't as bad at being snotty as she always thought. Margo left the table slightly deflated, but Jordan wasn't naive enough to think it would last any longer than the trip back to the kitchen. A fleeting thought about spit in her shake made her question the wisdom of her shallow victory.

"Well, she's certainly a shining light. Is she a friend of yours?" Charlotte asked. The ladies were so intrigued by Jordan's relationship with the offensive waitress that no one noticed one of the twins' eyes fly open and fill with blood.

"No, definitely not. We went to school together, and for some reason she's always hated me. As far as I know, I never…" Jordan's story was cut short by a piercing scream from the kitchen.

"Oh, my God, I wonder what in the world is going on." Their heads turned quickly toward the kitchen then immediately to the babies.

Both Jordan and Charlotte's hands went instinctively to the stroller in an act of protectiveness. Jordan looked inside to see that both boys had their eyes closed in sleep, undisturbed by the screams.

Most of the wait staff was hurrying into the kitchen as customers exchanged glances of confusion and fear. Amid the screams and commotion from the back, someone was yelling, "Call 911!"

A waitress hurried across the restaurant from the kitchen to the front counter looking white as a ghost. Apparently she was the one in charge of making sure business continued as usual. She announced to the room that there was a slight accident in the kitchen, but everything was under control. Within seconds, several customers approached her to pay their bill and inquire about the emergency.

The ambulance arrived at the back door, so none of the customers saw the paramedics come in with the gurney or leave with their patient. Customers only knew the emergency was over when they heard the sirens of the ambulance pulling out of the parking lot.

Employees must have been told to get back to work, because they all came into the main dining area at the same time, talking amongst themselves and shaking their heads.

It was several minutes before someone made her way to Jordan's table but it wasn't Margo. "We're so sorry for the disturbance. The waitress from your section had an accident in the kitchen. It's all taken care of now, but I'm afraid we're going to be closing for the rest of the day. Here's a certificate for 20% off your next visit and again, please accept our apologies." The bright, young waitress did her best to appear cheerful, but it was obvious she was still quite upset.

"No problem at all," Charlotte consoled. "The young lady who was injured, Margo, she is actually an old friend of my companion here." She gestured towards Jordan. "Could you tell us what's going on?"

The young girl apparently only needed someone to ask. "I guess she was bent over to get some malt glasses out of a cupboard when one of the cooks was taking the broaster to the sink to clean it. He didn't see her crouched down and I guess she didn't see him walking towards her. Anyway, he tripped over her and lost his grip on the pan." She paused. "I was in that cupboard myself a few minutes before Margo.

"It was weird, like a freak accident or something because when Josh ran into her, she fell over sideways. He was trying not to step on her but he dropped one side of the pan and the boiling oil spilled right on her face and chest." The girl shook her head to demonstrate how tragic the event was while Charlotte, Jordan, and Anna looked at her in horror.

Wipe the smirk off her hateful face rang through Jordan's mind.

Surely though no one would ever think she would wish something like that on another person, even if they could read her thoughts. She shook her head to dismiss her ridiculous train of guilty thoughts, and the waitress continued.

"The manager put a cold towel on her face right away, because I guess hot oil is hardest to cool down or something. Then someone said that might be bad if she started to get blisters, so they took her into the walk-in freezer until the ambulance got here. She was awake and everything and at first it didn't look too bad, but it kept getting worse." The girl put her hands to her face to cover a sob. "I don't really know how she's doing. The manager said she was going to be fine but I think they have to say that." The girl's tears started to build again. "They're taking her to the Kindred Hospital on El Cajon."

"Thank you for letting us know. We will certainly keep her in our prayers. My husband is a doctor and I know they've made great advances in burn care. I'm sure she's going to be fine." Years of being a doctor's wife had trained Charlotte in the art of reassurance, but it also taught her that burns of that nature rarely ever turn out well. She turned to her companions.

"Why don't we get our things together and head back to the house for now. I don't know about you two, but I've certainly lost my taste for a milk shake." The others nodded in agreement as they gathered their belongings.

They rode in silence for most of the drive. Each lost in her own thoughts about what had just happened. Jordan's feelings were bouncing all over the place. She certainly would never have wished something like Margo's accident on anyone, but for some reason she couldn't shake the feeling that someone had, in fact, granted her wish. She couldn't deny the fact that she was thinking terrible thoughts about her long-time arch nemesis, but it wasn't like there was someone out there granting her wishes, was there?

Margo had been cruel to so many people, not only Jordan, but everyone who wasn't in her little circle of acceptance. Maybe justice had been served.

It was the twins who finally broke the silence. Hayden woke up first, looked around for a second, before full out wailing. With a start, Hudson woke and joined his brother in the scream fest. They were hungry, but fortunately they were almost home. Jordan did her best to console them by singing the ABC song.

Chapter 14

Months flew by as the twins continued to grow and learn new things every day. All too quickly, they were getting ready to celebrate their first birthday. Both boys had started crawling at around eight months, but after eleven months Hudson started walking around furniture. It didn't seem like it would be long before both were up and running. Jordan, Anna, and Charlotte were always joking about how much trouble they would all be in when the boys were fully mobile, but there was more truth to it than any of them knew.

Each of the ladies settled into her role in the boys' lives early on. Charlotte was the loving grandmother who played with them and rocked them. Anna was the one who did most of the cleaning and cooking in the house, but she was also the one who took care of the boys when Jordan needed to get something done. And Jordan was... Mom. She was the one who fed them and bathed them. She was the one they would reach for at the slightest injury... at least most of the time.

Jordan had planned their birthday party with excitement, but realized she was still just as anti-social as ever. The sparse guest list consisted of Charlotte, Dr. Shapiro, and Anna.

She really didn't mind the short guest list and actually felt very fortunate to have such wonderful friends, but she did feel a little bad for the boys. They had each other but no other children for friends. They were both so independent when they played that she never really thought about them needing other people. They never even played with each other. Still, she thought socializing with others might be good for them. She decided after the birthday excitement faded she would look into enrolling them in daycare one or two days a week.

On the day of the birthday party, Anna and Charlotte had gone out shopping for some last minute things while Jordan dressed the boys. They looked like such little men in their matching suits, and for the millionth time she was shocked at how fast the time had gone.

It seemed like only a couple of months ago when she brought the babies into the house for the first time. They had both seemed so aware as they looked around the room from the security of their car seats. At the same time, she also couldn't remember what life had been like before the boys were born. Her life had become so completely filled by their existence that she finally realized how empty it had been before they were born.

Jordan thought back to her pregnancy. It certainly wasn't her first choice to be a single mother at 21, and yet it turned out to be exactly what she needed. She had no idea how her babies came to be, but for whatever reason, it didn't matter. While fate can sometimes be unbelievably cruel, it can also be undeniably kind. She smiled down at her boys.

As they sat side by side, looking at her like they'd been modeling for years, she couldn't help but chuckle at their puffed chests and perfect posture. They knew how cute they were and that made it all the more adorable. Jordan wrapped her arms around both boys for one big family hug. The doorbell sounded.

"It looks like someone is here to tell you both 'Happy birthday!'" It took some maneuvering but with their recently perfected skills of standing on their own, she was able to pick up one twin in each arm and carry them down the main staircase. Jordan hollered, "Come in!" from the middle of the stairway and by the time she set the boys down on the marble floor of the foyer, the front door was swinging open with force.

"Sorry about the door!" Dr. Shapiro used his knee to open the door too hard and it flung wide with surprising speed. Fortunately, the doctor noticed it swinging back towards him and was able to brace the ball of his foot against the backlash.

Jordan was surprised to find the doctor, Charlotte, and Anna all struggling under the burden of what seemed like a hundred presents. The boys were so excited they immediately dropped to their knees to speed crawl.

She greeted everyone with hugs, as she tried to lighten their burdens equally. Meanwhile the boys tugged at pant legs and put their arms up to be held. Jordan realized it would have been more help if she'd just corralled the boys.

With significant effort, the group made their way to the living room and Jordan set her armload on the coffee table. She took the presents from the doctor so he could be the first to pick up the boys. He was the only one at the party who didn't see them daily.

Charlotte wasn't joking when she said he'd been working long hours. Jordan saw the bags under his eyes and wished he was able to delegate more responsibility at the hospital. His exhaustion didn't dampen his spirits, though, and he seemed genuinely excited to see the boys. The boys loved playing with the only man in their lives and the infrequency of his visits only made them more excited to see him. The doctor was always the one to throw them in the air or bounce them on his knee. When they saw him they immediately thought of fun.

He spun around in a circle with one twin under each arm until Jordan and Charlotte started to worry about his balance. There probably weren't a lot of patients in his hospital who would believe the image of the highly respected doctor spinning around and making helicopter noises, like it was his own first birthday.

Eventually they all settled into the living room and Roger set the boys down in front of a mountain of presents.

"I don't think I'll be able to do that move much longer," he managed. Winded but smiling, the doctor dropped into the chair that was always reserved for him. Whether he was there once a week or once a year, it would always be his chair. It was a simple, square shaped, dark brown leather side chair with overstuffed arms. It didn't specifically have a place in the room but at the same time, there was nowhere in the world it wouldn't fit in.

The boys weren't phased as they continued their helicopter spins, made a b-line for the coffee table, and started pulling at brightly wrapped presents. An avalanche seemed certain. The birthday party wasn't Jordan's first day with the boys, though, so she anticipated their moves just in time. She set Hudson on Anna's lap and Hayden on Charlotte's lap, then handed the camera to the doctor. Jordan assumed the job of present sorter and handed each boy a present to unwrap.

Everyone watched as the toddlers tried to figure out what in the world the brightly colored boxes with dangling ribbon were all about. Hayden was busy playing with a bow he had pulled off his package, while Hudson used his box as a drum.

They all laughed at the entertainment until the doctor suggested the twins find out what was actually inside some of those boxes.

The doctor was busy zooming in and out to feature each boy, without missing much of what the other one did. He seemed a natural behind the lens. Actually, it didn't much matter what the task at hand was, the doctor always seemed to master things immediately. Well... almost everything.

"Ok now, which one is Hayden again? You'd think by now I could tell these two apart but I still have no idea." He didn't say it in a way that undermined his intelligence or apologized in any way. It was simply a statement. That was, perhaps, the trait Jordan loved most in the doctor. His world was based on fact and fiction. Emotion was reserved for his wife.

Jordan pointed to the appropriate twin and chuckled because it still seemed that only she could easily tell who was who. The doctor put his arms out to Hayden who reached out, showing his approval for the doctor to steal him from Anna.

Settling back into his chair while adjusting Hayden on his lap took place in one fluid movement. Roger proceeded to show Hayden how to open his first present.

The lesson seemed completely under control until Hayden discovered he could put the bow in his mouth. The doctor seemed more excited about what was inside than Hayden did, but the birthday boy was definitely curious. What in the world could his crazy friend be up to by tearing that paper?

They all laughed when Hayden looked at Jordan with his eyebrows raised to verify that ripping paper was now allowed.

No one noticed how closely Hudson had been watching his brother's lesson in present opening. He studied in silence, then, as if he had done it a hundred times, he peeled back a section of the paper until a piece came off in his hand. He seemed to take to the idea of ripping paper a little easier than Hayden did. He was tearing and throwing scraps all around. The little group laughed as the doctor ducked from the flying paper as if it were an air raid.

"Isn't it amazing how quickly they learn?" Anna posed the question to no one in particular. "They're both so smart but in such different ways. That's the only way that I can tell them apart and I see them every day!" She continued, "Hayden is so much more physical, but Hudson seems to be the studious one. It will be interesting to see if that stays the same as they get older."

"They really are amazing aren't they?" Jordan wasn't really looking for support on the subject but the group echoed its agreement just the same.

After the presents were opened, it was time for cake. Charlotte, in her eternally fair manner, made a tiny cake for each boy. They sat in their booster seats with colorful cakes only inches away. Hayden was the first to succumb to the temptation. He reached out a chubby little arm and basically clubbed his cake to death. As Charlotte and Anna were laughing, Jordan was trying to get him to stop pounding his frosting-covered fist.

"Oh no!" Jordan exclaimed. Just as Hayden discovered the mess on his hand was edible, Hudson followed suit and reached out for a handful of his own cake.

"No, no, boys. We're supposed to do the candles first. Oh gosh, the cake is getting everywhere, it's…" She knew she was fighting a losing battle and couldn't think of anything to do but laugh.

The quick-thinking doctor had caught most of the scene on camera, but by the time Jordan realized she was the star, she was covered in as much cake as they boys. The adults were laughing so hard that the twins, covered in cake, stopped what they were doing to watch.

"That's why they each have their own cakes, my dear," Charlotte interjected. "I'll go get the grown-up cake out of the refrigerator."

The rest of the afternoon was spent watching the twins play with new toys and sipping lemonade by the pool. By the time the sun started to disappear beneath the evergreens along the fence line, both boys had collapsed from exhaustion.

"Thank you all so much for making this an absolutely perfect birthday for the boys. They are so very lucky to have you all in their family. I can't thank you enough. They're only one-year-old and I think I'm already going to have to worry about spoiling them." Jordan intentionally lightened the conversation with her joke because she knew that the slightest sentiment from anyone else would surely send her into emotional meltdown. The last thing she wanted to do was start sobbing.

As the sun officially set, the Shapiros began preparing to leave. The boys lay sleeping on their own padded chaise lounges, but Charlotte could never leave without a proper goodbye. She bent over and kissed each one on the forehead carefully, so as not to disturb their slumber. After hugs and thanks, they headed into the house to gather their belongings. Jordan followed them out, while Anna stayed behind to keep an eye on the boys.

It was sad to see the day end, but as she watched the Shapiros drive off, Jordan had to admit she was pretty beat herself.

Chapter 15

A week after the twins turned one, Jordan kept her promise to herself and began researching daycare centers. She had already talked to both Anna and Charlotte about it because she didn't want them to think the decision had anything to do with the care they gave the boys. They were both extremely supportive and agreed that the twins were ready to spend time with other kids.

She had the names of several highly regarded centers that Charlotte had put together and set out to visit each of the top five personally. By the end of the day she had found the one she felt most comfortable with and enrolled the boys. She had been impressed both by the staff and the agenda of activities that were laid out. They would spend Mondays and Wednesdays, from 10 am until 2 pm, at the daycare.

As she drove back to the house, she couldn't help but feel a little sad about the time she would be spending away from them. She knew the socialization would be good for them, and based on what she saw from the other children at the center, she knew they would love going there. But still she couldn't help but miss them, and they hadn't even had their first day yet!

The change would also mean spending more time alone with Anna each day. As Jordan pulled into the middle stall of the garage, she thought about how strange it was that even though she had spent most of the last year with Anna - and completely considered her a part of the family - she barely knew her.

No reason not to remedy that immediately, Jordan thought. She decided she would invite Anna out by the pool after the boys went to sleep, and see if she could talk her into sharing a bottle of wine. It turned out it didn't take much convincing.

Conversation had always come naturally for Jordan and Anna because they were both so absorbed in the boys. It was easy to let them be the center of discussion, but that day Jordan wanted to find out about Anna. She never would have guessed the deep history that went into making her friend.

Chapter 16

Anna's grandmother had been one of the first children placed by a German orphanage that was founded by Roger Shapiro's father, Dr. Hiram Shapiro. She was adopted quickly but stayed in close contact with the Shapiro family all of her life. It was only a couple of years before she died that she told Anna their full history.

Dr. Hiram Shapiro was a brilliant young surgeon in pre-war Germany. He saw the writing on the wall and had successfully moved his family to the United States right before the Nazi party made the official "request" that citizens no longer visit Jewish doctors.

His Jewish associates called him a reactionary. They had endured prejudice before and found the best thing to do was ignore it. They lived in small towns where neighbors knew each other. World affairs wouldn't affect them. They even appealed to his practical side in an effort to convince him to stay.

Dr. Shapiro's practice was the largest of anyone from their medical school. How could he give up everything he'd worked for and move to America?

At the end of all conversations, neither side had convinced the other. Dr. Shapiro stayed in contact through letters until, one-by-one, each of his associates... each of his friends... fell off the face of the earth.

Hitler's reign took the majority of Jewish Germans but not all of them. And, of course, not all of Hiram's associates were Jewish.

Anna's grandmother had told her that Hiram spoke of his friend Josef every day of his life. He bludgeoned himself daily with the regrets of his former indecisions.

Josef was a mediocre doctor but a fascinating man. He believed that the answers to creation lay within the actual genes of our bodies. He also believed that manipulating those genes would be the perfect way to remove undesirable traits.

He recounted thinking it was wonderful to dream of a world where physical weaknesses, paralyzing deformities, and crippling diseases could be eradicated. How amazing would it be to live in a world where he, himself, would never have to tell parents that their newborn baby was ruined? What a world it would be if every child could run and jump and see and hear!

"But, of course, that was not God's plan for the world." Anna continued on with the story to explain how Hiram took the conversations as simply imaginings of men who spent more time in the operating room than they did with their children. The talks were just impossible dreams imagined after long shifts. But they weren't only imaginings for Josef.

Hirem wasn't surprised when Josef moved up the ranks in the Nazi organization. Hiram wasn't surprised when the media deemed Josef the "Angel of Death" years later. He had watched Josef's mind turn from curiosity to a hunger for power, long before his affiliation with Hitler began. Hiram knew that Josef's mind had rotted away with greed. He knew, but he did nothing.

Josef Mengele would be known to the world through all histories for his genetic experimentation on living souls. Hiram had seen enough of the world that he knew the newspaper coverage would never include the most horrific of Josef's experiments. But Hiram had seen some of his work first hand. Every day, for the rest of his life, Hiram thought of Josef spewing lunacies, while Hiram and his associates treated the matter as a joke.

The fact that he could have stopped Josef became the haunting regret of Hiram's life. When he spoke of his regret, people always assured him that the good he brought to the world outweighed the bad that Josef brought to it. But Anna's grandmother knew Hiram's response all too well. "I could have prevented so much death."

When the smoke cleared and sense was restored to the world, Hiram Shapiro still owned property in Germany. There were entire years where his family didn't see him because he was busy building his hospital and orphanage in Germany.

Mrs. Shapiro had no interest in ever returning to Germany, so she spent most of her marriage as a single parent to Roger. Anna's grandmother had started working for Mrs. Shapiro when she was 12 years old.

From the stories her grandmother told, Anna imagined Mrs. Shapiro as a sort of Southern belle pioneer woman who wasn't afraid of hard work, but also had a flair of elegance. Anna remembered her grandmother saying, "If there was royalty in this country, there wouldn't be nobody better fit for the job than Ms. Shapiro."

The absent doctor's wife had been a young midwife when she first met Hiram. While he was over-seas, she was able to turn their large Victorian home into one of the area's first birthing centers. Sometimes at night she would read Anna's grandmother the letters she received from her husband.

Hiram's life abroad was considerably less refined. He had no idea how much the human body could endure, until he began seeing concentration camp survivors. Hiram thought of Josef as he performed the surgery to separate twin sisters who hadn't been conjoined until they met Mengele. He thought of Josef when he delivered set after set of twins in the same small geographical area. A frequency of multiple births that was statistically impossible… until he thought of Josef.

Anna's great grandmother Mara was one of the twins in Josef's experiments and Hiram wrote about them often. She was dying when he met her but desperate to ensure the story of her ordeal didn't die with her.

Mara and her sister Mary were beautiful girls who possessed the ideal characteristics for the up-and-coming Arian nation. They had long blonde hair, blue eyes, and blossoming figures. They felt special when they were selected from the ranks that were filed into the gas chambers. They realized all too soon, the "ranks" were the lucky ones.

When they were taken to meet Dr. Mengele, they knew immediately that he was immensely pleased to see them. He checked them over the way their father had checked livestock he was purchasing. Throughout the examinations, the doctor made flattering remarks which convinced the girls his inspections would be the worst part of their confinement. Again, they were wrong.

After their first examination, the doctor injected each of the girls with something that burned their arms for more than a day. As they sat consoling each other in a cage while the sun set that first night, neither girl had any idea how soon they would look at that evening as the pleasant one. It would be the last night of their lives when parts of their bodies weren't burning yet.

The girls were given to soldiers as a reward. Of course, the soldiers also had characteristics desired by the Arian nation. The first children were born nine months later.

Both babies were born with dark hair and were taken away before either mother could see them. The girls were told the infants weren't viable and given another injection.

Dr. Mengele's objective was to find a way to create the perfect person faster and better than God Himself could do.

Growth hormone experimentation led to full-sized newborns in as little as one month from conception, but the outcome was... not viable.

Neither Mary nor Mara kept count of the miscarriages, stillborns, or births. The pain from the theft of their first children was the final loss of hope. Both girls retreated into their minds. The distancing of thought from body was necessary to survive if they were to maintain the ultimate hope that someday God would free them from their torture.

Dr. Mengele knew enough about genetics to know that injuries acquired in life didn't affect the physical traits passed to offspring. For that reason, there was no need to apply rules or restrictions to the soldiers who were rewarded with the twins. Some of the men were kind, in the beginning, but most of them were sadistic savages.

As broken bones twisted their bodies into different shapes and lack of treatment froze them into contorted positions, the soldiers became less sympathetic. That was when Dr. Mengele started to wonder if body parts could be taken from one twin and transplanted into the other. From there the experiments were unspeakable.

Mary died a month before the Allied troops arrived at the camp. Her remains had been burned long before the first soldiers would have found what little was left of her. Mary had been the donor, and Mara had been re-built.

When the troops stormed the camp, Mara was found in her cage. The left arm had been transplanted from Mary and was badly infected. It was ultimately lost to them both.

One month after Mara was taken from the concentration camp, she was delivered to the clinic of Dr. Hiram Shapiro. He had heard of her situation and knew there were no other doctors willing to donate their time or facilities for such a hopeless case. To Dr. Shapiro, it was a long-awaited opportunity for redemption.

Between treatments and operations, Hiram sat by Mara's bedside and took notes as she painstakingly recounted the things she was afraid the world would never know. In addition to her left arm, she had lost her eyesight and both legs, to infections that continued to spread. By the time she had finished the stories she was driven to tell, there was nothing anyone could do to save her. The twins she was carrying, however, were perfect.

Doctor Shapiro wired his wife immediately to see if she might be able to place the twins with a suitable family. One of those twins was Anna's grandmother.

Two generations later, it would be Charlotte who brought the families back into contact.

While researching Roger's genealogy, Charlotte discovered the connection between Roger's father and the young orphans. In tracing their lineage, she found that one of the descendants was a member of her own congregation.

Charlotte was active in the church and recognized the girl she saw pictured in the church directory. Anna never missed service, but she always attended by herself. She was friendly and polite and seemed particularly interested in children. One morning Charlotte invited Anna to help with the "quiet room" during service and found Anna happy to serve.

Over the next few years Anna taught Sunday school, helped with Bible school, and assisted in the Christmas program. She never accepted requests to be the leader for a particular project, but she was always happy to help where she could. Anna blushed as she talked about Charlotte praising her for her "soothing personality," but Jordan had certainly witnessed that first-hand.

Anna became the "baby holder" for their church. It didn't matter how mad or upset an infant was when he was handed to Anna, he was calmed almost immediately. Her inability to accept the limelight made Anna virtually invisible in any room, but yet she was pivotal.

Charlotte was fascinated by the fact that Anna was the first single birth in the generations since Mara. She imagined the peace Mara must have felt in heaven knowing that the curse of the holocaust was over. "That is exactly what Anna is," Charlotte stated when she was recommending Anna, "peace personified."

As Jordan listened to Anna tell the story of her great grandmother and the horrors Mara endured, she finally understood what Charlotte meant.

She thought back to her first feelings about Anna and deeply regretted her assumptions and jealousies. The more Jordan thought about Anna's family, the more she wanted to know. She had always thought about writing a book, and Jordan couldn't imagine a story more interesting than Anna's grandmother's. Maybe that would be her new hobby. Jordan had been so deep in thought, she didn't realize Anna had stopped speaking… and she didn't know when.

"I just… wow, Anna." Jordan saw the worried look fade from her friend's face. "How do you even know all of those things?"

"Dr. Shapiro, Hiram, that is, felt that the only people who had a right to tell her story were her family members." Anna stretched her back as she sat up. "He gave all of his notes, photos, and files to my grandmother before he died. He told her

- 148 -

how important it was to Mara that her story be told. Over the years, my mom and grandmother put everything together in a kind of a scrapbook." She looked at Jordan with a slight touch of humor in her eyes. "In our family, it's more sacred than the Bible."

"Have you ever thought about publishing it?" Jordan wondered if she might follow in her father's footsteps after all. "I could go through my father's Rolodex and come up with at least ten people I could call."

Anna's posture stiffened. "No. It's not that kind of book. The world would look at it for the macabre details and that isn't her story. Great-grandmother's story is one of survival and faith." Anna smiled and looked at her watch. "I didn't realize how late it was getting! I'd better start dinner."

Jordan stayed by the pool after Anna went in to fix lunch. The story of Mara's determination and legacy left Jordan pondering her own future.

Since the twins arrived, every breath she took revolved around them in some way. She wouldn't change it for the world, but she knew it couldn't stay that way forever. She sighed at the thought of having them start school, fall in love, get married, have children! Time just went by so quickly! She wanted nothing more than to hold her babies and rock with them, but they were napping so she might as well do something productive.

Jordan went into the house to help Anna in the kitchen and tell her every miniscule detail about the daycare. She'd been so engrossed in the subject of Anna's family that she had all but forgotten how she'd spent most of the day.

Jordan explained a little about how she was feeling and found that Anna completely understood. As they talked through the illogical fears of bumps and bruises, Jordan thought, *Charlotte was right, Anna really is a reassuring presence.*

While Anna finished making lunch, Jordan went up to the nursery to wake the boys from their naps. As she stood over their cribs watching them sleep, she wished there were some way for her to still pick up and cradle both of her babies at once. She stared at their faces trying to memorize every crinkle and every pore as they slept. She wanted to burn the memories into her mind so, regardless of the years that passed, she wouldn't forget a thing. For the first time in a long time she thanked God for the precious gifts He had given her.

In synch with her silent prayer of thanks, Hudson stirred in his sleep and started whimpering. Jordan reassured him as she lifted him easily from his crib. At least she could still pick up one at a time, she thought. Hudson snuggled into her arms as he yawned the biggest yawn she'd ever seen. He was waking up, but content with being held. She sat down in the oversized recliner that separated the cribs.

As they rocked, Jordan stared into Hudson's eyes in adoration. He tried so hard to keep his eyelids up to watch her too but in the end he couldn't hold them up. She had come upstairs intending to wake them up, but decided instead that lunch could wait. She held Hudson tightly as they rocked and hoped she would always be able to comfort him so easily.

Chapter 17

The twins' first day of daycare came too quickly for Jordan's comfort, but she stayed strong and took them in. Anna offered to come along, but Jordan felt it was something she needed to do by herself. She knew that having Anna along would have made the entire event easier, but Jordan didn't want easier. She wanted a little alone time to cry after she trusted her babies to strangers.

All-in-all it went better than she expected. She did wind up getting emotional when she hugged each of the boys goodbye, but she couldn't deny they were excited and ready.

The twins immediately occupied themselves with different toys, and Hudson was already beginning to make friends. She hoped Hayden would do the same before the day was over. She couldn't put her finger on it, but he seemed to be the more sensitive of the two. Her maternal protectiveness wanted to make everything perfect for both of them. She reminded herself that it was only two days a week and it was obviously harder on her than it was on them. They would be just fine, and she would simply have to suck it up.

She drove back to the house wondering what in the world she was going to do with herself for the next four hours. Anna did an excellent job of keeping the house picked up and she didn't feel like spending another day lazing around the pool. Her thoughts went back to writing.

She had thought many times growing up that she might someday be an author. *Why not give it a try?!* She liked to write and she certainly had the time. Jordan started to get excited about the whole idea of having a project. She would start cleaning out her father's study as soon as she got home and turn it into a writing den for herself.

When she arrived back at the house, Anna was anxious to hear how everything had gone. They sat at the kitchen table and drank cups of coffee as Jordan filled her in on every detail, her writing career thoroughly side-tracked. It was obviously as hard on Anna to have the boys gone as it was on Jordan.

Then she told Anna about her plan to turn the study into a writing room. Anna thought it sounded like an excellent idea and asked if Jordan had any story ideas. A small part of Jordan was hoping that Anna would have re-thought making her great-grandmother's story public, but she knew how selfish it would be for her to push it.

"Not yet, but it will probably take me a few days to get Dad's study cleaned up anyway. I thought I'd start by going through some of the things I came up with when I was younger. I know Dad kept everything I ever wrote, but I have no idea where he would have put it all." Anna was nodding her agreement as she picked up the dishes.

"Thank you so much for the coffee. I'm going to go in and get started." Jordan took her cup to the sink before heading off to the study.

As she walked through the double French doors, she wondered where to begin. The circular room was lined with bookshelves that stretched from the floor to the 20-foot-high ceiling. Hundreds... no, thousands of books filled the shelves, separated only by an occasional duck decoy or nautical decoration. It may have been her father's study but her mother's taste was definitely represented too. Jordan craned her head back and realized most of the books were only accessible with the help of the rolling ladder that was affixed somewhere high above her head. Her fear of heights would likely prevent her from ever reading most of the books, but she really did like the look of the room. She couldn't imagine a more perfect "author sanctuary."

What do I need to have to become an author? She thought for a second and couldn't come up with anything other than a computer. That's it then. Start with the desk.

Her father's desk had been his pride and joy. It was seven feet of solid mahogany with ornate detail on every surface area except the top. The top was perfectly finished and polished meticulously. It looked like a piece of glass. She loved the desk as much as her father had. It would be the perfect spot for her to write.

She walked behind the desk and sat down in her father's chair. She had been in it plenty of times before… when her father was alive, but she hadn't ever noticed how comfortable it was. The leather was perfectly worn in without looking even a little worn out. She wouldn't have any problem spending hours on end in her father's chair. Her excitement to begin writing swelled.

When she opened the top drawer, she realized clean up might be a bigger project than she had anticipated.

The drawer was crammed full of old checkbooks, receipts, scraps of paper, and who knows what else. She had never thought of her father as the pack rat type but apparently he had some secrets. *No wonder his study was always immaculate; his desk was a mess!*

She rifled through a few of the papers but didn't find anything she thought she needed to keep. The estate had all been handled by lawyers and accountants so she assumed they had any of the papers they needed. She didn't see any mementos or pictures so she guessed most, if not all of it, would wind up in the trash.

She pulled the drawer out as far as it would go, thinking it might be easier to sort through if she actually took it out of the desk. When it reached the end of its rollers, something solid dropped onto her lap. She pushed the drawer back in as far as it would go and looked down to see a bound leather book with no markings. She opened the cover and immediately recognized her father's handwriting.

It was a journal. She had no idea her father even kept a journal and was a little surprised it hadn't been discovered during the police investigation two years ago. She debated whether she should actually read any of it. *Would it be an invasion of his privacy?* After weighing the question carefully, she decided it wouldn't. He had been gone over two years and even if he had deep dark secrets in the book, none of them mattered now.

October 1, 1988

The studios rejected my latest screenplay, again. If something doesn't happen for me pretty soon, I'm going to have to give up and go find a real job. Beverly has been working double shifts at the factory to get our savings built up a little before the baby arrives...

Jordan did some quick math. She hadn't been born until December of 1989. *What baby was he talking about?*

...but she isn't going to be able to do that much longer. The doctor said she needs to take it easy if she's going to carry this baby to term, and I just don't think she could handle the loss of another child. She's been through so much. The three miscarriages were hard but when our son was born

still last year, I thought for sure I was going to lose her. She looked like an empty shell when we buried the baby. I should have been more attentive. Maybe then she wouldn't have tried to kill herself. Even now I can't stand the idea of living without her. I've failed her in so many ways. I can't allow myself to do it again, even if it means giving up my dreams. She's the only thing that really matters anyway.

Jordan couldn't believe what she was reading.

I had a brother? And there were more? She had always assumed her parents only wanted one child. Apparently that wasn't the case at all. She thought of what her poor mother must have gone though, losing so many children. She couldn't imagine going on if something happened to her boys.

And her poor father, how difficult it must have been to blame himself for something that was so obviously out of anyone's control. She continued with the next entry.

October 15, 1988

I finally sold the screenplay! The production company would only pay $1500 for it but that's more money than we've seen in a long time. Maybe things will start turning our way now.

November 2, 1988

Devastating day! We found out that Beverly lost the baby. She hadn't been feeling well this morning so I took her into the emergency room. After a few tests they told us the baby had died. They had to keep her overnight to make sure everything takes care of itself the way it's supposed to. She looked so hopeless when I saw her. I would give anything if I could take this pain away. The hospital wouldn't let me stay with her, but they said they would keep a close watch over her, just in case.

The sale of my screenplay will get us through a little while but not very long. There doesn't seem to be many opportunities for us here in Detroit and the weather is starting to turn so gloomy.

Detroit? My parents had lived in Detroit?

I think a change of scenery would be good for both of us, maybe it will help Beverly forget some of her heartache and I'm hoping it will be a good career choice as well. We're moving to California as soon as Beverly is able to travel. I haven't told her yet but she loves sunshine. I believe she will be happy with the decision.

Neither of us has any family anymore and there doesn't seem to be anything but sorrow for us here.

December 6, 1988

We've settled in San Diego and although we don't live in a very nice area of town, the weather is beautiful. Beverly has taken a job at a local diner and I've started working on my latest screenplay. Moving turned out to be the best medicine for Beverly. It feels like things are almost back to normal. She still has frequent bouts of depression and I would give anything to be able to help her. I suppose it's a matter of time.

January 1, 1989

A new year! I have great hope that this year will be better for Beverly and me. We don't celebrate the holidays anymore. I've never believed in any of that anyway but in the past Beverly always wanted to celebrate, so we did. This year she said that since God had forsaken her, she would forsake Him. My personal feelings are that she gave up something that was never there to begin with, but I know it's just another sign of how difficult things have been for her.

I've finished my latest screenplay and it looks like the same production company is interested in buying it. This time they're only offering me $100 but half of the profits from the movie as well. The first one isn't doing well at all so it's definitely a risk, but what have I got to lose?

January 6, 1989

I think today was perhaps the most bizarre day of my life. Beverly brought home a man that some new doctor she found recommended. The guy introduced himself as "Bub" Beleez and seemed pleasant enough. His real first name is Tanas, but apparently everyone calls him "Bub." Bev invited him over to the apartment for dinner and I don't know what to make of him. I think he might be insane. As far as looks go, he's a very striking man with his dark wavy hair and chiseled features. I would guess him to be in his mid-thirties. He asked a lot of questions about our lives, but he knew way more than either of us told him.

At the time I thought it was because Beverly had already talked to him but she assured me after he left she hadn't. He knew about the children we'd lost. He knew about the screenplays I've had rejected. He knew about things from our childhoods!

The evening got even stranger when he said that he could make all of our problems go away. At that point I really wanted him to leave but Beverly begged me to hear him out.

He said he could make it so that she would be able to carry a baby to term and we could have financial rewards beyond our wildest imagination. He spoke very cryptically and literally made my skin crawl with every word. I asked him if he was trying to tell us he was the devil or something because I thought seriously about calling the police.

He didn't actually say he was, but I remember his answer exactly. He said, "I so hate to assign labels to anything or anyone. I am simply a person who can offer you what you want and you, in return, are in a position to offer me what I want."

I didn't really believe any of his ramblings but I could tell by the look on her face that Beverly did. Maybe having faith in something again will help carry her through, at least for a while.

There was definitely something that made her invite the man into our home. She has never done anything like that before! I listened to the guy for her sake, and there's no doubt he was convincing. I asked what would be in it for him and that's when he explained the conditions of his "deal."

"Jordan, it's time to pick up the twins." Anna's announcement startled her back to reality. For some reason she felt like a snoopy teenager who was about to be busted.

"It's been so strange here today without…" Anna was so excited about getting the boys it never occurred to her she might be interrupting until she saw how startled Jordan looked.

"I'm sorry! I didn't mean to interrupt you," Anna apologized. "I should have knocked first."

"No, not at all, Anna." Jordan's calm crept back. "I was reading through some old paperwork of my father's and I guess I got a little caught up in it."

"Would you like me to go pick up the boys by myself?" Anna asked.

"No way!" Jordan smiled and Anna's face relaxed. "I can't wait to see how their first day went. Are you ready to leave?"

Jordan truly was excited to get the boys, and as they got ready to leave, she realized how anxious she was to see them. She had been so wrapped up in her father's journal the time had flown by. With most of her mind back in the here and now, she realized how much she missed them.

Her thoughts kept going back to the journal. Already there were so many things that she hadn't known about her parents, but deals with the devil?! It was like some bizarre fiction novel.

Of course! She felt stupid for not thinking about it earlier; the guy *was probably just trying to sell Dad on a screenplay. But he hadn't ever done anything in the horror genre as far as she knew.*

Chapter 18

The boys had a wonderful first day of daycare. When she and Anna arrived, both boys were playing games with other kids. Jordan was a little relieved to find that even though the boys didn't care when she dropped them off, they were very glad to see her when she came to pick them up.

After exchanging long bear hugs with each of the boys, Jordan talked briefly to one of the staff members. She wanted to find out how the day had gone while Anna got her turn at hugs and kisses. Neither of the boys was saying more than a couple of words but the ride home was abuzz with conversation anyway.

Jordan and Anna asked questions about the day and the boys answered with what could best be described as gibberish. They all laughed and both Jordan and Anna were surprised at how "talkative" the boys were.

By 8:00 the boys were ready for bed. Their big day had worn them out a full hour earlier than usual. As much as she had enjoyed the evening with them, she was also grateful for the extra time. She wanted to get back to the journal.

After tucking the boys into bed she returned to the study and opened the journal to the page where she'd left off.

I asked what would be in it for him and that's when he explained the conditions of his "deal."

It sounded like something right out of a horror movie, which is probably where he got it. He's obviously a nut case but I figured what would it hurt? I'd agree to his Boris Karloff conditions, and maybe it will buy enough time for Bev to pull out of this depression. After all, it's not like I'm really making a deal with the devil. What can it hurt right? Besides, everything he wanted has to do with our daughter and it's not like we have any children.

Jordan felt a chill run down her back.

Weeks passed before Jordan could bring herself to go back into the study. She wanted to know what else the journal said, but not nearly as badly as she wanted to pretend it didn't exist. What if it had something to do with the boys? After countless hours of imagining the worst... and occasionally best possibilities, she decided she needed to know.

January 12, 1989

After the weird meeting with Bub last week, Bev made an appointment with Dr. Shapiro. He told her again that my tests were conclusive and there was no way I would be able to father a child. He also told her again that Bub was our only choice if she wanted to have a baby naturally.

We've talked about adoption, but the idea seems to make her sadder than ever. Since the day I told her I wasn't comfortable with Bub or any of his wild ideas, she's sunk down into depression again. Maybe after she's had a little time to accept the news she'll reconsider, but I know she has always dreamed of carrying her own baby. I only hope she can pull through this new disappointment.

February 3, 1989

I can't handle it anymore. I'm going to agree to Bub's terms.

June 1, 1989

I hadn't realized how long it had been since I've made an entry in this journal and so much has happened I hardly know where to begin. The month following my refusal to accept Bub's offer was too difficult to write about. It's simply exhausting to even remember it. As soon as I agreed to Bub's terms, Beverly snapped out of her depression.

It was right after that when Dr. Shapiro confirmed that Beverly is expecting. The change in her has been extraordinary. The stress she felt with the other pregnancies is non-existent and she has been busying herself with preparations for the baby's arrival. It seems that every fiber of her being is confident she will carry this baby to term.

The screenplay I sold was made into a movie! It was filmed in record time on an extremely low budget. For whatever reason, audiences have responded like nothing I've ever seen before. It's been in the theatre for two weeks and has broken every record in existence. The studios are regretting the deal to share 50% of the profits but they've already signed me for projects I haven't even started! We have literally become millionaires overnight. Beverly quit her job at the diner last week and has been spending her free time house hunting and preparing for the baby.

It really does appear that all of our dreams have come true. The only downside, whether it's real or imagined, is the nagging thoughts in the back of my mind over our conversations with Mr. Beleez. The logical side of my brain can easily dismiss the "deal" we made with him but it doesn't provide an alternate explanation for our new found fortune.

My deepest hope is that the baby Beverly is carrying is a boy. If we did strike a deal with the devil, he didn't mention any repercussions to a son. The idea of writing the conditions down terrifies me, perhaps because it will somehow *make it all more real, but who knows, maybe I'll turn it into a novel someday.*

I've already specified the benefits to Beverly and me in this arrangement, so I'll skip over that part. I think I remember nearly word for word what he had said, so rather than try to make sense of the nonsense now, I'm just going to write it down as he said it.

Without realizing it, Jordan sat straighter in her chair, intent on the details that were negotiated about her before her birth.

"In return for these favors, I ask only for the opportunity to have a son of my own. If your daughter achieves the age of maturity in a pure state and has not chosen a life with my... counterpart, you hereby promise her to me. Up until the age of 21 she will have free will to follow the teachings of her choice. You may in no way influence or persuade her towards Christianity, but if she should find it on her own, well, I guess that would be my loss."

Jordan felt the blood rush from her face and arms, leaving a clammy feeling in its place. She was almost 23!

Chapter 19

Jordan leaned back in her chair lost in a swirl of disbelief and understanding. Could this have something to do with her parents' deaths? Could this have anything to do with the mystery surrounding her babies? She flipped quickly through more than a decade of entries until she found the last one. It had been written the day before her parents were killed.

October 17, 2008

Jordan called today to let Beverly and me know that she has scheduled her baptism next month. There are no words to explain the joy that is filling our house right now, but I do know we haven't felt jubilation like this since the moment Dr. Shapiro announced, "It's a healthy baby girl."

Even as I write this I can't hold back the tears of relief. Our daughter is free! So many times we wanted to tell her about the deal we made so many years ago. To encourage her towards faith in God, but we knew that if we did she would be taken from us and neither of us could bear the thought of that. Oh how I wish I could go back to my agnostic ways. All

I can think about are the countless nights that Beverly and I have spent praying for Jordan's future. And now, our prayers have been answered! We knew if we waited long enough that God would win!

Beverly and I are going out to find a gold crucifix to give Jordan after the ceremony. At this point she must be thinking her parents have gone insane. We have never been able to discuss religion in her presence for fear of breaking our deal, so she's got to be wondering why we were both blubbering about how proud we are of her. It would be nice if we could tell her everything, but it will be nicer to just put all of this behind us forever.

She hadn't gone through with the baptism.

After her parents were killed, Jordan turned her back on God. *Ok,* she thought. *Push aside all the judgments of reality vs fantasy and just see how this all fits together.*

She allowed herself to think the unimaginable and her entire life fell together like pieces of a puzzle.

She remembered walking in on her parents one night when she couldn't sleep. She had found them both kneeling beside the bed with their hands folded together but they said they were straightening the sheet. She had no reason to question it.

She thought about a telephone call she had heard her father make one night when she was about nine.

"So how did you know that her faith would be enough to break the deal?" She heard her father say the words and assumed they probably had something to do with his work. She'd always wondered what kind of a deal he was trying to break, though, because it seemed like something *she* would have gotten in trouble for.

She remembered how strange it was that her parents were so excited when she found religion. She couldn't understand why it would be important to them that SHE found God when they themselves didn't appear to have any interest in religion. Everything finally made sense. When they encouraged her on the phone the day she told them her decision, they broke their end of the agreement. That was the reason they were killed.

But why would the devil take them rather than her? Wasn't that what he had threatened to do? *He knew.* He knew that taking her parents would cause her to turn her back on God. But even so, she had never chosen a Satanic lifestyle in any way. Even when she was filled with anger at God, she never considered devil worship.

Choosing nothing leaves the window to your soul wide open. The thought ran across her mind like someone had whispered it into her brain.

But even though I turned my back on God, I still believed in Him. I was confused and hurt but I still can't believe that God wouldn't be there to protect... The mental debate ended.

"Oh, dear God," she said aloud. Jordan thought back to her dream. The alternating images? The conflicting feelings of pure love and pure lust? God was there!

Her heart raced at the thought that one of the men from her dream could really be the father of her children and what would it mean for her babies?

But she had made no deals with anyone and they were her children, too. It didn't make any difference who their father was. She was the only person in the world with legal rights to the boys. The only way anyone would be able to get to them would be over her dead body. But no one had ever even tried to get to them... had they?

She had two healthy, happy little boys who were completely normal in every sense of the word. Even if their conception was the result of some supernatural struggle, their lives certainly hadn't been. How they came to be didn't matter. She was the single parent of two beautiful children and she would protect them with her life... with her soul.

"I choose God," Jordan whispered into the journal and decided to start taking the boys to church.

She couldn't turn back time or change her own indecisiveness, but she had made no deals with anyone. Her children would be raised to believe in God and Jordan knew immediately who could help.

Chapter 20

Anna had been a devout Catholic her entire life, so Jordan wasn't surprised at her excitement when asked if she would mind some tag-alongs at church. What would have surprised Jordan would have been to find out how very much it meant to Anna.

It bothered her tremendously that the boys hadn't been baptized. She would never dream of overstepping her bounds with Jordan but it meant enough to her to sneak a vial of holy water into the babies' nursery one night when they were only a few months old.

She knew it would be wrong to impose her own will on someone else so she didn't go through with it, but the overwhelming urgency that the babies needed to be baptized lingered for months. In the end, good sense won out and Anna left their religious choices to their mother.

When Sunday morning arrived, Anna seemed as excited as a kid at Christmas. While Jordan was packing a bag of snacks in the kitchen, Anna was putting the finishing touches on Hayden's outfit. "Look at you in your Sunday best. You're so handsome I just have to kiss you!" Hayden giggled as Anna took him by the shoulders and kissed his cheek.

"Your turn, young man," Anna turned to Hudson who had been watching intently from his crib. "Let's get you dressed and…" Terror filled Anna's face as she watched Hudson's eyes fill with blood. "Oh, dear God! Hudson, are you alright?" As she approached his crib, Hudson sat down hard in a trance. His muscles strained as if he were carrying a burden a hundred times his size. His eyes were pleading for help but Anna couldn't understand what he was struggling against.

Anna ran out of the room and leaned over the railing that overlooked the foyer. "Jordan, come quickly! I'm afraid something is happening to…" With a loud crack, the rail gave way. Anna scrambled to find something to hold onto, but wound up impotently flailing her arms in the rush of air that swept past as she fell. Anna landed in a crumpled heap 25 feet below on the marble floor.

Chapter 21

Everything had settled to stillness by the time Jordan came out of the kitchen drying her hands. She saw something on the floor as she ran past, but her eyes were focused on the broken railing high above her head. Her mind was still trying to process what had happened when she saw Hayden walking towards the broken rail.

"Hayden, NO!" She had no idea she could travel 37 steps that quickly, but she reached her son before he took another step. She scooped him into her arms and held him tightly as she tried to piece together what happened. She carried Hayden into the bedroom and gave another sigh of relief when she saw Hudson standing up in his crib trying to peek around the door. She put Hayden in his crib and kissed them both on the forehead before heading back to the hallway to find Anna and see what happened.

"Anna?" She looked at the broken rail, then towards the hallway where she knew nothing waited. There was no sign of anyone.

"Anna?!" She said it more urgently but still heard no reply. Jordan walked a little closer to where the rail had been and saw the crumpled pile of clothing amid debris from the fallen rail. There was no longer any denying what had happened. The crumpled pile wasn't moving.

"Oh, God, no. Please don't let that be…" Jordan ran back down the stairs two at a time. Even standing next to the body, it was hard to tell she was looking at a person. Anna's head was completely folded under her body. Her back was arched into an unnatural position and the debris from the rail, wall, and parlor table were scattered around and on top of her. Jordan reached out to touch her friend but it was more out of instinct than a misguided belief that something could be done.

"Anna, dear God, Anna!" When Jordan's hand touched Anna's back, the fragile balancing act was disturbed. The body rolled over to its side. Anna's unseeing eyes were wide open, frozen forever in the terror she must have felt at the end.

"Oh, God, Anna… no! I'll call for help. You're going to be alright now. Don't move." A part of Jordan knew the obvious, but a bigger part of her needed to hold on to denial like a life preserver.

She ran to the phone and dialed 911. When the operator answered, Jordan didn't even let her finish the greeting before she started in. "I need an ambulance right away! My nanny fell from the second floor and… oh, God! She landed on… she's not… Oh, God, this can't be happening! The address, you need the address. It's…"

The operator interrupted, "It's ok, ma'am, I have your address up and I've already dispatched an ambulance. They should be there in the next few minutes. Is it just the two of you in the house?" The calming voice of the operator helped soothe the hysteria a little.

"No, my sons are here. They're only a year and a half old. Anna was getting them dressed and, I don't know… I heard her holler for me and I came as quickly as I could from the kitchen but… I don't know what's going on. Please hurry!!" Uncontrollable sobs overwhelmed Jordan as the operator tried to keep her calm and focused.

After a few minutes that felt like an eternity, Jordan heard sirens outside her door. "They're here; I have to go." Jordan tried to hang up the phone but only succeeded in dropping the receiver to the floor. She threw open the front door as two paramedics were running up the walk with a stretcher in tow.

"This way!" Jordan barely noticed two more paramedics behind, as she rushed the first arrivals to where Anna lay motionless. She stood far enough back that they would have room to work, but close enough to see a little too well. The sense of urgency they had coming through the door disappeared almost as soon as they saw the body.

They went through the motions of checking for a pulse, but the paramedics no longer rushed. One of the attending medics shook his head in answer to a question that no one asked.

Jordan saw the unspoken gesture of hopelessness and her eyes darted among each member of the ambulance squad.

"NO!" She screamed hysterically, rushing towards the body. "You have to do something! Please!! She needs CPR or we have to get her to the hospital so they can get her into surgery. Please, you have to do something! I have a friend who's a doctor; we could call him… PLEASE!" One of the paramedics walked over to Jordan and gently pulled her into a hug.

"I am sorry, ma'am, but there isn't anything that can be done. She's gone."

Jordan suddenly remembered what she'd heard about dealing with neck and back injuries. "Oh, God, I moved her! She was lying on her stomach with her head tucked under and I touched her back and made her roll over. It's my fault! I shouldn't have touched her until you got here!"

The paramedic held Jordan's upper arms firmly but gently and forced her to look him in the face. "Now, listen carefully. Your moving her made no difference whatsoever. Your friend died on impact and there's nothing anyone could have done."

One of the twins began to cry and all heads immediately looked up at the broken railing.

"The boys." Jordan said it more to herself as a prompt to get it together than as conversation to anyone in particular. She wiped her eyes and tried to compose herself as well as she could. Her children needed her.

"My boys are in their cribs. They're probably terrified. I think Hayden saw her fall. Oh, God, what must be going through his poor little mind?" Jordan turned from the ambulance personnel to care for her babies.

As she climbed the stairway she noticed the section of rail that jutted out into mid-air. It was too long. The pieces of railing that were broken off were stretched. It looked like the whole thing had been pulled… or pushed… until it broke. *Pull yourself together… your children need you.*

Chapter 22

The next seven days went by in a whir. The Shapiros came over the night of the accident, and Charlotte had been with her virtually every minute since. The doctor promised Jordan he would run every test he could think of on the boys to make sure they didn't have any indications of Post-Traumatic stress.

As much as Jordan wanted to make sure neither of her boys would be mentally scarred in the future, she worried that all of the stress might be too much for the doctor. He looked exhausted already and now, in addition to his work at the hospital, he had Anna's death to deal with.

For Jordan it seemed like everything was taking place inside Jello or something. She couldn't think straight. She was able to go through the motions of the day but it was purely out of robotic routine. Everything was all much harder without Anna.

Now here she was, standing at the cemetery barely hearing the words that Father Hannigan was saying about her friend. The light drizzle coming down added to the gloominess of the day. As she looked around at the small group of black umbrellas, she felt that she might actually be in a movie. The distinct feeling of déjà vu hit her and her eyes wandered to the section of the cemetery where her parents were buried.

"Ashes to ashes, dust to dust," the minister read while shaking some kind of a rattle with smoke coming out of it.

So that's it then Jordan thought. *That's what we all come to in the end.* There was nothing left to do, nothing left to say. Anna was gone, and she was not. The only things that really mattered were her boys and she needed to pull herself together to care for them.

The small group who braved the weather to attend the interment broke apart and headed to their cars.

Only Jordan and the boys lingered at the coffin to say a final goodbye. Her mental voice was screaming at her again, but she had no idea what it was about and no real interest in finding out. It was time to go.

Jordan led the boys to the minivan and buckled them in for the ride home. She felt like every person in every vehicle was staring. Of course, she was leading the funeral procession back to her house for a small gathering so they probably were.

On the drive, Jordan couldn't help but think about how Anna's absence would affect the boys. She had been a huge part of their lives since the day they came home from the hospital almost 16 months ago. Now she was gone and they were too little to really understand why she wasn't with them anymore.

Over the past few days they had both called out for Anna several times. Each time, Jordan's broken heart cracked a little more. She consoled herself with the fact that they were very young and wouldn't remember anything about the accident or their friend. Instead of helping, the realization they might not remember such a special person created a whole new sadness.

For now, they would take it one day at a time and get through it together.

She pulled into her driveway, followed immediately by the other cars from the funeral. She was grateful that the Shapiros would be helping her with the guests and the luncheon. Once again she could only come up with one word to describe them, Godsends.

Charlotte, in her usual fashion, jumped in and saved the day about a hundred times in the last week. Jordan wanted everything perfect when Anna's family arrived, but as she saw the looks of awe on people's faces when they stepped out of their vehicles, she hoped her intentions didn't come across as ostentatious.

Anna's family hadn't experienced the wealth that Jordan had always taken for granted. When she realized how difficult the expense of a funeral would be for the family, Jordan insisted on paying for everything. They had, of course, refused vehemently, but Jordan convinced them that it was an employment benefit and therefore something Anna had already earned. *Sometimes it's kinder to lie*, she told herself.

Anna's mother seemed more like a grandmother. She worked as a seamstress out of their home while her husband worked in a factory. Anna was their only child, born just before they celebrated their 25th wedding anniversary. They were both conservative Catholics who believed God had His reasons for not blessing their marriage with a child. They had even come to look at it as a blessing because of the "curse" that had been inflicted upon their family by Dr. Mengele.

When Anna was born, her parents felt as if they'd finally been favored by God. The way they talked about their daughter made Jordan wish she had taken more opportunities to spend the day talking with Anna.

The family put together albums of pictures from Anna's childhood that even the boys seemed fascinated to look through. She had been a beautiful child who loved absolutely everything. While they were working on the obituary, Anna's mother reminisced about the daughter she'd lost.

"I remember how excited she was the first time she saw a butterfly. She marveled at the creature when it landed on her finger, and I would have sworn she was talking to it." Jordan saw reality wash over her fragile face and the impossible grief returned. Anna's mother summed everything up perfectly when she said, "I can't understand why God would take her so early when she brought so much goodness to the world."

Not a single person could come up with an answer.

Dr. Shapiro had been at the hospital late again, analyzing all of the boys' test results. He said several times that everything he'd looked at appeared normal but he was still waiting to hear from a friend who was an expert in child psychiatry. Jordan appreciated his concern over the boys tremendously but they really did seem fine. Why was he killing himself over questions that hadn't come up? The bags under his eyes were darker than when they'd left the house for the funeral that morning. Jordan promised herself to catch him alone after everyone was settled and make him lie down in one of the guest rooms. He had been so quiet the last couple of days, but she imagined they were all a little lost in their own thoughts since Anna died.

Jordan and Charlotte were busy giving last minute instructions to the caterers and adjusting table linens. Mostly they were just doing busy work. Charlotte started putting ice in the punch bowl while Jordan removed plastic wrap from various bowls brought in by the caterer. The doctor was manning the front door and ushering new arrivals to the backyard. The morning clouds were replaced by a beautiful blue sky.

The ladies worked without speaking, but neither felt uncomfortable in the silence. Eventually there was nothing left to do.

"It was sure a lovely service, wasn't it?" Charlotte asked rhetorically. "I thought it might be strange to have the service in the rain at the cemetery but it really worked out beautifully. It was fortunate they thought to set the canopy up."

"It sure was," Jordan answered for none of the questions in particular. "It still feels really strange not to have her in here helping us doesn't it?"

Charlotte nodded her agreement and the two went back to working in silence.

"Ok, I think that's everything," Charlotte said as she slapped her hands together. They both understood the universal signal of finality and Jordan had to swallow a lump in her throat. It was time to get down to the difficult part of the day, acting like their worlds weren't shattered. Jordan's biggest fear was facing Anna's mom's question again. "Why would God take her?"

Conversation hadn't progressed beyond surface niceties before the caterer wheeled the two carts into the foyer and announced that lunch was served. It may have been Jordan's imagination, but it seemed that at one point or another, every individual had cast, then immediately averted, his eyes from the newly-repaired railing above their heads.

She wished now that they had chosen a better location for the serving tables but it probably wouldn't have mattered anyway. You can't even enter the house without seeing the railing and it's not like people would be eating in the foyer. Jordan's mind was flooded with thoughts of things she should have done or could have done to make Anna's final sending a little closer to perfect. Anna deserved for it to be perfect.

After people filled their plates and glasses, they settled into the various seats around the living room. There were only 34 guests so they didn't even use all of the folding chairs Dr. Shapiro had set up that morning.

Jordan thought about how sad it was that a person as wonderful as Anna would have so few mourners. Then she thought about her own death. How many people would be there to see her off? She knew that if she died right then, it would probably be a minister, the Shapiros, and her sons. Thinking of it that way made Anna seem pretty loved after all.

Chapter 23

When the guests were gone and the boys were down for their afternoon nap, Jordan sat at the kitchen table, sharing a cup of coffee with the Shapiros.

"Why do you think that God allows stuff like this to happen in the world?" Jordan asked the question without looking up from her coffee.

Charlotte sighed and turned to Jordan. "I'll tell you a story that my mother used to tell me when I asked that same question.

"God gave man dominion over the earth when He promised free will. Each generation of man believed he could do things better than God, that we could somehow learn from God's mistakes. Earth became the battleground between good and evil. For every person who agreed to keep God's laws, there were a hundred who refused."

Charlotte took a sip of her coffee before continuing.

"The angels were angry. They couldn't understand why God would give such dominion to a race full of greed and hate like humans. God's decision was final and He sent the angels to live among mankind to influence us and protect us." Charlotte lifted her coffee cup to her lips but didn't drink. "I think maybe Anna was one of those angels," she finished.

"Like my Charlotte." Roger smiled at his wife, the light of his life.

Jordan thought about Charlotte's story and imagined ordinary people taking off their coats to reveal grand sets of wings. It was nice to imagine guardian angels watching over her and the boys, but she'd already lived through enough tragedy in life to know it didn't work that way.

"This may not be the most appropriate time to bring this up, but have you thought about whether you plan to hire another nanny?" The doctor's question took Jordan off guard.

"Oh, Roger," Charlotte scorned, "now is hardly the time for her to worry about something like that. There isn't any reason at all I can't start coming over more often again. I miss seeing those boys as much as I used to." Since they started daycare, Charlotte had only been coming over about once a week.

"I really don't want to impose any more than I already have." Jordan had the distinct feeling the doctor would prefer his wife hadn't offered her help. "The boys are in daycare two days a week and I think I can handle most everything on my own. You've done so much for us already."

"Nonsense," Charlotte said matter-of-factly. "I enjoy spending time with the three of you, and I won't have you chasing after two little boys all by yourself. If you get sick of me, you can always say so, but in the meantime I'd like to come over during the day when the boys aren't in daycare."

Jordan noticed the look of disappointment on the doctor's face and wondered why. There was no question in her mind that he had been uncomfortable around the boys since Anna's death. What she didn't understand was how or why he would connect the boys to the accident. Was there something he knew that she didn't?

On the other hand, Jordan had seen the doctor overly protective of Charlotte on numerous occasions. And then it hit her. Maybe he was afraid it had something to do with the house itself. That would make sense, especially considering what had happened to her parents.

As Jordan tried to figure out what was going on with the doctor, he was trying to console himself with the fact that Charlotte would only be in the house during daytime hours. That reasoning didn't work anymore, though. Anna had died during the day.

Chapter 24

Two days after Anna's funeral, Jordan decided she needed to get back to being a grown up and figure out what she was going to do with her life. She and the boys needed to get back to the world of the living. She had kept them home from daycare the entire week after Anna's death. It would have made funeral preparations easier if she had just taken them for a few hours, but she couldn't stand the idea of being away from them.

Now it was time to get back to their normal routine. She would take them to daycare and get the house back in order.

Neither of the boys had been very anxious to get up that morning. She gave in and let them sleep an extra half hour while she enjoyed a cup of coffee on the patio. By the time she went back to their room, Hayden was sitting up in his crib rubbing his eyes and Hudson was beginning to stir.

"Good morning, sleepy heads. Today is the day that we all start getting back to normal."

When they walked into the daycare, it was Laura who greeted them. She was usually the one working up front so it wasn't out of the ordinary. What was out of the ordinary was her pitying tone. Jordan had come to hate that sing-songy tone after her parents were killed.

"Hiiiii Jordaaaaaaaan, how are ya dooooiiiing?" Laura frowned as she added "boo" and drew imaginary tear streaks down her face.

"As well as could be expected, I guess. Thank you for asking. The first couple of days were pretty hard on the boys but you know how resilient children are. Right now we're taking things one day at a time. Did the boys miss anything exciting last week?" Jordan thought changing the subject might get rid of the pity voice. She was right.

"Well," Laura was back to her perky self, "on Monday we went to the zoo and had a wonderful time." She turned her attention to the boys. "Do you guys like animals? We've been learning about them all week. Today we're going to watch a movie and play games that are all about zoo animals."

The near schizophrenic switch to perkiness confirmed Jordan's disgust for the earlier fake sympathy. At that moment she felt a deep loathing for the stupid girl leading her children away from her. Jordan even started to leave before she had an epiphany.

As Laura walked the boys to the play area, Jordan realized it was Laura's job to be perky. Would she really want the person caring for her children to be anything less? She decided to wait like she normally would to make sure the boys settled in alright and say a decent goodbye.

Back at the house Jordan decided to blow off responsibility and take advantage of the backyard. She changed into her bathing suit and grabbed the pool essentials: a beach towel, a glass of soda packed to the top with ice, and her sunscreen. It was a beautiful California day and she was going to take full advantage of it. She turned her favorite lounge chair strategically towards the sun and settled in. The water, the landscaping, and the warm sun made her backyard feel like paradise and it wasn't more than ten minutes before she was sound asleep.

Jordan felt like a helpless spectator in the dream that began to unfold. Hudson and Hayden were standing on a stage with about 500 other graduates. She wanted to scream out for the dream to stop. She had missed everything! Where was the rest of their childhood?

Out of nowhere the front of the stage burst into flames. Jordan couldn't tear her eyes from the scene but quickly realized she wasn't a spectator in this dream. She wasn't there at all! She was a helpless voyeur of an event she wasn't attending.

She watched as the flames crawled toward Hayden and all of the other young adults standing around him. She heard them scream and saw them flail their arms futilely, only to succeed in fanning the flames. She scanned the group and found

Hayden smiling and unaffected. He stood frozen in place. Jordan realized as she watched him melt that it was only a wax figure of her son.

Then there was Hudson. His arms were raised to his sides and he was screaming. His head was back at first but when he leaned forward she saw the blood spill from his eyes and down his cheeks. The flames surrounded him and all of his muscles were tensed almost to the point of explosion. The pain struck her heart like a knife as she thought of the amount of pain her baby would have to be in to look that way. Jordan saw nothing but flames and somewhere alarms were ringing.

Not alarms, a phone… her phone. The connection between the dream world and reality seemed to take forever for her mind to process, but once it did she sat up fast. She hadn't heard the house phone ring since her parents were alive and her sense of urgency was automatic. She swung her legs over the side of the lounge chair and hurried through the sliding glass doors into the kitchen before she was even fully awake.

"Is Jordan Sullivan there?" She didn't recognize the voice on the other end of the line but she recognized the sense of urgency that usually started bad news. Her heart sank to her feet.

She thought about hanging up. Could not hearing bad news make it go away? Fighting her instincts, she answered, "This is Jordan."

"Jordan, this is Ellen Donovan from the Child's Play Daycare." Jordan felt a wave of nausea strike her stomach, threatening to turn it completely over. *The boys!*

"Would you be able to come and pick the boys up right away? We've had an accident and will be closing for the rest of the day."

"Are the boys alright?" There was no question that Jordan was now fully awake.

"Yes, yes, the boys are absolutely fine. I'm sorry; I should have said that right off the bat." *Uh... yeah!* Jordan guessed that she must have been one of the first parents Ellen had contacted.

"I'm on my way. I can be there in ten minutes." Jordan hung up the phone and ran up the stairs to grab a shirt and jeans. She could throw them on over her bathing suit on the way to the garage.

A million questions ran through her mind on the drive back to the daycare. *What in the world could have happened there today and why in the hell is every single light changing to red right before I reach it?* She fought the urge to floor the accelerator by continually reminding herself that the boys were alright.

She pulled into the parking lot and hit the speed bump she'd forgotten about going way too fast. The boys would have loved the jostling and bouncing the car went through. Jordan? Not so much. She pulled into one of the few empty spaces, threw the van into park, and ran through the front doors of the daycare. The face at the desk was not one she recognized.

"Uhm, hi." Jordan felt for a moment like she was in the wrong place. "I'm Jordan Sullivan?" Even as she was introducing herself, her eyes were scanning the emptiness beyond the windows where her children were usually playing.

"Yes, hi, Jordan. I'm Ellen Donovan, the one who called you? I'm one of the owners here. We really appreciate you coming so quickly. The kids are all in the movie room watching cartoons with the rest of the staff." She could see through the glass window to the movie room and saw Hayden's face fixated on the screen. A little more of her anxiety floated away.

"So, what exactly happened here today?" Jordan couldn't see anything broken and the roof certainly hadn't fallen in. Once her heart started to slow, she was curious about what could have caused the impending doom she heard in Ellen's voice earlier.

"Well, I was working in my office, so I didn't actually see anything first hand, but I've spoken with all of the staff members. We've all spoken with the police already, so I don't see any harm in telling you what I know."

The police? What in the hell is going on here?

Ellen continued, "The children had been separated into small groups. We had an animal theme today, so the kids were sitting in circles pretending to be their favorite animal. The group that your boys were in was being led by Natalie Michaels. Have you met her?" Jordan nodded, anxious for Ellen to get to the point.

"Well, apparently one of your boys was pretending to be a wolf and when it came to his turn, he growled or something. Several other children had already done their animal imitations so I really don't know what could have happened, but one of the little girls in the group became startled. She got up and ran out the front door before anyone even knew what was happening.

"Our front receptionist, Laura, had been on the phone but as soon as the little girl darted past, Laura dropped the phone and went after her. She was so concerned about Ashley that she didn't even think to look before she ran into the parking lot and she was struck by a speeding truck. I tell you, it never ceases to amaze me that people will speed like that in a parking lot. And right past a daycare no less!" Ellen shook her head in disgust.

"Is Laura alright? What about the little girl? Was she hurt?" Jordan thought about her own speed as she pulled into the parking lot only a few minutes earlier.

"Ashley is fine. She's obviously very shaken so her mother came right away. Unfortunately, Laura... Laura was killed. The paramedics told us that she died instantly. The paramedics didn't want us to call any of the parents until after they had everything taken care of and cleaned up here."

Jordan could tell that the businesswoman in Ellen was taking the lead, probably for fear of potential lawsuits, but the underlying emotion did seem genuine. Jordan recognized her tendency to pre-judge people kicking in again. *Oh my God!*

She had been thinking terrible things about Laura right before she dropped the boys off... It wasn't much different than when she thought terrible things about Margo right before her accident! Jordan looked up and through the window to the movie room.

She saw Hudson standing on his chair looking at her. She could worry about black magic another time. At that moment all she wanted was to get her babies home and snuggle with them. She was so thankful they weren't hurt.

"The staff is obviously shaken, and we feel it would be best if the children were at home right now." Too quickly, again probably out of fear of a lawsuit, Ellen added, "I want to assure you, though, neither of your children saw anything that happened. The police questioned the driver outside and talked to all of the staff members privately in the office."

"Could I speak with Natalie for a minute?" Jordan suddenly realized she should probably know if there was anything else that happened in the circle.

"Oh, I wish you could. Natalie went into shock or something. They took her to the emergency room but we haven't heard any news yet." Ellen the executive seemed to turn into Ellen the gossipmonger as she confided the rest of the story about Natalie.

She leaned in like she was sharing a juicy little secret. "It's very bizarre actually. From what the other staff members have said, Natalie didn't even turn around when Ashley broke from the group, so no one can figure out why she would be so traumatized. She was still sitting on the floor with the children after Laura was hit. I guess the paramedics know more about medicine than I do, but it sure didn't seem like it was shock to me. She seemed like she was hypnotized or something. Anyway, hopefully we'll hear something later this afternoon." Jordan wondered if her earlier impression of Ellen might have been correct after all.

"Thank you for telling me what happened. I normally just bring the boys on Mondays and Wednesdays, but I'll give you a call before I bring them in next. If you don't mind, I'd like to get the boys and head home now."

Chapter 25

After Jordan returned home she kept a close eye on the boys. She wanted to see if there were any negative effects from the morning's events. Either Ellen was right and they were completely sheltered from everything that happened, or they were too young to comprehend such things. Whatever the reason, they both seemed fine.

She decided it would still be a good day to spend at the pool, and a picnic sounded like a fun thing to do with the boys. She packed enough food for at least eight people into a picnic basket while the boys played with trucks at her feet.

Sitting in the grass, under the biggest tree in the yard, made the morning events seem distant. That was good. Jordan had been having feelings of guilt on and off since they left the daycare, but they seemed pretty unimportant as she sat with her sons. It wasn't like she was an important person in Laura's life or anything. All she did was think mean things about her. Like she had with Margo...

The girl was only trying to be supportive when she asked how things were going. Jordan had no right to be frustrated just because there was a certain tone in her voice or because her mannerisms were irritating. *On the other hand, it wasn't like I yelled at her or anything. Do I really have to feel guilty about a fleeting thought?*

There in the grass, the mental tug-of-war was suspended and she could allow herself to enjoy having lunch with the boys. They were safe there, away from the world. For the moment that was all that mattered.

It was truly a beautiful day. The boys were fascinated with nature and she was fascinated with the boys. Hudson had picked a few blades of grass and was trying to get them to stay in his nose. He giggled as the pieces tickled his face. Hayden had found a caterpillar and was entertaining himself by poking the creature with his finger. He touched the tip of its furry covering then clutched his hand close to his chest and laughed as the creature rolled into a ball.

For the millionth time since they'd been born, she realized how incredibly fortunate she was to have them. They were her life. And then it struck her. Suddenly she knew exactly what she needed to do. She shouldn't be involving them with more people. She should be involving them with fewer! The world was a dangerous place waiting to hit them with heartache. But in their own little world, in their own home, they would be safe. There really weren't that many reasons to leave anyway. Between the telephone and the computer, she could do almost everything she needed to do right from the house. Why couldn't they create their own fortress?

After the lunches were devoured and the caterpillar had crawled away to safety, the boys started rubbing their eyes. She stood up and brushed away the left over nose grass that Hudson had thrown across her legs.

Jordan held out a hand to each boy and both gladly took it. The three walked hand-in-hand into the house, through the kitchen, and around to the stairs. It took longer to walk next to them than to just carry them, but it was still so new to have them walk next to her. It was worth the extra time. Besides, it was getting harder and harder to pick them both up.

When they reached the stairs they each looked up to her and raised their arms wanting to be held.

"I don't blame you guys. Sometimes when I'm exhausted I don't feel like climbing these stairs either." She knelt down and both boys immediately grabbed a shoulder, ready for their lift. "Ready? Jump! Wow, you're getting heavy! At least I have both of you to counter balance though, huh?"

Before they were even half way up the stairs Hayden laid his head on her shoulder and started to drift. By the time she reached the top step, Hayden was sound asleep and Hudson's head was getting wobbly.

She had to set Hudson down to get a good enough hold of Hayden to lay him in his crib. Tears of exhaustion and rejection immediately started, along with some very loud screams.

Fortunately, it only took a second to lay Hayden down and he stayed asleep through his brother's conniption. Jordan pulled Hudson into a hug as she lifted him out of his crib.

"Shhhhh, sweetie, I'm right here." Hudson clung to her neck like he was afraid she would disappear. She bounced a little and rubbed his back while she sang a soft lullaby in his ear. Within seconds his grip loosened and his head relaxed on her shoulder. His weight told her he was asleep, but she wasn't quite done holding him yet.

She sat down in the recliner and thought about their futures. She loved them both the same amounts but for entirely different reasons. She rocked and hummed as she watched her baby fall into a deep, peaceful sleep. When her arm started to fall asleep she placed him carefully in the center of his crib.

Before leaving the room she stood in the doorway a moment. She looked at the matching cribs that contained the most precious things in her life and hoped their lives would never be touched by tragedy again.

Jordan wanted their lives to be choreographed with happy endings at every scene. For the first time, Jordan understood why her parents kept her sheltered.

Chapter 26

The next morning the boys were sitting in their high chairs having breakfast when Charlotte walked into the kitchen carrying a paper bag. "Good morning!"

Jordan found Charlotte's cheerfulness out-of-place before she remembered, Charlotte knew nothing about the accident at the daycare. Jordan decided not to ruin the day by telling her.

She turned around and greeted Charlotte with a smile. "Well, good morning to you. What in the world have you got there?"

"I brought some special treats over for my two favorite boys and a little something special for their mommy." The boys were jumping in their seats and squealing with joy. They didn't seem to notice the package she set down. Grandma was here and breakfast was over!

Jordan lifted Hudson out of his chair first and before his feet even hit the floor, he was making a b-line to Charlotte's legs. She bent down and scooped him up while he smothered her face with kisses.

"My goodness, you'd think they hadn't seen you in a year!" Jordan held Hayden to make sure that their combined force didn't wind up knocking Charlotte on her butt right in the middle of the kitchen floor. When the excitement died down, Jordan decided it could possibly be a normal day after all. The accident at the daycare was terrible, but it didn't really have anything to do with her or the boys. Would it be so wrong if she pretended it never happened?

"Well, I think that may very well be the best greeting I've ever received in my life," Charlotte said. "So who would like to see what we have for treats?"

In unison the boys nodded their heads and shouted, "Me do!"

Regardless of what she tried, Jordan couldn't shake the feeling that she needed to find out more about what happened at the daycare. Her maternal instincts were screaming that she needed to protect her children, but from what?

After enjoying the surprise pastries, Jordan asked if it would be alright if she ran a few errands. As expected, Charlotte had no problem being left alone with the boys. A half hour later Jordan was walking out the door.

The only thing she really wanted to do was go to the hospital to visit Natalie Michaels. She hadn't told Charlotte anything about what had happened at the daycare and it wasn't just because she didn't want to ruin the day. She had a nagging feeling that it all had something to do with the boys.

Jordan called the daycare before Charlotte arrived to find out where she could send Natalie flowers. They gladly told her the name of the hospital and Jordan thought how easy it was to manipulate people. Before she really even knew what she was going to say, she was pulling into the parking lot.

The front desk receptionist directed her to the third floor and pointed out the nearest elevator. On the short trip up to third, she was trying to think of ways to broach the subject. Whatever happened had frightened the woman enough to put her into shock, for crying out loud. On the other hand, maybe it was something entirely different like Ellen had suggested. Was Natalie a hypochondriac who wanted attention from someone else's tragedy? Maybe she had some kind of medical condition that no one knew anything about. Jordan had no idea what to expect. The elevator bell sounded and brought her out of her contemplations. As the doors opened she decided she would have to play it by ear.

The nurses' station stood guard over the patients, so she thought it would be best if she checked in. She stopped at the desk and asked directions to room 304. Without even looking up, the charge nurse pointed her arm straight out to the left, obviously irritated by the stupid question Jordan hadn't needed to ask.

Must not have gone into nursing because of a love of people, Jordan thought. She was surprised at how nervous she felt walking up to the door and suddenly realized she should have brought flowers. *Oh, well, too late now. Go in and get this over with.*

The door to room 304 was braced open. She walked in. As soon as she entered Jordan could see that Natalie was alone. That was good. The head of her bed was raised to the 45-degree mark, perfect for watching television, and that's exactly what Natalie was doing. Apparently she hadn't heard Jordan come into the room. She was obviously engrossed in whatever she was watching.

"Natalie?" Jordan spoke softly so as not to startle her. Natalie didn't even flinch. "Natalie?" Jordan said it a little louder, still nothing. She walked over to the side of the bed and for the first time since arriving, saw Natalie's face clearly. "Oh, my God!"

Natalie's eyes were wide open, too wide, in fact, and she had a look of terror frozen on her face. Other than the occasional blinking of her eyes, there was no movement. She looked like a wax figure frozen in horror.

Jordan stood with her hand over her mouth, unable to believe what she was seeing. She was so engrossed in Natalie's face that she didn't even hear the nurse walk through the door and up to her side. When she saw the nurse out of the corner of her eye, she let out a short scream that scared both of them. Natalie remained motionless.

"Oh, geez, I'm sorry about that," Jordan apologized. "I didn't see you come in. This is the first time I've seen her since the accident and... I... I guess I just didn't know what to expect."

The nurse looked to be about 60 and seemed as though she had probably seen a little of everything in her day.

"Yes, it's haunting, isn't it? I can assure you, she isn't in any pain, though. We're monitoring all of her vital signs and they're completely normal. It's basically like she's sleeping right now. Are you another family member?"

"Uh... no." Jordan couldn't help feeling like a kid caught in the teachers' lounge. "I'm a friend from her work. Do you have any idea how long she'll be like this?

"Unfortunately, there's no way to tell. She could snap out of it any moment or, in the worst-case scenario, it could be permanent. Physically there isn't really anything wrong with her. We'll be transferring her to the seventh floor this afternoon." From the way the nurse said it, Jordan knew the seventh floor must be the psychiatric ward.

"Her family stepped out to get a bite to eat, but they should be back any minute. You can have a seat over there if you'd like to wait for them." Jordan definitely did NOT want to wait for Natalie's family to return.

"Actually, I've got a couple of errands to run but maybe I'll stop back later." The lie was working well for her, might as well stick with it. Trying not to seem like she was in too much of a rush, Jordan left the room and headed back to the elevators.

When the doors opened and the elevator was empty, Jordan breathed a sigh of relief and stepped in. After the doors closed her body broke into convulsive shakes. Fortunately they passed before the elevator signaled the first floor and the doors opened to a crowded reception area. All she wanted at that moment was to be out of the hospital.

Outside in the parking lot she sat in her car and tried to collect her bearings. The image of Natalie's face petrified in terror monopolized her thoughts. *What in the hell could have happened that would scare someone that badly?* As much as she dreaded the thought of it, Jordan needed to talk to the little girl. She needed to find Ashley.

Chapter 27

A full twenty minutes passed and Jordan was still sitting in her car at the hospital. She was wracking her brain to remember Ashley's last name or any other piece of information that might lead her to the little girl. She was drawing a blank. The boys were too little to talk beyond one or two words, and it wasn't like there was a directory of four-year-olds anywhere. Unless…

Jordan dialed the number to the daycare and hoped it wasn't one of the sharper employees who answered the phone. For that matter, she hoped there would be someone there to answer the phone at all.

"Child's Play Daycare, may I help you?" The voice on the other end of the line was unfamiliar. That was good.

"Yes, this is Lieutenant Lacey from the San Diego Police Department. I was typing up the report from yesterday's events over there and there are a few things that I can't read. I keep telling those officers that they need to print clearly but do they listen? No. Anyway, I've got to get this done today and I just need to verify the spelling of a few things with you. Its Child's

Play, P-L-A-Y, is that correct?" She held her breath, hoping the person on the other end of the line didn't catch on that the only police officer's name she could think of was one from an 80's television show.

"Yes, that's correct."

So far, so good. "And the employee who was taken to the hospital is Natalie Mitchel?"

"No, it's Michaels. M-I-C-H-A-E-L-S."

"Man, I'm going to have to give those guys a talking to. Last thing, I can't make out the little girl's last name at all. It looks like her first name is Ashley, though, is that right?" Again Jordan held her breath.

"Yes, it's Ashley Jorgenson. J-O-R-G-E-N-S-O-N." It seemed almost too easy so Jordan decided to press her luck.

"I need to verify a couple of things with her parents, but I don't see their names written down anywhere. You wouldn't happen to know them, would you?" Jordan hoped she hadn't gone too far with that one.

"Let's see, oh yes, Mark and Amanda. What did you say your name was again?" Jordan could detect the growing suspicion. She had gone too far but that was alright. She had everything she needed.

"It's Lieutenant Lacy and for my records, what is your name?" She hoped she could turn the tables back in her favor one last time.

"My name is Maureen, but I'm just a temporary employee. Oh, here. One of the owners just walked in the door. Would you like to speak to her?"

"No, that's fine. Thank you for all of your help." Jordan hung up but not before she heard Ellen's voice in the background asking who was on the phone. Apparently luck was with her!

Jordan called information from her cell phone and got the number for Mark and Amanda Jorgenson. Now, how should she go about contacting them? Ashley was only four, so there certainly wouldn't be an opportunity for Jordan to speak to her without her parents knowing. On the other hand, the reason she wanted to know what happened was because her own children were involved. Certainly any mother would understand that!

Jordan decided to call the Jorgensons directly and see what she could find out. She dialed the number and crossed her fingers that someone would be home.

"Hello?"

"Hi, could I speak with Amanda Jorgenson?"

"This is she."

"Amanda, hi, this is Jordan Sullivan. I have twin boys who attend Child's Play Daycare with Ashley. I guess they were in the same group as your daughter Ashley the day of Laura's accident. From what I understand, it was one of my boys who scared her. They're only a year and a half so they can't tell me anything about what happened, but I was hoping maybe Ashley could shed some light on things. Would it be possible for me to come over and talk to her or meet you somewhere?"

"Jordan, is it?" Amanda waited for a positive confirmation on the other end of the line. "Ashley is with her grandparents today, but I don't really think she needs to re-live it all again. She's only four and she's already had to go through talking to the police and about 20 other people at the daycare. At this point I'd like to just let her forget about it. She had nightmares all night. I don't think she needs any other reminders about what happened."

Dead end. "I understand. I certainly don't want her to go through any more than she already has, but I want to make sure that my own children aren't traumatized too. Did she say anything to you about what happened in the circle?"

Jordan heard an exasperated sigh on the other end of the line then, after a short pause, Amanda spoke. "The only thing she said was that one of the twins turned into a monster and growled at her. There were a couple of kids who had gone before your son. One had picked a kitty and one had picked a cow, so my guess is that she was taken off guard when he started growling. She doesn't usually scare easily but she is quite imaginative. She's always been scared of wolves in story books. I really don't think you have anything to worry about, though. From what I understand, both of your boys stayed in the circle when Ashley ran off. I don't think they saw anything that would have traumatized them."

"Has she ever mentioned the boys before?" Jordan searched for some logical explanation for Ashley's fear.

"No, I think they're usually divided into similar ages for activities, so I don't think she's spent much time with them. I'm sorry but I really need to get going. If you'd like, I can give you the name of the child psychologist that the police gave me. If you're concerned about the boys, he would certainly be more helpful than I would."

"That would be great, if you wouldn't mind. I have a pen right here." Jordan thought if nothing else it might not be bad to have the name of the doctor who would be seeing Ashley. Jordan thanked Laura and ended the call.

She hadn't learned any new information, but the nagging warning in the back of her mind seemed vindicated.

There might be a logical explanation for everything that was going on. Four year olds are probably very likely to get scared at the idea of a monster. And maybe Natalie had entered some kind of catatonic state for a reason completely unrelated. Stranger things had been chalked up to coincidence, and the police hadn't spoken to her or the boys at all. No one else seemed worried about her son's involvement, so why was she?

Because no one else knew the whole story.

Chapter 28

Jordan spent the drive home reassuring herself. "So what?" she asked out loud. "What difference does it make if one of the boys is able to growl realistically and make a snarly face at a year and a half? There are child actors who make millions of dollars for doing the same type of thing." By the time she pulled into the driveway she had almost convinced herself.

Jordan walked through the front door and gave her most cheerful, "Hellllllloooooo." Charlotte answered back from the kitchen but was mostly drowned out with squeals from both boys. She laughed out loud as she heard the stampede of four little feet heading her direction.

Jordan crouched down and allowed them to tackle her with hugs. "It isn't going to be long before I can't even defend myself against you two. I can't believe how strong you're getting!" Jordan looked up to see Charlotte in the kitchen doorway drying her hands on a dish towel and smiling. She had made the right decision, not telling Charlotte about the accident. There was no reason to tell her bad news if it wasn't absolutely necessary.

"Now that's a greeting!" Charlotte's maternal smile always made Jordan feel like nothing in the world could hurt them. "They had macaroni and cheese for lunch so that probably pumped their muscles right up. Would you boys like to have some M&Ms?" The mention of chocolate was all it took to bribe the boys off their mother and back into the kitchen. Jordan picked up her purse and phone and followed after them.

"What about me? Do I get some M&Ms too?" Jordan was only half joking but was nearly as delighted as the boys when Charlotte tossed her a bag of her own. No matter what happened around them, the house would always be a safe haven for her family as long as Charlotte was around.

"So…" Charlotte began in an *I-know-something-you-don't-know* kind of voice. "Is there a new gentleman in your life you've neglected to tell me about?"

"Yeah, right," Jordan laughed. "If there were a guy in my life, you'd be the first to know about it. Actually, you'd probably have to introduce me to him! What makes you ask that?"

"Because a young man stopped by today while you were out. He's probably a little older than you but quite handsome. I thought maybe he was a new flame. He said his name was Tanas and you would know who he was."

Charlotte was loading the dishwasher and didn't see the blood drain from Jordan's face. Or hear her heart stop. After a moment of silence, Charlotte looked up and saw Jordan's face.

"Oh my goodness, what is it, Jordan?"

"I… I'm fine," Jordan stammered. "Did he give you a last name?"

"Why no, and I didn't think to ask since he said he knew you. What on earth is the matter?" Charlotte had instinctively moved closer to Jordan. "Come here, my dear. Sit down at the table. You look like you've seen a ghost. Who is he?"

"I don't actually know. My dad wrote about a gentleman named Tanas in his journals, but I don't believe I ever met him personally. If I did, I would have been too young to remember I guess. What did he look like? How old is he?"

Charlotte tried to remember everything she could. "Well… let's see, he had dark wavy hair and brown eyes… striking features, very chiseled, very handsome. I would guess he's in his early thirties." Charlotte studied Jordan's face as she gave the description.

"Did he leave a message of any kind?" Charlotte's description matched the one her father had written decades earlier. Matched it exactly!

"No message. He said he would stop by another time. Do you think there is a reason to be concerned about him? Should we call the police?" Charlotte's concern was growing.

Jordan wanted more than anything to spill her guts to Charlotte. To tell her everything she knew and everything she suspected. It was too ludicrous to even say it out loud. Charlotte would certainly think she was insane, and at that moment she couldn't stand the idea of risking the loss of her only friend. Jordan tried to compose herself as much as possible. She was preparing to lie to Charlotte for the second time that day.

"No, I'm sorry. When you said the man's name, it made me think about Mom and Dad and having to tell someone else what happened to them. It just kind of freaked me out, I guess." Jordan smiled as she shook her head. She watched Charlotte's reaction and saw the concern disappear.

"Oh, thank goodness! You had me worried there for a minute... Not to say that it isn't concerning that you're still haunted by what happened to your parents. Anyone would be, dear. Have you ever thought about talking to a professional about it?"

The diversion had been successful. Charlotte's new concern took her focus off Tanas. Jordan wished she could get her own mind off of him as easily.

Chapter 29

A week had come and gone since Charlotte passed along the news of Jordan's unexpected guest. Even though she couldn't say he was the furthest thing from her mind, at least he wasn't monopolizing every waking thought like the first few days.

It was possible, after all, that the man her father wrote about had a son. Maybe he came by to clear the air and tell her his father was in an asylum somewhere. Obviously it couldn't be the same guy. It had been more than twenty years. A few more days and she might actually convince herself.

At the moment, her biggest concern was making sure she had everything the boys would need for the day packed and ready to go. Dr. Shapiro had taken the day off so he and Charlotte could take the boys to the San Diego Zoo. It would be their first visit there, and as much as Jordan would have liked to see their reaction to the animals, she had promised herself to sort through the rest of her father's study. Without Anna around, her free time became a thing of the past.

Jordan had been alone in the house for a half hour and all she'd managed to do was drink two cups of coffee. There was time. The boys were going to be out with the Shapiros all day.

She had started to make her way to the study when she heard the doorbell. She was expecting a UPS delivery with some educational videos she'd ordered for the boys.

She opened the door and momentarily lost her breath. The gentleman standing before her may or may not have been the person her father described. He might or might not have been the man Charlotte met. It didn't matter. He was definitely the man from her dream.

She stood speechless as he smiled confidently and even bowed slightly before speaking.

"Good morning, Jordan. I would imagine that no introductions are necessary, but since this is our first official meeting I feel it's best to adhere to the rules of proper etiquette. I... am Tanas Beleez." He paused for a moment, allowing Jordan the opportunity to return the introduction. She stood frozen and speechless. Tanas's confident, patronizing smile never changed.

"And you, of course, are Jordan Sullivan. We have a great deal to talk about, you and I. Shall we move into the sitting room and make ourselves a bit more comfortable?"

Still dazed, Jordan allowed her visitor to enter the house and lead the way to her sitting room. The role-reversal seemed perfectly normal when he escorted her to a chair and only slightly out of the ordinary when he excused himself, leaving her alone as he meandered somewhere in her house.

With Tanas out of the room, Jordan realized how assumptive his forwardness had been. Even stranger was the fact that she could think clearer when he wasn't in the room. She was trying to decide if it was fear or surprise and realized it was both. She was contemplating ways to banish him from her life when he returned with a tray of coffee and two cups. Her mind started to fog over, but his inappropriate familiarity with her home helped her regain a little of her composure.

"And what, exactly, is it that we have to discuss, Mr. Beleez?" She tried to sound as confident as possible, but the quiver in her voice gave her away. She knew he could read right through her façade. She also knew the answer to her question scared her to death.

"Oh, Jordan, there is no reason to put up a false front for me. After all, it is you and I who know the true situation we are in here. I feel it would be best if we spoke candidly so as not to waste time." If his motive was to make her feel like an incompetent child, he succeeded.

"Then how about this?" she said. "What do you want with me?"

"Ahh, to the point at last. Very soon our son will reach his second birthday and…"

Jordan cut him off. "Our son? What are you talking about? You and I have never met so don't try to pretend you have any legal rights to my children!" Jordan found strength she would never have guessed she had when it came to protecting her boys.

"Tsk, tsk, and here I thought we had agreed to speak truthfully." The look of disappointment did nothing to convince her he was capable of emotion.

"Your denial of the facts does not negate the reality that they are indeed true. But don't worry, Jordan, I have no intention of involving the legal system. I do find it humorous that you think they might have some influence though." His patronizing chuckle made the hair on the back of her neck prickle. He kept talking. "You know as well as I do that our paths have not only crossed, they are forever entwined. However, I will give you the benefit of the doubt and piece together the puzzle for you." He leaned back in his chair and looked perfectly comfortable as lord of the house.

"As you learned when you found your father's journal, I am your biological father. When you met me at the door a short while ago, you learned that I am also the father of one of your boys. May we now dispense with discussions of the obvious and move forward?"

The maternal strength Jordan found earlier disappeared. She was a chastised child who nodded agreement.

"As I began to say, very soon our son will reach his second birthday. He has a great gift that must be refined. He's a chip off the old block you might say. Now, personally… I have no issues with mass destruction, but it does tend to draw unnecessary attention." Jordan held up her hand, signaling him to stop speaking.

Tanas was both perturbed and fascinated by her audacity to give him instruction, but it was early in their conversation. He would forgive her insubordination. He stopped speaking and simply raised one eyebrow. "Yes?"

"First of all, you say our son but I have twin boys. Secondly, why in the world do you think I would allow you to have anything whatsoever to do with either one of them? You claim to be my father, but you didn't have any rights to seeing me grow up. Why would you assume you have some kind of right with my children?" Jordan's fear was gone. She wanted to throw him out of her house but had a feeling that would accomplish nothing - even if it were possible.

"Perhaps I should start at the beginning. When I agreed to give your mother a child, it was with the intention that the daughter would bear me a son. You have had one purpose in this arrangement and you have fulfilled it. Our son, however, has an entirely different purpose. Obviously his blood is purer than yours. You were a third generation but he is a fourth. As for the lineage of the other child, let's just say his father is… of no consequence to me."

Jordan interrupted, "So basically you're trying to tell me that evil is stronger than good? You're trying to tell me that even though I have two sweet little boys, one of them has no choice but to become evil?"

Tanas smiled the same patronizing smile she was growing to hate. "Everyone has a choice, Jordan. You ask who is stronger? Strength is such an intangible notion. Who is more likely to be the victor in a fist fight, the individual with the greater physical strength or the individual who brings a hand gun? My counterpart is governed by a great many rules. I am not. I have but one rule to adhere to, and that is the right of free will."

Jordan felt a glimmer of hope and the return of her strength. "Then my will is that you leave my home and stay away from my children!"

His patronizing smile never faltered. "You are still confused, dear girl. You have and have always had free will over your fate. You very nearly chose to follow my counterpart at one point in your life. That would have ended my involvement with you forever… and what a shame that would have been." His feigned sadness was brief, replaced by what could only be described as jubilation.

"This time in history has yet to see a fourth generation anti-Christ. Even history is too new to have heard of such power. It will be so very entertaining." He clapped his hands as his head bowed down towards his lap. "And it very nearly didn't happen, Jordan, but… alas… the tragic demise of your parents ended your faith, did it not?"

Jordan saw the pieces of her mystery fitting together.

"So you killed my parents to keep me from getting baptized?" She was enraged, mortified, and deeply sorry, all at the same time.

"And still you do not see the full picture." He continued, "All I ever did to your parents was give them what they wanted... you. With that as a motivator it required nothing more than basic illusions to... shall we say 'manage' their behavior?

"I think it's important that you understand something. I do not cause tragedy and I do not take lives. What I do is very much the same as my counterpart. We simply do our best to influence free will. He promises rewards in a land no one has ever seen. I promise rewards... and punishments... in the real world. How do you think I got your mother to kill your dad? I'm an illusionist, Jordan. I simply paint the scene. It's you... humans who provide the action. All I had to do was show her the right thing at the right time and your mother easily made the decision to take a life.

"Oh, I may have led her to believe that I was your father, and that he was me, but I showed her who was who in the end. She made the decision to murder your father and take her own life entirely on her own.

"Now... I may have posed their bodies for effect," a sinister chuckle escaped his mouth, "but I can assure you, it was done entirely post mortem. The life and death decisions were hers, alone. I had no guarantee that you would blame my counterpart for the loss of your parents, but Jordan…" He brought his foot up onto his knee and his stare intensified. "I have been playing with human nature for centuries and suffice it to say, you did not disappoint me. You see, you have always had free will to choose your own path, as your parents did… as your children do."

"Then I'm going to take the boys to be baptized as soon as possible." Jordan's conviction was faltering but there had to be a way to beat him at his own game.

"I believe you already know that the time for that has come and gone. First and foremost, it would still be your will, not the child's. Can you not see the signs that our son has already made his choice? Can you not see the tremendous power he already holds?" He paused for a moment, knowing full well she wouldn't answer. Jordan sat looking at her lap. "I see by your silence you need no reminders of the incidents that have already occurred. Our son has inherited a great many powers, but he has an advantage that even I lack. He is not governed by the restriction of free will."

Jordan interjected, "I haven't seen either of my children do anything to hurt another human being but I've seen BOTH of them show love. And as for me, I can't say I've never sinned, but I've certainly never done anything so unforgivable as to deserve this! I did NOT make any deals with you!"

"Again you confuse me with my counterpart. I'm not here to punish or forgive transgressions." A low giggle shook his shoulders and his voice was almost a whisper. "I celebrate them." His chuckle brought the hairs on the back of her neck back to attention. "As for the love you believe you've seen from our son, until you have the ability to look directly into someone's heart, you cannot accurately evaluate his ability to love. He does not feel what you believe you're seeing; however, he is very aware of his dependence on others around him. There will come a day when that dependence no longer exists, and even you will not be immune to his abilities. Even you will be unable to turn a blind eye to his true appearance."

As much as Jordan didn't want to believe his words, she felt in her heart they were true. What she didn't believe was that there was no way to prevent it. Tanas had to be wrong about that.

She had no clue which of her sons could be evil, and she didn't even consciously decide she wanted to know. Her question came out anyway. "Which of my sons do you claim is yours?"

Jordan was startled by his eruption into a roaring burst of laughter. "Surely you must know. You have been the one who has been able to tell them apart from the beginning. Are you so incapable of seeing their true selves?"

She didn't know, and now she wondered if she ever wanted to. If Tanas told her which son he was talking about, she would have to choose differently for him. What did that mean… home schooling? She could handle that. Then she thought of the things that had already happened and the unbelievable power it would take to be able to bend physical objects with only your mind, to be able to influence someone's decisions without making a move or a sound. She had never seen anything that would be a sign of the things Tanas was talking about. Could it be because she was their mother?

Jordan thought about Adolph Hitler. He was an innocent toddler too at one point in life. If she had the chance to go back in time and kill him while he was just a baby, she could have prevented the deaths of millions. When she thought of the atrocities she'd heard about in history classes, she could certainly see the honor in it.

But what if he were her baby? Couldn't she love him enough to prevent that from happening? Neither of the boys had ever done anything but love her. There was no way that either of them would hurt her. There was good in both of them. Tanas had to be wrong.

"All I see are two beautiful, innocent children. If what you're saying is true, there should be a birthmark with three sixes on one of them, right? Neither of them have anything like that anywhere!"

"You, my dear, have read too many fiction novels. Do you really think I would mark my child in such a pedestrian way? Mark him in a way that he, or she, could be identified so easily? Lest you forget, you too are one of my offspring. Where is your birthmark of sixes?"

Tanas moved his foot down from his knee and placed it squarely next to the other. "No… I would never resort to such elementary tactics in order to recognize my own children. It's not so much different than your own ability to tell them apart I suppose." He leaned forward and lifted his cup of coffee from the saucer.

"Suppose you knew… then what? I can assure you that you are incapable of performing the only act that would save the child's soul."

"Maybe you underestimate me." Jordan tried to sound more confident than she felt. She began to hope that his arrogance would be enough to make him just tell her. "What exactly would I have to do?"

"To take what you have given, of course." His smile disappeared and was replaced by a somber look. "You, and only you, have the power to save his soul by taking his life before he reaches the age of reason."

Jordan stood abruptly. "Never! I don't know how, but I won't let you near either one of my babies! I will figure out some way to save my children or I'll die trying. Now get out of my house!" She held her arm straight out in the direction of the door. She waited with a feeling of joyous triumph at her new found conviction. She waited for him to rise with slumped shoulders and exit in shame. She waited until she felt stupid standing there with her arm hanging out in front of her.

"Such dramatics." Tanas's calm was unaffected by both her outrage and her defeat. When he continued he sounded bored.

"We both know your inability to face choices, Jordan, but don't worry. Your role will change back to mere spectator very soon.

"It's really quite simple... somewhat more within your capabilities, at this point. You are troubling yourself with thoughts of how our son's future unfolds, but that has already been determined. What you must decide now is whether you would like to live long enough to see it. The time has come for you to make a choice, Jordan. You have wavered without particular loyalties your entire life. Today you find yourself in the middle of two equally powerful forces that repel each other. As their strength grows, you can either be crushed by it or benefit from it. All you have to do is choose which son to keep. Once the decision is made, I will walk away from this house forever - with my son.

"Think about it, Jordan. You could live your entire lifetime before the two of them meet again... As always, the choice is yours." He picked up his coffee cup and sipped the last of the remaining liquid. After carefully returning the cup to its saucer, he stood.

"The Shapiros will be returning shortly with the children. As much as I would like to meet our son in person, I feel it would be best to take my leave of you now. And don't worry too much, Jordan. You can always choose to do nothing… again."

With that he was gone.

Jordan remembered what her father had written about how meeting Tanas made his skin crawl. Hers was doing exactly that and she needed to take a shower.

Her mind was spinning so quickly that the thoughts jumbled together into a blur. She changed her mind from a shower to a bath and as the water ran into the tub, her random thoughts began to separate into coherent trains.

She could save one of her sons, but it would mean handing the other one over to Tanas. She thought about Hudson and the dimples that only came out when he smiled. He was her studier and she imagined having deep philosophical discussions with him someday when he was older.

She thought about Hayden and the way his eyebrows gave him away emotionally. He was already learning how to win people over with different facial expressions. She remembered that morning when he looked at her with a raised eyebrow when she asked if he wanted a bite of her oatmeal. He was her entertainer and she imagined watching him in sports and plays when he was older.

The idea of life without either boy wasn't something she could fathom. There had to be a way to beat Tanas!

As Jordan climbed into the water that was much hotter than she could normally tolerate, she realized she needed to talk to someone. There had to be something she could do to save her children, and she knew she couldn't come up with it on her own. The big question was how to explain the situation to an outsider without winding up in the mental ward.

For Jordan the choice of who to go to was simple. She had no one in her life except the Shapiros; it would have to be them. She felt immediately reassured and realized she would have chosen them out of a field of a thousand possibilities anyway.

Chapter 30

As Jordan stood on her bathroom mat drying off, she heard distant voices and knew the Shapiros were back with the boys. She had a sudden twang of anxiety at the idea of discussing the lunacy that had become her life. Would they think she was crazy and make an excuse for a quick exit?

She could not allow herself to chicken out. She threw on her sweatshirt, pulled on her jeans, took a deep breath, and reached for the doorknob.

Jordan enterred the foyer as Roger and Charlotte finished removing shoes and jackets from two very tired little boys. Even in their exhaustion they were excited to see their mother. She greeted them both with huge hugs as she stooped down to their height. The hugs loosened slightly as two little heads came to rest on each of her shoulders. *He's just got to be wrong about them,* she thought.

Jordan strained at the weight of the boys but was able to stand up without letting go of either twin. "It looks like you've pooped them out. I'll take them up to their room and put them to bed. Could you guys stick around for a while?" Jordan watched as the Shapiros engaged in a silent conversation about their agenda and gave her nods, signaling that they could indeed stay. "Great. I'll be right back. Go ahead and make yourselves comfortable."

By the time Jordan returned, Roger and Charlotte were settled into the sitting room. Whatever they had been talking about stopped when they saw Jordan enter the room. She noticed that the bags under the doctor's eyes were a little lighter than last time she'd seen him. Lighter, but still obvious. She still had no idea how she was going to start the conversation but hoped the words would come to her at some point.

"So how was the zoo?" Small talk seemed like the best place to start.

"We were just talking about that," Charlotte's answer clearly signified the lead into a story. "It was a beautiful day and we certainly got our fill of exercise, but neither of us has ever seen the animals act so strangely. They ran away or hid every time we got close to their cages. Unfortunately, the boys didn't get to see very many. Maybe it's mating season or something."

"Have you ever noticed other strange things happening around the boys?" Jordan had found her opening.

"Like what, dear?" Again it was Charlotte who spoke, but the doctor was looking down at his hands as if he hadn't heard the question.

"Well, I don't know really. I guess it would be best if I start at the beginning and actually, Doc, you will probably know more about this than I do." His head snapped up quickly.

"Several months ago I found my father's journal. There were a lot of things that I didn't know about my parents but nothing earth shattering. It was things like where they had lived and the fact that my mother had lost children before having me. Anyway, he wrote about their first appointment with you, and how the tests showed he was sterile. Then a short while later my mother became pregnant. Do you remember that?"

"Yes," the doctor answered in a way that almost seemed like relief. The funk she had noticed during Anna's funeral hadn't left him but she could swear she saw it lifting now. He went on, still guarded. "I had no idea that you knew anything about that. Are you wondering if your father was your biological father?"

"Unfortunately, I know that answer too." Jordan continued, "He wrote about that in his journal. My biological father's name is Tanas Beleez. He's the man you referred them to." Jordan searched their faces and saw no reaction from Dr. Shapiro but understandable confusion from Charlotte.

"Do you mean the man who stopped by here the day you were out?" Charlotte asked. "That hardly seems possible. He can't be older than 35."

"Well, that's just it. My father described Tanas in his journal as being around 35 when they met him. He came back,

Charlotte; he was here today and he hasn't aged or changed in more than 2 decades. And he told me things." Jordan shook her head.

"He told me unimaginable things that I wouldn't believe for a second under normal circumstances, but when you put it all together... well, I just don't know." She took a deep breath and braced herself. "How about if I tell you everything I know; then we can debate the sanity of it afterwards."

Jordan spent the next hour telling the Shapiros everything she knew, from her father's first dealings with Tanas to her meeting with him earlier in the day. She explained in great detail everything she knew about what had happened at the daycare and even told them about Anna calling out to her before falling.

There were several times during the recounting when Charlotte shook her head and tried to interrupt. She wanted to argue the lunacy of what she was hearing, but Jordan asked her to listen first. The doctor, however, never tried to interrupt and showed no disapproval whatsoever, not during Charlotte's protests or Jordan's explanations.

Finally, Jordan had told them everything she knew, well... almost everything. She couldn't bring herself to tell them what Tanas said would prevent the inevitable.

"I hadn't put this together when I read Dad's journal but it came to me today. His name is an anagram. Bub Beleez is Beelzebub and Tanas is Satan."

She studied their faces for signs. Were they leaning towards thinking she should be committed or did they believe her? She couldn't tell.

Charlotte ended the suspense. "My dear, no one can argue the fact that there have been some horrendous things that have happened in your life, but I'm sure there has to be a logical explanation for all of this." Charlotte looked to her husband for support and was surprised to see him staring down at his lap, cleaning his glasses.

"Darling, you're the scientist in the group here. Tell Jordan that everything she's talking about has a logical explanation."

Roger was silent for several moments leaving both women wondering what he could be thinking. He held up his glasses, carefully inspecting his polishing job, put them back on and took a deep breath. His exhale of breath came out in a sigh and he spoke.

"Being a scientist has made me overlook, for many years, several of the things Jordan is talking about. I have searched for logical explanations and come up blank, so I've chosen to ignore them. I don't know for a fact that Jordan had a meeting with the devil today, but there are things that I've seen that cause me to believe she very well may have."

Roger told Jordan and Charlotte about what he had seen before the lights went out when the twins were born. Charlotte looked at him as if she were viewing a stranger and Jordan looked at him in horror.

Jordan was mortified at the realization that instead of having her fears taken away, they had actually been confirmed. Her heart sank at the idea of what might become of her children. "Do you know which twin was born first?" She couldn't look him in the eye as she waited for the answer. She concentrated on holding back her tears.

"No. I'm sorry but I don't." Dr. Shapiro looked down to his lap again. "We didn't take the boys' foot and handprints until after they were both delivered. Normally that wouldn't be a big deal with fraternal twins but none of us could tell the boys apart, so I can't say for sure which one was born first." The doctor started to say something else but stopped himself. The bags under his eyes were darker again.

The three of them sat in silence for several minutes. Jordan broken hearted, Roger deep in thought, and his wife lost in disbelief. Charlotte watched the others' faces like a tennis match in extremely slow motion. Finally she couldn't stand it.

"Well, I can't believe any of this. They're just little boys… little boys whom most people can't even tell apart. If one of them were evil incarnate, I would certainly think there would be some drastic differences between them." Charlotte shook her head again but couldn't dismiss the fact that the most rational person she knew, her husband, DID believe it.

"There's so much I haven't told you, my love. Remember the other day when I was talking about men wanting to play God? Well, I have firsthand experience with that. It was I who gave Edgar to Tanas." The doctor rubbed his forehead hard and continued. "I didn't know the Sullivans when I made my deal with Tanas, so when he gave me the chance to settle my debt once and for all just by sending a couple of strangers to see him, I took it." He looked up at Jordan. "I didn't know them then. I'm so very sorry. I had no way of knowing that he had ties back to your great-grandmother. I had no way of knowing he was continuing experimentations he had started in concentration camps. Hell, who knows! Maybe it's a plan he put in motion way before THAT even. I know it shouldn't have mattered that they were strangers, but I was desperate. Looking back, I see now that he engineered that part as well." The doctor exhaled deeply. It seemed to Jordan that the weight of the world had left his shoulders.

"I justified my actions by doing good things with the money we made and I watched you closely when you were growing up, for any... signs. There was never anything. For 21 years there was never anything. Then when the signs started... I didn't have the courage to face the truth." He looked down at his lap.

"In the beginning I thought I'd rigged the game, having Charlotte as my ringer and all, but he kept coming back into our lives."

More than ever before, Roger Shapiro wanted a cigarette. He pushed through it and continued. "When Rog was baptized, it was supposed to be game over. I had won. I had everything a man could ever dream of having. I was arrogant. I truly believed that I knew how to beat him but he kept coming back. Remember when my friend Daniel died, Charlotte?" The doctor turned his eyes to Jordan. "He was supposed to be Rog's godfather, but he was killed in a car accident on the way to the church.

"I didn't realize until it was way too late that I never won any of the battles. I wasn't a brilliant strategist with a secret ringer. He had choreographed the entire thing. I didn't out think him. He was playing a game much bigger than mine and I had no way of knowing. My strategies were for a moment but his were for a millennium. I didn't think far enough ahead, and I had no way to imagine what he might be planning. I didn't fall into his path, Charlotte; I helped him build it." He took a deep breath.

"I couldn't see beyond my own lifetime any more than my father could. We were just pawns as he 'line bred' his way through Jordan's family tree."

Charlotte looked at her husband with undeniable love and compassion. "You've carried so much all these years." Roger weakly held a hand up to silence her.

"I found the connection when I was studying everything I could about the twins. Jordan's great-grandmother's name was Mary. She was a twin sister to Anna's great-grandmother Mara." When he took a breath, his shoulders slumped even further.

"So… Anna and I were related?" Amidst Jordan's confusion was a touch of anger. If the doctor had known that she and Anna were related, why wouldn't he have said something? She had lived an entire year before the twins were born, believing she had no living relatives. Her mind was still spinning with what if's when he continued.

"They were 14 years old when they were taken by the Nazi soldiers. Their family had no idea that there was a plan to build an Arian nation. They didn't even know what was going on when they were led to the gas chambers. There was no way to predict that someone like Josef Mengele would actually do those kinds of experiments." The doctor looked up at his wife and then to Jordan. He realized that he must sound like he was losing his mind. He made a concerted effort to pull it back together. He took a deep breath and started to fill in the gaps.

"Mengele and my father knew each other before the war. He talked about conducting genetic experimentation on living people even when they were in medical school together. He had introduced his friend Tanas to my father once." The doctor shook his head and laughed weakly. "My father was smart enough not to get involved with him though. Shortly after that Mengele joined the army and fell into Hitler's favor from the start. I don't know whether Tanas put the idea of playing God into Mengele's head or just used it to his advantage, but they were a match made in hell." He paused, "It's almost ironic. He couldn't get my father, so he waited for me.

"Anyway, Mengele manipulated the eggs, the sperm, the embryos, the infants, and yes, the parents in an attempt to create the perfect race." He looked at Jordan.

"Mary, your great-grandmother, died before the Allied forces arrived at the concentration camps. One of her children, however, was found alive.

"The little girl was barely more than an infant, but she had been the object of experimentation since before she was born. There were medical records showing that twin fetuses were detected early on but when Mary delivered, there was no indication that another baby had ever existed. Twin absorption, they would call it today.

"Mengele was convinced that he had discovered a way to make 'survival of the fittest' occur in utero. Jordan... that lone twin was your grandmother." The three sat in silence as the words sank in.

"She was taken to my father's orphanage when she was about one but her physical maturity was closer to eight. The growth hormones and accelerators that she was given, well... who knows. With all of the mix-up and confusion of the war no one kept accurate records, but my father knew Mara and he wrote down her story."

"Suppose that all of this is true." Charlotte interrupted. "There still has to be something that can be done. You were going to have them baptized the day that Anna died. Let's do that, let's get them baptized." Charlotte's ever hopeful spirits tried to lift the room.

"I threatened Tanas with that this afternoon," Jordan said. "He said that it wouldn't make any difference because it would be my choice, not the boys'."

"Well, why should we trust him to tell us if it would work? He lies." Charlotte reasoned. "If nothing else, it certainly couldn't hurt anything."

"That's what Anna and I thought," Jordan said sadly. "How could we make sure that something like that wouldn't happen again?"

"Well, what about an exorcism then?" Charlotte was running out of ideas but then Jordan's head tilted at the possibility of hope.

Even if only a part of the things she'd heard about possessions were true, the boys were nowhere near that far gone! "Yes, that's a great idea! Do people really do those kinds of things? Who would I call?" Jordan was ready to put the ball in motion but had no idea where to start. Charlotte was about to answer when Roger interrupted.

"I think we are forgetting something. An exorcism, if the movies hold true in any way, is done to drive out evil spirits that possess an individual. What we're talking about is evil incarnate, not a possession." Dr. Shapiro paused briefly, "What is left when you drive out the whole of something?

"Jordan, did Tanas give you any type of indication about what could be done? Maybe something you said that made him nervous or defensive?"

Jordan sat silently for a moment as a mental debate raged within her. How could she tell them what Tanas had said? How could the doctor have figured it out so quickly? What if they actually wanted her to follow through and kill one of her children? On the other hand, how could she expect them to help her if they didn't know everything? She had to tell them.

"He told me… He told me that the only way to change the outcome would be to take the child's life." Upon saying it out loud Jordan burst into tears. Charlotte rushed over to her side and put her arm around Jordan's shoulder.

"Shhhhh, he's lying, Jordan. There has to be another way and we will find it together." Charlotte pulled her tighter as she continued to reassure her. "Try to be strong, my dear. We love those children too and together we will do whatever needs to be done to save them. Both of them." Jordan turned towards Charlotte and wrapped both arms around her. As Charlotte sat holding and consoling Jordan, neither noticed the extreme look of concern on the doctor's face.

When Jordan had mostly composed herself, Charlotte brushed her thumb under Jordan's eyes to wipe away the last of the tears. "I have to be honest with you, I'm having a hard time believing everything the two of you have been talking about, but there are things that have happened to completely convince me of God's involvement in my life. How could I deny the existence of a devil He warned us about?" It was obvious that the words she would choose next were vital.

"I saw Rog's face when he was born. I felt uncomfortable with him from the first moment I held him. Do you remember, Roger? Do you remember how the doctors thought I had post-partum depression?" She exhaled in relief. "I had Rog baptized as soon as possible because I was afraid of him.

"The feelings all went away as soon as he was baptized, so I haven't thought about it in years. I'd always told myself the doctors were right and it was depression. I knew it was more than that."

Charlotte straightened in her seat and returned to her take-charge self. "Now, let's put our heads together and figure out the first step. I think we need to go ahead and have both boys baptized." Jordan reluctantly nodded her agreement.

"To be on the safe side, I think it would be best if we ask the priest to come here. I don't think we would need to explain anything to him other than that we would like the ceremony to be private and to take place in your home. I will contact Father Hannigan in the morning and make the arrangements. I think I will tell him that we're afraid one of the boys is ill so you would like the baptism done as quickly as possible. As for any further steps, let's see how the baptism goes and then decide from there. Does that sound like a good plan to everyone?"

Jordan enthusiastically nodded her agreement and Dr. Shapiro shrugged his. Their relationship seemed to undergo a shift in power but then she realized, the only thing that changed was her perspective. The doctor always seemed so sure, so determined, she never questioned his authority. Now he just looked lost and defeated. His strength had always come from his wife.

On the drive home, Roger desperately wanted to ask Charlotte to distance herself from Jordan and the boys. He ran over different options in his mind: take her on vacation, tell her they had to move out of state, anything!

Roger knew he was the one responsible for perpetuating the mess in the first place. He knew he should want to help as much as his wife did, but he was old. He was tired. He'd fought the battles he chose when he was young enough to win.

He was also more frightened than he'd ever been. He loved the boys like they were his own grandchildren, but Charlotte was his life. He would do whatever he had to do to protect her.

His thoughts wouldn't matter in the end. Neither hell nor high water would keep Charlotte from doing whatever she could to help Jordan and the boys. As much as he hated it sometimes, it was the main reason he loved her so deeply. It was also the reason he had gambled their family's future on the strength of her faith. There was only one thing he could do. He would simply have to protect her while she helped.

As the Shapiros were driving home, Jordan carefully took each boy from his crib and put them into her bed. She crawled under the covers between them and slipped one arm behind each of their heads. At least for now she would make sure that nothing touched their little worlds.

Jordan had ultimately confided everything to the Shapiros except the deadline. She had no idea when the age of reason occurred but until she knew a little more, she was afraid that confiding it to anyone might put the boys in even more danger.

She fell asleep thinking about decisions and the age of reason.

Chapter 31

The next morning, Charlotte was at home trying to track down Father Hannigan by phone. Jordan was on the internet searching for information about the "age of reason."

Jordan was becoming frustrated with site after site dedicated to Thomas Paine's book with the same name. She scanned the summaries, hoping they might mention something about Tanas's reference, but she was having no success. Finally, she stumbled upon a website called the Catholic Encyclopedia and found exactly what she was looking for. She began to read the main page as her heart beat wildly in her chest. It read:

"Age of Reason

The name given to that period of human life at which persons are deemed to begin to be morally responsible. This, as a rule, happens at the age of seven, or thereabouts, though the use of reason requisite for moral discernment may come before, or may be delayed until notably after, that time. At this age Christians come under the operation of ecclesiastical laws. "

The words she read afterwards could have just as easily been in a foreign language, but she understood the part that mattered. The age of reason happens around the age of seven. That is, of course, from a Christian standpoint.

Even if it happened much earlier, she would still have years before a decision would have to be made. She would have lots of chances to try to change fate. She still had no idea how to accomplish the task, but at least there was a glimmer of hope with the gift of additional time.

So why had Tanas referred to their second birthday? Even if the Satanic age of reason is half the time of Christianity, I should still have nearly two years. What was it he had said? She tried to think back to his exact words and couldn't remember. She wished that she had been as wise as her father and written them down while they were still fresh in her memory, but she hadn't. She did remember the context of what he had said and guessed that the age of two was a critical time to begin mentoring whatever powers might exist.

That could mean that he would try to kidnap one of her sons before then, or it could mean that the powers would begin gaining strength at that age. Either way, their second birthday wasn't far away. Hopefully one of the solutions she and the Shapiros discussed would work before then.

At that same moment in the Shapiro household, Charlotte was thanking Father Hannigan and hanging up the phone. With surprisingly few questions, he had agreed to conduct a private baptism at Jordan's house the next morning. Apparently the lie about a potential health concern was enough to satisfy the priest's curiosity and perk his sense of urgency. Charlotte immediately dialed Jordan's number to make sure she and the boys would be home and ready the next morning at 9:00 am.

Charlotte had started to wonder whether Jordan was even home when she finally picked up after six rings. "Hello?"

"Jordan, thank goodness. I was beginning to think maybe you weren't at home." Charlotte didn't introduce herself but Jordan knew immediately who she was.

"Sorry about that. I was doing some research on the internet and I left my phone in the kitchen. Were you able to get a hold of Father Hannigan?" She may have several months, but Jordan didn't want to waste any time, even in conversation.

"Yes, I did and he is available tomorrow morning. He said he can be at your house at 9 am. Does that work for you?" Charlotte asked.

"Absolutely! Are you kidding? Thank you so much for arranging this with him!" Jordan's hope began to mount. Everything was working out perfectly. Surely this had to be a sign that things were going to be all right.

"Why don't I come over around 8 to help you get the boys ready?" Charlotte hadn't completely finished her thought when Jordan interrupted abruptly.

"No! Please don't come over until 9:00. I'm sorry but as much as I would love to have you here to help me get them ready, I don't want to put you in any kind of danger. Remember what happened to Anna? We were taking them to get baptized that day too." Jordan felt sure that she herself would die if something happened to Charlotte. It felt like forever before Charlotte finally spoke.

"Do you really think either of the boys would do something to hurt me?" Charlotte sounded more hurt than concerned.

"A part of me doesn't think so, but there's another part of me that just doesn't know, and I don't want to take any chances. Remember how much they loved Anna?" Jordan wanted to reassure her friend but not at the expense of her safety.

"Alright then. I will see you at ten to nine." Both women laughed a nervous chuckle at the compromise. They said their goodbyes and Jordan set about cleaning the house in preparation for the big day. Regardless of what she was doing, she kept at least one eye on the boys. If something were going to happen, she would be watching.

Never before could Jordan remember an evening that dragged on more slowly. She had taken the boys to the store and bought three movies she thought they might like. They were completely engrossed in a cartoon about two dogs on a trek across the country, and she was completely engrossed in them.

She hadn't said anything about the baptism in front of the twins. It was still hard to imagine they could actually understand what she was saying anyway, but there was too much at stake to take chances.

She was excited, nervous, scared, and curious plus about every other emotion humanly possible. She imagined she probably felt like a kid the night before Christmas on a year when he had been very, very bad. She found herself checking the clock every ten minutes and realized she needed to do something to occupy herself before she completely lost her mind.

The Bible! That would be a perfect way to bide time until a baptism. She would read her Bible.

The amount of dust she had to brush from the pages when she took it off of the bookshelf was embarrassing, but at least she knew where to find it. She settled into the overstuffed lounge chair while the boys watched their movie.

She had finished reading, well, mostly scanning, Genesis when the DVD she had put on for the boys went to the menu screen. They were wide awake and not very happy when she shut off the cartoon they were ready to watch again. Deciding it wasn't going to hurt anything to let them veg out in front of the TV for one night, she pushed play. The disc started over at the familiar menu page. She pressed play and the boys immediately quieted down.

Jordan settled back into her chair and picked up at the start of Exodus. What she hoped would be soothing reassurance of a forgiving, all-powerful God, was instead a frightening look into a vengeful, punishing one. She thought about the treatment that God's son received the last time he came and wondered which of the boys' fate would actually be worse.

By the time the movie ended for the third time, both of the boys' heads were bobbing. Hers was threatening to do the same.

She had read quite a few chapters of the Bible and although the words hadn't necessarily comforted her, the act of reading them did. She held onto the boys' hands as they walked upstairs together. She was relieved they didn't need her to carry them. The day had taken all she had to give, and it was enough to drag her own feet up the stairs.

Rather than heading for their cribs to the left, both boys turned right and made a b-line for her bed. She laughed out loud at how they were suddenly opposed to sleeping on their own. She didn't mind a bit. She actually welcomed the chance to keep them safely next to her for another night.

It seemed that Jordan had barely lain down when the alarm started signaling 7:30. Still half asleep, she reached over and shut it off, hoping to prevent the beeping from waking the boys. They were both still sound asleep. She propped pillows around the sides of the bed in case either of them started rolling and headed in to take her shower.

The warm water felt good against her skin and helped wake her up. There was a big day ahead of them and she hoped to God nothing tragic happened. With that thought, she decided to say an actual prayer and ask God to watch over them. It had been a long time since she'd prayed and she hoped God wasn't keeping a score card.

After she was as ready as she was going to be for the day, she went back to the bedroom to wake up the boys. Hayden was starting to stir and greeted her with a big smile when he saw her. She woke Hudson and took both boys into the nursery to pick out the clothes they would be wearing. It felt more like she was dragging them than carrying them. Fifteen minutes later they were on their way downstairs for some breakfast.

Jordan had just settled the boys into their high chairs when the phone rang. She felt a twinge of anxiety that it might be bad news. Her anxiety showed when she answered the phone.

"Good morning, it's just me," Charlotte said on the other end. It seemed she knew exactly how Jordan was feeling. "Roger was called into the hospital this morning, so he isn't going to be able to join us, but I wanted to see if there was anything I could bring over before I left the house."

"Oh, thank you so much, but I think we have everything we need. I picked up a coffee cake last night when we went out to get movies so I thought we'd have that for lunch while Father

Hannigan is here." Jordan looked to the boys when the priest's name slipped out. Both boys seemed intent on eating their Cheerios.

"That sounds wonderful," Charlotte replied. "I have a couple of things left to do before I leave. I should still be at your house by a quarter to nine." The two women said their goodbyes and Jordan breathed a sigh of relief. Everything was going fine, and very soon her children would be baptized.

The boys finished their breakfasts and were playing with their own toys in the sitting room when the front door opened at exactly 8:45. Even though she knew in her heart that the boys loved Charlotte and would never do anything to hurt her, Jordan was still relieved to see her walk through the front door intact.

"Good morning, Sunshines! How are my favorite little boys in the whole world doing today?" She held her arms out as she stooped down. Both boys came running into the hug. Jordan stood in the kitchen doorway smiling as she watched them greet each other. Things were going to be alright, she knew it in her heart.

Jordan offered Charlotte a cup of coffee, which she gratefully accepted. They sat down at the kitchen table by the boys and made small talk about everything except their plans for the day. The boys raced toy cars around the kitchen.

"It's funny, isn't it?" Jordan wondered out loud. "They never actually play together. They can play the same game and be in the same room, but they never actually play anything together."

"Yes, it is. I noticed that a long time ago but never really put a lot of thought into it. If what we were talking about the other night is actually true, I guess it would make sense, wouldn't it?" Charlotte seemed sad that there was further confirmation of the ludicrous assumption they had all reached.

"You know, now that I think about it, the nurses in the hospital even commented on how they wouldn't tolerate being in the same bassinet together. My God, it's hard to imagine that even as newborns they could be..." Jordan's thoughts trailed off and Charlotte nodded. Neither woman was truly prepared to accept the potential ending to that sentence.

"Jordan, Roger has been berating himself about introducing your parents to Tanas. He was moaning in his sleep about it last night. I know it doesn't..." Charlotte's explanation was interrupted.

"Charlotte, if Tanas told me he would leave us alone forever if I just told a stranger to go and talk to him... well, I would jump at the chance. I wish I could say differently and I'm sure he does too, but he had no way of knowing. It wasn't his fault." Jordan wasn't trying to make her friend feel better. She truly meant what she was saying. In fact, she wished she really could have the opportunity to pass her problems off on a stranger.

They sat in silence for a few moments watching the twins. It was Jordan who eventually broke it. "It probably doesn't mean anything but it's after 9:30 already. You don't suppose something's happened to Father Hannigan, do you?" Charlotte looked at her watch for confirmation and found that Jordan was right. Their eyes met but neither held any reassurance.

"Oh, I'm sure he must have been delayed, nothing to be concerned about. I'll call the church and see if the secretary knows what's taking him so long." Charlotte walked over to the phone and picked it up while Jordan stared in horror at the boys.

Something was wrong. She knew something was wrong, but the boys had been with her all morning. Surely they couldn't have that kind of power, even if Tanas was right.

Her maternal instincts were stronger than ever as she rushed over and scooped each boy off the floor. She boosted them up onto the counter and wrapped her arms around them. Jordan watched Charlotte finish her conversation while holding her sons. It seemed like forever before Charlotte turned to face them.

"I spoke with Margaret; she's the secretary there. She said the Father left the church around 8:30, and as far as she knew he was coming straight here. She's going to do some checking and then call us back if she hears anything. I gave her your number."

Charlotte tried to make her voice light but it only partially worked. "Try not to worry, my dear. I'm sure he got tied up in traffic or something. I'm sure he carries a cell phone. His office would know if something had happened. He's fine." Charlotte moved closer to Jordan.

"Why don't you let me take one of the boys?" She reached out her arms and raised the pitch of her voice to a range that was as close as Charlotte got to baby talk. "You two are getting way too big for momma to carry by herself."

Jordan handed Hayden to the only other person in the world she would trust with his life.

Both women stood in the kitchen rocking back and forth with a toddler's head resting on their shoulders and tiny arms wrapped around their necks.

Not ten minutes later the phone rang. Charlotte looked at Jordan, "Would you like me to answer it?" Jordan nodded and Charlotte placed Hayden on the floor.

Jordan went to the kitchen table and sat down but even before she was completely in her seat, Hudson was scrambling to get out of her arms. Both boys were anxious to return to their games.

Jordan listened to Charlotte's end of the conversation. It consisted mostly of "I see's" and "Oh dear's." Jordan knew they weren't signs of good news. The phone conversation lasted less than five minutes. Charlotte hung up the phone and took a chair at the table next to Jordan.

"I'm afraid there's been an accident. Now, I'm sure it's a coincidence, but right after Margaret and I got off the phone the first time, she received a call from the police. Apparently Father Hannigan was on the freeway when a drunk driver jumped the median and hit his car head on. I can't imagine what type of person is driving drunk at 8:30 in the morning but it does happen, Jordan. Father Hannigan died instantly." Charlotte tried her best to be reassuring but was struggling to convince herself.

"I appreciate what you're trying to do, but you know as well as I do it's no coincidence." Jordan was bordering on hysterics. "I've been trying to believe that all of the things that have happened are coincidental too, but we both know they're not! I was so careful not to say anything around the boys, just in case, but this morning when you called I mentioned Father Hannigan's name! That's all it took, just his name! What am I going to do?" Jordan placed her head in her hands and sobbed.

"I'm here and we're going to figure this out together." Charlotte took Jordan's hands in her own.

"They're only babies, Jordan. Even if one of them IS actually the child of the devil, he's also half yours. I know there is love in both of these children." Charlotte's own eyes filled with tears. "They are just babies. We will not allow Satan to have either of them." Roger Shapiro was wise to bet his eternity on Charlotte. She wasn't afraid. She knew she could win. She had beaten him before.

Jordan put her arms around Charlotte's neck and the two women embraced... and sobbed.

When they pulled apart, they both noticed they were being watched.

"What am I missing?" Jordan wondered aloud. "If one is the child of the devil and one is the child of God, why can't I tell which is which? Why doesn't God help me?"

Charlotte shook her head. "I don't know, Jordan. I don't know. I don't think any mother sees evil in her children, but it's more than that. None of the rest of us sees a difference either." The boys lost interest in the women they loved and turned their attention back to their toy cars.

After a long pause, Charlotte broke the silence. "I have an idea. Contrary to what Tanas told you, baptism must have some kind of effect or Anna and Father Hannigan wouldn't have paid the ultimate price to stop it from happening. The most important ingredient in a baptism is the holy water!"

Charlotte spoke a little faster as her excitement grew. "We can do it right now... by ourselves. There is a font right inside the doors of the cathedral down the street. Anyone who enters can dip his fingers in holy water and genuflect as he enters. I'll run over there and fill a vial with holy water. I may not be a priest, but if the water is blessed, I can read the words out loud as well as anyone else. While I'm gone do you think you could find the wording for the baptismal service on the internet?"

Jordan was still tentative. "I don't know, Charlotte. I believe the boys love you very, very much but assuming what Tanas said is correct, one of them isn't capable of feeling love. If that's true, we would be putting you in as much danger as Anna or the Father. I'm their mother and according to him, even I'm only safe until they reach the age of reason." Jordan suddenly remembered she hadn't mentioned that part to the Shapiros. She saw the look of confusion on Charlotte's face and knew she had to fill in the blanks.

"I'm sorry I didn't tell you this the other night. I guess I was... afraid. Anyway, he told me that one of the twins was incapable of feeling love. He said that what appeared to be love was actually a manipulation brought about out of dependency. He said that dependency ends at the 'age of reason' so I looked it up on the internet and found out it's around the age of seven." She surveyed Charlotte's face for an indication of her feelings, but there wasn't any. Jordan continued.

"Now, that's the Christian definition, so I'm assuming the Satanic age of reason would happen a little earlier. I didn't find anything that talked about a difference. Anyway, he said that at that point, even I wouldn't be safe." Jordan felt better now that Charlotte knew everything.

Charlotte looked to the boys, unable to believe that anyone so tiny could possibly be dangerous or manipulative in that way. "Alright then, it can be done while they're asleep. It's almost 11:30 so it will only be a few hours before the boys are ready for their naps. After they're asleep in their cribs, you can perform the service. I won't even be in the room if it would make you more comfortable."

Jordan thought for a moment and couldn't see any mortal danger that could affect Charlotte in a short walk on a quiet street. She agreed to the plan with a nod and handed Charlotte a spill-proof cup from the cupboard to demonstrate her support.

While Charlotte walked the two blocks to the church, Jordan prepared sippy cups for the boys. She was hopeful that full tummies might put the boys to sleep early. She took them to their room to read a story while they worked on their warm milk.

By the time she finished the book, both boys were nodding off. She'd hoped to have the opportunity to shop for big boy beds soon. She hoped to have lots more opportunities to watch them grow. After both boys were settled in, she quietly walked out of the nursery.

Jordan still walked as far away from the railing as possible. While she didn't believe either of the boys would hurt her, she also didn't believe theirs were the only forces at work.

She began descending the steps, more aware of how many there were than she'd ever been in her life. It wasn't until she reached the bottom step that she began to worry about Charlotte.

How long had she been gone? How long did it take to walk two blocks? Would anyone want to talk to her while she was there? That's when Jordan remembered she was supposed to find the words for a baptismal service.

She walked quickly to the study, sat behind the desk, and logged onto the internet.

She searched first on "baptismal service" and found only news stories of baptisms that had recently been conducted. She revised her search to "baptismal vows" then to "baptismal sermons" but still didn't find the exact wording. Like Charlotte said, it was the holy water that really mattered. Jordan had been to a couple of baptisms when she was going through her own religious training and remembered some of the words: "I baptize you in the name of the Father, the Son, and the Holy Ghost." That would be enough.

She logged off the internet as she heard the front door open and Charlotte call out, "Hello". *Thank God!* She was back!

Jordan practically ran to the foyer. Charlotte barely had time to close the door before Jordan got to her.

"How did everything go? Did anything happen on your walk to the church? I couldn't find the exact words but I think I can wing it." Jordan felt like she was talking a mile a minute. She couldn't help it.

"Not at all, everything went fine. There wasn't anyone around so I grabbed a mistral as well. I'll return it when we're finished, but it has the baptismal service in there." Charlotte handed the book to Jordan who took it and immediately started flipping through pages. Jordan was focused on her search of the index for the word baptism, so she barely noticed Charlotte's hand fly up to her chest.

Jordan looked up in time to see the cup that wasn't supposed to spill explode on the tile floor. She watched the plastic fly and the holy water run onto the tile floor as if it all happened in slow motion.

She instinctively reached in the direction the glass had fallen, even though it was too late. As Jordan moved, she saw Charlotte out of the corner of her eye. She turned as her friend started to fall. She watched it in slow motion, but she was in slow motion too and it was over before her lethargic limbs could move her body.

Jordan dropped the mistral into the pool of now tainted water, but it was too late. All she accomplished was to reach out to her friend who was already sprawled out on the floor.

Charlotte's eyes were wide open as she lay on her side. She didn't respond as Jordan screamed her name. Almost afraid to discover the truth, Jordan took one of Charlotte's wrists in her hands and searched for a pulse. There was nothing.

"NOOOO!!!!!!"

Jordan didn't specifically remember doing it, but at some point she had called the ambulance. She remembered going through the motions of the basic CPR skills she had been taught in high school PE class.

The fog of disbelief surrounded her mind again and she barely remembered letting the paramedics in when they arrived.

Jordan watched as the experts tried similar CPR moves but from that one step back it was obvious they were working on a dead body.

Charlotte was dead. Jordan was still watching when they loaded Charlotte into the ambulance. She had watched when they draped the sheet across her face. She remembered telling them Charlotte's name and that her husband was a doctor. She remembered giving them the name of the hospital.

She remembered pleading with them to check who was on duty before taking Charlotte anywhere. Her husband absolutely could NOT find out about this by pulling back the sheet as an attending physician. She thought she remembered them confirming that they knew Dr. Shapiro. Would they really take care of it? Should she call the doctor herself? She couldn't even think the words, "Charlotte is gone." She knew she couldn't say them.

Jordan remembered closing the door behind the paramedics but didn't remember collapsing to the floor in gut-wrenching sobs. Never, not even when her parents died, had she felt so utterly and totally alone. She didn't even know what to wish for anymore. Everything was hopeless.

When the sobs weakened their hold, she wished she had the strength to get up off the floor and get her mother's bathrobe. Her last hope was gone and she was out of ideas.

She sat in the same position sobbing and rocking for over an hour. Eventually there was nothing left.

When Jordan composed herself enough to at least speak, she dialed the number for Dr. Shapiro's office. Surely he would be aware of what had happened by now. She owed it to him to at least see if there was something she could do to help.

Dr. Shapiro's nurse answered his private line. She explained that he had a personal emergency and wouldn't be seeing patients for at least a week. Jordan only had to mention her name for the nurse to immediately soften.

"We are all in shock and, of course, our hearts go out to all of you." Jordan interrupted to ask if the doctor had gone home but the nurse wasn't finished.

"The doctor wanted to be here when the medical examiner arrived, and I believe they're still together. I'm not sure if he will be finished before I leave today, but I will make sure he gets the message that you called."

There was nothing left to say but goodbye.

"Yes, thank you," Jordan said. "Please let him know it doesn't matter how late it is. I'll try him at home later, too." Jordan hung up the phone and went to wake the boys from their naps. They had been sleeping far too long and she was afraid that if she didn't make herself get moving she might give in and lose the last of her mind.

Jordan tried to reach Dr. Shapiro at least half a dozen times that night and the next morning… he never answered.

Chapter 32

Roger Shapiro sat in his study. He was in the exact same position he had occupied since he got home from the hospital around five. It was hard for him to really think about anything. All he knew was that his wife was dead.

Oh God, how can my Charlotte be gone? his mental anguish screamed. His brain would race ahead and think, b*ut if I would have stayed home this morning. If I just would have told the hospital that I couldn't come in, I could have been there. It would have turned out completely different!* His heart felt a fraction of a micro-second of hope, before it was shattered again by reality.

He could not turn back time. He could not bring her back. His thoughts went to deals with the devil.

Roger was a young doctor just finishing his residency when he met Tanas for the first time. He and Charlotte had been married since he started med school and those were difficult days for his young wife. She had worked as many jobs as they needed in order to pay the bills and keep him in school.

He had wanted so badly to pamper her, to give her everything she ever wanted. The day he passed his medical boards Roger promised Charlotte she would never again have to work. She had, as usual, pish-poshed his concern.

He had known Charlotte since second grade and had never once heard her complain about anything. She was the reason he became a doctor. She was the one who taught him how to care about someone other than himself.

When Tanas came into the clinic where Roger was working, it seemed odd to everyone that he asked to speak with the doctor alone. At the doctor's assurance, the nurses disregarded policy and showed him in. They assumed the dark handsome stranger was some kind of a supplier and hoped they would see him a lot more often. No one could have guessed why he was really there or what Roger would gamble that day. But what did it matter now? The only thing that mattered was Charlotte and she was gone.

No matter how often his mind wandered to distant memories, the reality that his wife was dead always came back like a punch in the stomach.

Roger's sons were on their way home. There were probably some things he needed to do to prepare the house for their visit but he had no idea what it would be. He didn't really care enough to even come up with the things that should be done. Charlotte always took care of all of that. "Oh, my darling Charlotte," his painful wail couldn't be held inside.

The sound of the doorbell startled the doctor out of his misery and his hands instinctively went to his face to wipe away his tears.

It was too early for his sons to be arriving and he wasn't expecting anyone else. Word had probably begun to spread and the casseroles would be arriving. He didn't want to eat and he didn't want to visit. He would simply have to tell whomever it was to go away.

His skin started to crawl even before he opened the front door to see Tanas standing on his stoop.

The doctor lunged forward at the sight of the man he wished he'd never met. He wanted nothing more than to wipe the smug look off his frozen face. "You son of a bitch; we had a deal!" The doctor floundered forward when the air in front was suddenly nothing but empty space. He turned around to see Tanas standing in his own doorway.

"Oh, doctor," Tanas spoke cooly, "you know as well as I do that none of the theatrics are necessary. I'm sure we can figure out a solution that works for both of us. We always have in the past." He ghosted towards the doctor's front room without so much as a look back.

"I assume you won't mind if I make myself comfortable." Tanas chose the seat that was the obvious center point in the room - the chair traditionally reserved for the doctor when his family used that room.

Tanas spoke casually. "I did not break our deal, although I'm not sure at this point I would consider our agreement intact." He looked the doctor in the eye and immediately deflated the little bit of courage Roger had mustered.

"My son is a bit over-zealous. I cannot deny that." Tanas spoke with paternal pride that turned the doctor's stomach. "He will be coming to me soon. You see, he's already made his choice. Your wife really shouldn't have interfered again."

The doctor's conviction returned at the mention of his wife. "Charlotte is the same sweet person she has always been. She never made any deals with you and you had no right to break ours. This was between you and me, NOT HER!!"

"And that was your loop hole, wasn't it?" Tanas remained calm and unaffected. "You believed that your wife's faith would be strong enough to overturn any deal you and I made." He paused for only a second but his face was that of the victor. "It was difficult for me to act dejected and outplayed. It's so contrary to my genuine nature.

"You did prove yourself useful when you gave me the Sullivans. And that, my dear doctor, is the reason you were allowed to live out your trivial little life-span with your wife." Tanas rose and walked toward a better view through the front window. He stared out as if that were just another routine evening.

A loud clap startled Roger out of his daze. The burst of celebration came from Tanas as he turned back to face the

- 269 -

doctor. "Can you imagine? A fourth generation offspring! I've waited so long for this kind of opportunity to come again. The world is ripe for the taking, and my son will be ready to pick it." Tanas walked toward the doctor, took his chin in his hand, and raised the doctor's face up to meet his own gaze. "I can't help it that you couldn't control your wife."

Roger should have exploded with anger but he couldn't. "Is there anything you could do to bring her back? Is there anything I could do?"

"You knew the answer to that question before you asked it. I did not give your Charlotte life, nor did I take it from her. She is with *Him* now and there's nothing that I can do to touch her."

Although it wasn't the intent, Roger felt re-assured and peaceful in the knowledge that Tanas was right. Charlotte was where she deserved to be, and if he were honest with himself, he had to admit he was where he deserved to be as well.

Wishing that he could have died with Charlotte triggered an idea. It was like a mental wind that cleared the fog from his thinking. "I could kill him." Roger looked up to see the fear wash over Tanas's face.

"You would never be able to do that," Tanas snarled back. "Already he is a million times stronger telepathically than any other soul on the planet. He would never let you get close enough to him to even try."

"I've been close enough to him a thousand times," the doctor smiled. "If you could have taken him already, you would have. But you haven't." The doctor's voice began to grow in strength as he realized he'd found a weakness.

Tanas's confident smirk came back. "You don't know which child is mine. Do you really believe you would be able to guess the right child, or are you simply prepared to kill both of them?" His arrogance was back and Roger hated him more than ever.

The doctor thought of the darling faces of each boy he had grown to love. He remembered the image of the monster he delivered and imagined that "being" with unstoppable power.

He wondered what Charlotte would think, if he ever got to see her again. What would she think of him if he were the one to kill the two babies she had given her life to save? He remembered her body lying on the cold metal slab in the coroner's office. He thought of his sons and his grandchildren whose lives had never become entwined with Tanas, thanks to his beloved wife.

"Yes. God help me but yes. If I can't figure out which of the twins is your spawn, I will not take the chance of having the anti-Christ live." The doctor's new found strength may have been the result of a death wish, but it was effective. In a puff of nothing, Tanas was gone.

The doctor fell to his knees with the knowledge of a force strong enough to break the bond that had tied him to Tanas all those years. "I am so sorry, dear God. I knew the strength you had given to Charlotte, and yet I still couldn't trust in you myself. I couldn't stand to watch her suffer in any way. I would have done anything to spare her the pain, and I did." Roger realized that he had worried so much about his wife's comfort and salvation that his own had never really mattered very much.

"I took the easy way out and I'm sorry, dear God. Thank you for coming back for me." The doctor bowed his head and folded his hands. "Tell me, dear Lord, what you want me to do."

Chapter 33

Twenty-six hours after Charlotte had collapsed in her foyer, Jordan was trying again to reach Dr. Shapiro at home. She had taken the boys to daycare in the morning in hopes she could reach him and help in some way. She was about to try his office again when the front door bell sounded.

Even before she reached the foyer, she could see through the front windows that it was the doctor. He had never been comfortable with letting himself in the way Charlotte had been. Jordan ran to the door and threw it open as quickly as she could. The man standing before her had a strong resemblance to her long-time friend and doctor, but he definitely was not the same man. Standing before her was an empty shell.

Jordan wrapped her arms around him, blubbering on about how glad she was to see him and how sorry she was about Charlotte. Dr. Shapiro's arms hung loosely at his sides. She offered him some coffee as she gestured nervously towards the kitchen. It was obvious he had been up all night. He refused the coffee and she walked with him into the sitting room.

"I know this is a stupid question, but how are you doing?" Jordan hated when people asked her that and now found herself doing the exact same thing.

He stared blankly at her for a moment that felt like eternity. Then he looked down at his lap. "I don't know. Just trying to get through each minute, I suppose." His voice sounded dead.

Jordan wished there were something she could say or do to console him. There were no words that could help. She waited for him to start.

"The reason I'm here is to talk to you about what happened." He had always been a serious man, but Jordan had never known him to be so completely distant. She reminded herself that he was obviously in shock and she shouldn't take it personally. She was having a hard time shaking the feeling that she was sitting with a stranger.

"The paramedics probably told you that Charlotte had a heart attack, right?" Jordan nodded. "They were only partially correct. The medical examiner is a close friend of mine so I asked him to perform the autopsy last night and he obliged." For the first time since he started speaking, Dr. Shapiro raised his head and looked Jordan in the eyes. "Her heart exploded, Jordan.

"When Frank told me what he'd found, I didn't believe him. I guess I thought he was just being descriptive in telling me that the heart attack was massive, so he clarified it. Then I looked for myself. Her heart literally exploded." His eyes returned to his hands fidgeting in his lap. "The only thing capable of causing injury like that would be a massive sonic blast. Of course, that wouldn't be pinpointed to just one organ. A force that strong should have exploded the entire house. There is no medical condition, no accident or precedent of any kind that would explain what happened to my wife. I need you to tell me exactly what went on here yesterday."

Jordan's heart started pounding. "I know what you're wondering, but the boys were asleep in their room when everything happened. There was no way it could have been their fault." She was becoming increasingly concerned and didn't like the look on the doctor's face.

"Tell me what happened," he demanded. Jordan proceeded to tell him everything that had taken place before and after Charlotte arrived at her house yesterday. She hoped that it would pacify him in some way, but his face showed it hadn't.

"I will tell you again," he said. "There is nothing humanly possible that can cause a person's heart to explode in her chest. Whether the boys were awake or asleep is irrelevant to me. We both know that one of them killed my wife." Tears welled up in his eyes as anger welled up in his heart.

"How many more people have to die, Jordan?" He paused. "One of your boys has taken my whole world away. I know it's probably my fault to start with. That's just more reason that it should be me who ends it. I don't know which one is responsible and unless you do, there isn't any choice but to get rid of both of them, before it's too late for anyone else."

Jordan was terrified as she watched him pull two small syringes from inside his coat. "If you aren't able to take care of it yourself, then I will," he said.

Thinking quickly seemed to come easily when her children's lives were at stake. Jordan put on the calmest face she could come up with and nodded, "I know you're right, but there's no way I can do it. They're in their room." Even the thought of what she was sending him to do made her eyes fill with tears and her heart ache. She followed him to the foyer and watched as he climbed the stairs.

When he turned to go into the nursery, she grabbed her keys off the table by the door and bolted outside to her car. She locked the doors and started the engine as quickly as she could. She was pulling out of the driveway when she saw him running towards the door. *Thank God I never got used to parking in the garage!*

She didn't know if he would follow her, but she didn't think he knew where the daycare was. She turned five or six corners in the neighborhood, just in case. There wasn't any sign of his vehicle and hadn't been since she left the house. Her heart might have slowed if she'd known his car was still parked in her driveway.

She debated whether she should go to the police or the daycare and decided the daycare was the only choice she could live with. She doubted that the police would believe her story when there were so many details she couldn't share. Even if she could get them to arrest the doctor, it didn't mean that they could hold him for very long.

She needed to get the boys and then take them away to a place where they would be safe. *Maybe that's what will keep everyone else safe, too.*

Chapter 34

After picking the boys up from daycare, Jordan had gone to the bank and withdrawn enough cash to live well for a year. Money wouldn't be a problem, but where would she go? She had no friends, no *known* family besides the twins, and no knowledge of any place more than fifty miles away from home. She decided to drive until she found a location that looked inviting.

After they'd been on the road about an hour, she stopped for lunch in Temecula. The boys were getting fussy and she could stand to stretch her legs. Just off the interstate they found a McDonalds, where no one knew or suspected they were running for their lives.

Jordan ordered a hamburger for herself and Happy Meals for the boys. The twins were hungry and ate everything in their bag, even though they each had an eye on the play area the whole time. How could they be so normal and still be cursed?

After their meals were finished, she moved to a table right next to the play room and let them go crazy on their own. She enjoyed watching them so much; it made everything else seem distant and unreal.

After almost an hour of play, both boys were clearly exhausted, and she was unbearably antsy to get back on the road. Would they ever get far enough away that she could feel safe again?

Jordan loaded the twins in their car seats, and both were fast asleep before she even left the parking lot. She got back on the interstate and continued north. Normally she would find herself lost in thought when she was driving, but that day had been quite different. Her mind seemed to be completely blank. Blank was good.

An hour and a half later they were nearing Los Angeles. That was about the time she realized that neither she nor the children had any clothing besides what they were wearing.

She saw a billboard advertising a shopping mall and figured that would be as good a place as any to buy new wardrobes. She took the appropriate exit and pulled into the parking lot near JC Penney.

Jordan looked around the parking lot to make sure there wasn't anyone who could see what she was doing. When she was certain she wouldn't be seen, she opened the glove compartment and removed a stack of hundred dollar bills.

The boys were still pretty groggy, so she rented a double stroller at the mall entrance. They both fell back to sleep almost immediately.

While the boys dozed in the stroller, she bought several outfits for all three of them. It might not be everything they would need, but it was enough to get them through a couple of days.

She also bought a new stroller. She talked them into giving her the floor model so she wouldn't have to hassle with assembly and, after checking out, transferred the boys to their new ride. She filled every available section of the stroller with bags and loaded the rest onto her arms. It was awkward but it worked. The feeling of being followed hit her again as she was packing everything into the van. She pulled the back closed and fumbled for her keys while she crawled into the driver's seat. Before starting the car, she locked the doors.

Seven hours and four pit stops later they were entering Sacramento. It was full dark and she was tired. After stopping at a convenience store for some basics, she found the nearest hotel and pulled in.

Jordan hoped the boys wouldn't be too wound up from sitting all day to sleep through the night but decided if they were, it wouldn't be a big deal for their days and nights to get mixed up. They were far enough away from San Diego that she knew they weren't being followed. She had used cash for all of their purchases so no one would be able to trace them through credit cards, even if someone did report them missing.

She had signed in at the front desk under the name Kathy Beverly but had to do more than a little explaining about why she couldn't use a credit card. Thinking quickly, she offered the excuse that her purse had been stolen, but her husband had wired her cash. She thought of how easy it was for someone to believe her lie but how impossible it would be to convince him of the truth. Ironic and sad, she thought.

She and the boys rode the elevator to the sixth floor and quickly found room 639. It was a nice enough room, but certainly nothing like they were used to at home. It didn't matter. Jordan was exhausted.

There was a queen-sized bed, an entertainment center with a television, and some kind of video game. The "living room" section of the suite had a small table, a chair, and a loveseat.

It may not be the Presidential Suite, but it was the perfect place to become anonymous. She took a few moments to baby-proof the room and put their new clothes in the closet. When she was satisfied that the boys couldn't hurt themselves, she turned on cartoons.

She had bought plenty of clothes in Los Angeles. The room was stacked full of snacks and diapers from the convenience store. The only things she hadn't thought to buy were toys. She hoped cartoons would be enough to keep them happy for one night. Tomorrow they would go buy a whole new supply of their favorite toys.

The boys made themselves comfortable on the floor with sippy cups and animal crackers. They were both glued to the television, mindlessly snacking. Jordan sat at the table watching them as intently as they were watching their show. Until that moment, she hadn't allowed herself to think about what might have happened if she hadn't taken the boys to daycare that morning, or if Dr. Shapiro had gone to the daycare instead of her house. His name was on the "approved for pick-up" list!

Tears began to well in her eyes at the thought of what nearly happened, but she stopped them before they were able to take control. She couldn't afford the luxury of a breakdown. Now more than ever, her children needed her. She had to come up with a plan.

She grabbed the pen and note pad, clearly marked with the hotel information, and began making herself a to-do list. At some point she would need to figure out if this was a permanent move or just an impromptu vacation. As it was, she felt like she should prepare for either.

Jordan thought about her house. For all she knew the front door was standing wide open and thieves had already cleaned the place out. Was there anyone back home she could call to help with things on that end? There was not.

The choices seemed endless and overwhelming. What she really wanted to do was climb under the covers and pretend none of it was happening. *Prioritize.* Everything else would be fine as long as the boys were alright. She needed to make sure they were safe.

"First things first," she said aloud. "Start with the list; then worry about how to accomplish it later." She looked at the boys. Neither of them seemed to pay any attention to her affirmation. She began the list.

To-Do
Buy new toys
Find place to rent for at least a month
Hire someone in San Diego to look after house…

Her home. Was there really any reason to keep it? It wasn't like there was anything in San Diego for her now.

These were the types of things Charlotte would have coached her through. She put the pen down and stared at nothing. Very soon, her last hope would be laid to rest. She could barely believe Charlotte was gone and now here she was, clear across the state, not even able to say goodbye.

Jordan didn't blame Dr. Shapiro, not really anyway. She understood what it felt like to have your mind snap away from reality. Jordan understood that Charlotte had meant the world to him. She also understood that he came intending to kill her babies. Taking her boys wouldn't bring his wife back or make any of what had been happening right.

She knew that the grief she felt over Charlotte was a mere fraction of the doctor's, but she did love Charlotte, too.

Tears filled her eyes again but this time she wasn't able to stop the flow. Charlotte had been like a mother to her in so many ways and now she was gone. And then the most unbearable thought of all, Charlotte's death was most likely caused by one of her own sons.

Whether it was because she didn't actually know which twin was responsible or because she was their mother, none of it changed the love she felt for them. As much as Jordan missed Charlotte, she could only afford one priority right now. Above all else, she would protect her children.

Chapter 35

The next morning, Jordan woke up disoriented. She sat upright and searched the room for the boys. They weren't on the bed next to her and her heart kick-started into frantic mode. It only took a second to find them in the small room. They were sleeping soundly on the floor next to the bed, as far apart as the floor space would allow, but in the same general vicinity.

She threw her legs over the side of the bed, stood up, and stretched the last remains of sleep from her body. She knelt down in the middle of the sleeping boys. It took even more stretches to give each of them a kiss on the forehead but neither stirred. She decided to take a quick shower and wash away the last remains of a day she would rather forget. She checked the door first, to make sure it was still locked. It never occurred to her that she could have been locking herself in with a monster.

After she was ready, she woke the boys and dressed them in one of their new outfits. She still couldn't get over how handsome they were. Granted, she was prejudiced, but they looked like perfect dolls.

The hotel served a continental breakfast, but Jordan wasn't in the mood for stale pastries and watered down coffee. She loaded the boys into their car seats and headed to the IHOP she'd noticed when they pulled into town.

No one looked up and pointed when they walked in. The waitress didn't whisper to the manager and point at them. The goal of anonymity had been achieved. Sitting with the boys eating breakfast made her feel almost normal again.

Jordan noticed a Toys-R-Us in the same strip mall as the restaurant, so after they had their fill of breakfast, she and the boys walked across the parking lot. It was a beautiful day, so they left the van where it was.

Halfway across the pavement Jordan realized it was a little chillier than she'd expected. She wished she had thought to buy some jackets and made a mental note to do that after toy shopping. There would be time.

It was a rare event when the boys got to go to a toy store. Usually the toys just came to them. As soon as they walked through the door their eyes grew huge with wonder. She couldn't imagine that their response was so different than other children who walk through the doors.

In nearly every way, they were normal, happy little boys. She knew she was kidding herself, but she wanted to continue burying her head in the sand. She wanted to pretend they were the same as every other kid on the planet.

Maybe if they only lived in places for short times and had limited contact with other people it could work. Maybe eventually things really would be normal. But would denying the truth about one put the other one in danger, like Tanas said? Her mind was as distracted as theirs but for very different reasons.

Each boy found the greatest thing he had ever seen within a few inches of the entrance and the area around the front door was becoming congested. A frustrated woman who hadn't heard that toy shopping should be fun, pushed into Jordan and snapped her out of her trance. Finally, amidst apologies to other customers, she was able to coax the boys far enough into the store that they weren't blocking anyone's way. It wasn't more than a second before they each found a new "greatest thing on earth."

She delighted in their joy and didn't even mind the fact that there was no way in the world they would get through the store in less than six hours. At least it was something to do. She hated the fact that she and her sons would have to live their lives like fugitives through no choice of their own.

A sudden realization hit her. Maybe she could reason with Dr. Shapiro! Certainly he would have been in shock over the loss of Charlotte. People act irrationally when they're trying to deal with a tragedy. He wouldn't be able to figure out where she was if she called from her cell phone but even if he did they could move to a new area easily enough.

She decided to call the hospital first. That might not give her clues about his mental health, but they would at least know if he had left town. She became hopeful over the possibility of having someone on her side again. At the same time, she wasn't overly anxious to make the call. She could wait until they got back to the hotel where she could place the call in private. It could wait. For now, the boys were normal children and the world could wait.

She wasn't far off on her six-hour estimate, but there was still time to call the hospital before the administration left for the day. She hurried the boys as much as possible by placing the toys they couldn't live without in the shopping cart. She added some Hot Wheels and crayons as an impulse and headed toward the checkout line.

A half hour later they were back in their hotel room. The boys were busy playing with their new toys, and Jordan was working up her nerve to place the call she was dreading. She took a deep breath and dialed the number.

The voice that answered was a familiar one. Would any of them know she was on the run? She hadn't thought about that before dialing the phone. What if the doctor was standing right there? She realized she was taking too long to answer.

"Yes… hi. Is Dr. Shapiro in?" She tried to sound casual. She wasn't succeeding. The nurse asked who was calling and after a brief pause about the wisdom of revealing her identity, Jordan gave the nurse her name.

"Oh, Jordan, we have been calling your house all day. I'm afraid I have some terrible news. The doctor passed away last night." Jordan sat speechless. After several seconds the nurse spoke up, "Are you there?"

"Uh, yes, I'm sorry. I'm here," Jordan stuttered. "I don't know what to say. I'm just shocked. Do you know what happened?"

"Well, you know how heartbroken he was about losing Charlotte. It was apparently too much for him. He committed suicide around 1:00 this morning. His sons came home yesterday evening because, well, you know Charlotte's funeral and everything." She seemed to pause for effect.

"From what I understand they could tell he was upset but didn't have any indication he was suicidal. They've decided to postpone their mother's funeral until the two of them can be buried together. I know they've been trying to reach you."

Jordan's mind whirled as she struggled to piece together this new information. Dr. Shapiro was dead? And his sons were there?

She knew the Shapiros had two boys, of course, but they spoke of them so rarely she had almost forgotten they existed. She needed to think. "I'm sorry; I just don't know what to say. Thank you for letting me know. I have to go now." And with that, Jordan hung up.

Dr. Shapiro was dead? She had never figured him to be the suicidal type... ever. She knew exactly what Charlotte meant to him but she still couldn't imagine him taking his own life. She looked at the boys playing happily on the floor. *Could they possibly?* She mentally debated the idea of returning home.

She had no idea what her next step should be, but she knew now they wouldn't be in danger if they went home.

It had been a long day and the last thing Jordan wanted to do was drive. Another night in the hotel wouldn't hurt anyone. A good night's sleep and a little more time to think. They would go home in the next day… or two.

Chapter 36

After an extremely long day of driving and about a dozen rest stops to calm restless toddlers, Jordan pulled into her own driveway with a sigh of relief. It had been two days since she learned of the doctor's death, but she was still afraid of what might be waiting at home.

She remembered now why she preferred to drive at night. The boys were wound up from too many hours of riding in the car, and it didn't seem likely they would be ready for bed anytime in the near future. It was getting dark and she was drained.

When she finally pulled up in front of the house, she was struck with a sudden fear that Dr. Shapiro would be waiting somewhere inside. What if he told the receptionist to give her the story about his death just to trick her into coming back? To be on the safe side, she left the boys strapped in their car seats as she went ahead to check the house. She felt like the rope in a tug-of-war. Her fear of the unsearched house battled with her fear for the unguarded car. Be fast.

The front door was closed but not locked. She opened it without stepping inside and called, "Hello?" to an empty house. There was no answer and nothing stirred. She ran through the first floor rooms as quickly as she possibly could, then sprinted upstairs to check her bedroom and the nursery. The house was empty.

Jordan raced back down the stairs with anxiety growing over leaving the boys alone in the car. Had she been afraid of the wrong danger?

By the time she reached the front door she was completely terrified and fully expected to see Roger Shapiro leaning against her car. She threw open the front door and saw both boys sitting peacefully right where she'd left them. "Thank you, God," she said aloud.

After getting the boys out of their car seats, she had each of them help by carrying a couple of small bags. In one trip they had the car mostly unloaded, and for the first time since Charlotte died, Jordan felt safe and sound in her own home.

She dropped the bags inside the door and noticed an envelope with her name on it angled carefully on the foyer table. Someone had been in the house.

Jordan made sure the sliding doors to the pool area were locked and the boys were occupied then sat down at the kitchen table to read the letter she'd been left. She opened the envelope and scanned to the bottom of the typed letter. It was from Dr. Shapiro.

My Dearest Jordan,

I am deeply sorry, but I am old, I am tired, and I can't help you fight the battle you are facing. This may be difficult for you to believe, but I do understand your love for your children. Remember, I have two sons as well. Right now I fear for their lives and the lives of everyone else in the world. I have weighed my options and know that if I approach anyone, ANYONE with the information I know, I will most likely be institutionalized.

I beg you to consider the only option that will save us all. I can only imagine the difficulty of the task ahead of you. It is my fault that you are in this position, my fault that you exist. I thought I was capable of ending it. I'm not. I've been haunted by the child's true face and I would suspect it's what the daycare worker saw as well. I know that what you see are the faces of angels. The devil was an angel once too.

God be with you, Jordan, but I cannot. You know what needs to be done and I cannot help you anymore. I never could. I feel that it would be best for both of us to sever our relationship now. Please do not contact me unless it is to say that you have completed what you know needs to be done. Perhaps if I had severed this relationship earlier my dear wife would still be by my side. In the end, no one ever wins against him, Jordan. No one.

Take care of yourself and please, do what is right.

Roger

She read the letter again and then a third time. No matter how she tried to slant the wording, it didn't sound like Dr. Shapiro was contemplating suicide. So what could have happened between the time he left her house and the time he took his own life? Jordan thought of her mother and how Tanas had explained he used people. Something or someone had persuaded the doctor to end his life. Who was it? Was it Tanas, or could it have been one of her sons?

Chapter 37

First thing in the morning Jordan called Dr. Shapiro's office to find out when and where the Shapiros' funeral would be held. She realized she'd reached the answering service when Jordan didn't recognize the voice. She was actually glad. It would be nice to get the funeral information without the chit chat.

The service itself was going to be held in the funeral home sanctuary and burial would take place at the same cemetery where her parents and Anna had been buried.

For a split second she wondered why they wouldn't have the funeral at Charlotte's church. She had been a loyal member for years. Of course, Jordan also knew that Dr. Shapiro had not been a member anywhere.

In the days before the funeral, she busied herself by cleaning the house and tripping over a never-ending barrage of toys. Bit by bit she stopped jumping at every sound. Bit by bit, she became comfortable again. She watched the boys intently and saw nothing. By the day of the funeral she had almost convinced herself it was all just mass hysteria.

On the drive to the funeral home, Jordan's mind went back and forth between scenarios of what might happen when she met the Shapiro children. As well as she knew their parents, she didn't feel like she knew the younger Shapiros at all.

Charlotte rarely mentioned her sons, but when she did it was obvious they meant the world to her. Jordan guessed the reason Charlotte didn't talk about them often was for her benefit. Charlotte was always so careful to make sure she felt like family. It would be like her to minimize her relationship with her sons to spare hurting Jordan in any way.

How would they react when they saw her? One of her imaginings had them screaming in her face that she murdered their parents. Another thought was that they would have no idea who she was and she would feel like a stranger at the funeral of her closest friends. None of the possibilities running through her mind were positive, so why, she asked herself, was she even going to the funeral?

Because Charlotte was always there for her, and she wanted to say goodbye.

When they arrived at the funeral home, Jordan was amazed to see the number of cars in the parking lot. Had she really been so self-centered to believe that she was the only person close to the Shapiros? She couldn't imagine the funeral home being large enough to accommodate the number of mourners who were filing in, but when she entered through the large double doors, the inside was much bigger than she thought.

The sanctuary was to her left. On the right side of the entryway was a double sized casket that looked like it could hold a piano. The huge lid was blocked open, making it look even more like a concert grand. As she walked closer she saw the faces of Roger and Charlotte Shapiro.

They looked like angels sleeping in clouds as their faces and hands stood out against their white satin pillows. Their hands were entwined forever, exactly how they would have wanted them.

Tears filled Jordan's eyes immediately. Even though the features and characteristics were easily recognizable as Charlotte, in some ways it didn't look like her at all. Her face seemed flatter and Charlotte never wore heavy makeup. Then there were the eyes.

The eyes seemed... well, the eyes seemed dead. The flat way the eyelids covered the eyes was the tell-tale sign of a mortician's handiwork.

Jordan bent down and scooped up one boy in each arm. They weren't tall enough to see into the casket, so it wasn't until she lifted them that they realized it was Charlotte. "Nanna!" Hudson shouted as Hayden scrambled to get out of her arms and go to his beloved grandma. It was hard enough to boost them when they were calm. It was impossible for her to hold them when they were squirming.

She nearly dropped Hayden when a strange voice from behind her asked if he could help. In the same instant he asked, he caught Hayden's head as he threw himself backwards.

When she had gathered her bearings enough to look at her savior, she found herself looking at a familiar stranger.

"You must be Jordan," the stranger said.

Trying to put her finger on where she may have met him, she replied, "Yes... I'm sorry, have we met somewhere before?"

"No, no, I've just heard so much about you I feel like I know you. I'm Daryl Shapiro."

Suddenly Jordan knew why he looked so familiar. He wasn't a dead ringer to either Roger or Charlotte but he had a strong resemblance to both. She liked him immediately. Daryl was smiling politely, but his eyes were filled with the same sadness she felt. Probably deeper, she corrected herself.

"I'm so sorry about your parents. They were wonderful people and I hope you don't mind me saying this, but I came to look at them as my own parents."

"Actually, it's very nice to hear that. They thought the world of you and the boys, too. Mom spoke of you every time we talked. She always had new stories about what the boys were up to. Which one do I have?" He looked to the toddler in his arms for a moment then back to Jordan.

"That's Hayden and this," she raised Hudson slightly as she spoke, "is Hudson." Tears welled in her eyes at the memory of

- 298 -

Charlotte playing with the boys. So much had happened since her death that it seemed like years ago rather than days.

"I don't know how to explain to them that she's gone. She was the only grandmother they've ever known. I guess you can tell by their reaction how much they love her."

They stood next to the casket in silence for several moments, until Jordan realized they were holding up the stream of mourners trying to get into the funeral home. "I guess we're holding things up and you're probably getting tired of holding Hayden. I'd better grab a seat while there are still some available. I can take him now if you'd like."

"If you wouldn't mind, I'd like to hold him a while longer, and we would love to have the three of you sit with the family. It's only my brother's family and me in the first pew." Daryl gestured behind him where the chapel was clearly visible through large etched windows. Jordan was touched and looked in the direction Daryl was pointing. She saw the huge golden cross behind the altar. She hadn't realized there would be an actual church inside the funeral home. What would happen when the boys went inside?

Anxiety hit fast like a fist tightening around her heart. She had never taken the boys into a church but Anna, Charlotte, and Father Hannigan died just from making plans to do it! She debated for a moment about taking the boys and leaving. Her answer took too long and Daryl noticed.

"I promise we won't bite. It would really mean a lot to us. Mom and Dad both thought of you as a daughter and your boys were so much like grandchildren." He smiled a tentative smile that convinced her. If nothing else, he had certainly inherited his mother's heart. *God help us if anything explodes.*

"That would be wonderful, thank you." Jordan followed feeling partly grateful to be included in the family and partly terrified of what might happen next. Much to her relief, they entered the chapel without event.

The service was short but filled with loving memories of the Shapiros. It was Roger's younger brother, Robert, who delivered the eulogy. He talked about the couple growing up, falling in love, and building a life together. He recounted memories from when his nephews were little that made everyone in the building smile. He spoke of the last conversation he had with his brother, which made everyone cry.

In the end it was a beautiful service that left everyone reminded there was a hole in the world where the Shapiros had been. There was an emptiness that could never be filled.

After the service, Daryl invited Jordan to ride with the family to the cemetery, but she declined. She used the difficulty of switching car seats and the room they require, as an excuse. In truth, even though she did feel that Roger and Charlotte were family, she didn't feel that same familiarity to their sons. As much as she liked Daryl, she'd barely met the rest of the family. It would be far too intimate to be in the same car with them all right after they buried their parents. As she drove along with the rest of the funeral procession, she reflected on her personal memories of the Shapiros.

Their involvement in her life apparently started before she was born, but they didn't really become family until after her sons were born. In so many ways it was the birth of her children that had brought Jordan herself to life.

It wasn't until she was pregnant that the Shapiros became more than friends of the family. Then out of nowhere they felt like her second parents. Jordan thought back to the tour Charlotte had given her of the house. Jordan thought about how Charlotte looked the first time she held the twins and of the way they nearly tackled her every time they saw her. Jordan thought of Roger fondly, regardless of their last meeting, but it was Charlotte she would truly miss.

Jordan continued down memory lane throughout the service at the cemetery. She and the boys stood outside the tent that had been temporarily erected around the extra large casket. If she had given it any thought, she would have been amazed at how well behaved the boys were being.

They both stood throughout the service holding her hands and watching the minister speak of their beloved grandparents. It was as if they knew they were there to say goodbye. Or maybe they were just apprehensive about being in a large crowd of people they didn't know. Either way, it gave Jordan the opportunity to lose herself in her thoughts.

The crowd began to move, snapping Jordan out of her flashback and she realized the service was over.

She turned to lead the boys back to the van when she heard her name. She turned around to find Daryl's now familiar face.

"We're having lunch at the house," Daryl said. "Just some sandwiches and coffee, but we'd sure like it if you could come over." He seemed nervous about the request and for the first time in her life, Jordan wondered if she might be being hit on.

"Thank you for the offer, but I think I'm going to take the boys home." Jordan was on uncomfortable ground and still overwhelmed with her own grief, regardless of how selfish that might be.

"The boys can play with my nephews. I'm sure they would have fun." He hesitated for a moment then continued, "Listen, the truth is, you were the last person, besides my brother and me, who saw our dad before he died. Rog, that's my brother, Roger Jr. Rog and I both felt like there was something strange going on with Dad for the last couple months, but neither of us believes he would kill himself." Daryl looked down at the ground like a nervous kid kicking a rock.

"We'd like to talk about what things have been like around here. We talked to Mom and Dad on the phone every week, but it's not the same as being here." Daryl's eyes met hers and she saw the pleading that his voice didn't convey. "Please? We just want to see what you thought about things."

Jordan felt a little foolish for thinking he was interested in her but hoped it didn't show. Her heart went out to him. She, better than anyone, understood the difficulty of dealing with unanswered questions surrounding a parent's death. She was a little afraid of the questions they might ask but was more afraid of raising suspicions if she declined. Certainly she could answer their questions. How likely would it be that they would ask about something she was still struggling to believe herself?

She herself wasn't convinced the doctor had committed suicide. Didn't she owe it to them to at least try to help? She agreed to go.

Chapter 38

Daryl had been right about one thing: the twins had a great time playing with his nephews. The last of the mourners left and the children had fallen asleep after an exhausting game of "chase" around the kitchen and dining room. The adults were feeling pretty exhausted themselves.

It was a draining day in so many ways, emotionally and physically. With coffee in hand, Jordan, Daryl, Rog, and his wife Karen went into the living room to talk. Jordan had grown quite comfortable around the three of them in the short time since they'd met. She no longer felt any of the earlier anxiety about impending questions. In a way she almost hoped they would ask the right questions, so she could let them into her confidence the way she had their parents. Then again, she considered where their parents were now. *No.* She would not confide her situation to anyone else.

"Sorry to keep you here so long, Jordan. We really didn't expect people to stay as long as they did," Daryl apologized.

"It's fine, really," Jordan said. "I didn't have anything else to do, and the boys had a great time playing. It was nice to see them having fun, and it's been great getting to know all of you."

Rog cut to the chase. "Daryl told you we had some questions." He was a great deal like his namesake, Jordan thought to herself.

"I guess I'll lay it on the line here. We're having a very hard time believing that our father would have killed himself. He was devastated when Mom died, there's no question about that, but he wasn't the type of person who would commit suicide. Daryl flew in the day after Mom died, but Karen and I didn't get in until the next morning, while Dad was at your house." He paused long enough for Jordan to feel that there may be a hidden accusation in there somewhere.

She began to feel uncomfortable again and was about to defend herself when he continued. "When he came home from visiting with you, he didn't seem himself, but we didn't expect him to - his wife had just died for Christ's sake." Karen reached over and placed a hand on his arm in silent comfort. He took a deep breath and continued, "I'm sorry. I guess this shouldn't bother me as much as it does, but our father was a highly respected individual his entire life. Now people are trying to tell us that he was someone we know he wasn't. I guess I feel like we need to defend his honor or something." He looked down and placed his hand over his wife's.

"I really do understand." Jordan's defensiveness was gone. "I can't speak for anyone else, but I know how I felt when your dad's nurse told me that he had killed himself. I couldn't believe it, and you're right, he wasn't the type. The only thing I could think of was that he was so lost without Charlotte, but I don't know. He didn't say anything at all about thoughts of suicide to me. There weren't even things you don't pick up until… after."

"So why was he at your house?" Rog asked. Jordan struggled with the emotions inside her. She felt pity for his grief, confusion over what he seemed to be thinking, and anger about what would be the most logical guess. She struggled to keep her emotions in check and succeeded.

"Your mom died at my house. She had become like a mother to me and was the only grandmother my boys had ever known. He was there because he had finished talking to the medical examiner and wanted me to know exactly what had happened."

Jordan paused for a moment while she studied the faces of all three Shapiros. "I didn't ask him why he was there. It would have been odd if he hadn't been… at least in my mind anyway." She looked down at her lap. She had nearly convinced herself that what she had explained was the only reason the doctor had come to her house that morning.

"I'm sorry, Jordan." She could feel Rog studying her face as he continued. "We know you left town right after our father left your house."

Jordan could feel the blood run from her face and her heartbeat quicken. Everything had happened so quickly after she and the boys returned that she hadn't even considered coming up with a reason for her sudden departure. In truth, it never occurred to her that anyone would notice she'd been gone.

Too long, she thought, *I've taken too long to answer the question. They're going to think I'm hiding something.* Then suddenly she had her alibi.

"Yes, the boys and I did leave town for a few days and yes, it was because I was upset." Jordan continued to look down at her lap. "Regardless of the medical reason for your mother's death, I still felt, I still feel… responsible. Maybe if I had given her CPR better or had her sit down as soon as she came into the house. I don't know, but maybe if I had done something differently, she'd still be here. THEY would still be here. I know how much your mother meant to your dad and… well, I just didn't feel like I would be able to face him again." Jordan pulled a tissue from her pocket and wiped her nose.

"I don't know what I was thinking, and I certainly didn't have a plan. I just wanted to run away from everything, so I did. I know now that it was stupid and immature and I should have done something to help support your dad." At that point the dam of tears broke free. Jordan placed her hands against her eyes and sobbed. Daryl went to her and put his arm around her shoulder for support.

"Why do you have to be such a jackass?" Daryl snapped at his brother, before turning his attention to Jordan. "There wasn't anything that could have been done to help Mom. The coroner said she died before she even hit the floor. As far as Dad goes, we were with him the night he died." He shot an angry look at his brother and sister-in-law then turned his attention back to Jordan.

"There wasn't anything that clued us in on the fact that he was in danger either. And that is why we're all sitting here tonight. We're trying to figure out what happened with Dad, so let's try to stay focused on that... Roger."

Jordan dried her eyes and realized Daryl was right. Even though her motives may be different from theirs, she too wanted to find out what had gone on with the doctor since she'd seen him last.

"How did he die?" She saw the look of confusion immediately pass over their faces. "What I mean is why was the coroner convinced he killed himself in the first place? Did he leave a note? Could it have been an accident?"

"There wasn't a note," Daryl answered, "but he had taken over 20 sleeping pills. The coroner said that if it had been four or five, he could consider the possibility of an accidental overdose but no one, especially a doctor, would take 20 by accident."

"But he was distraught," Jordan suggested. "Is it possible that he took a couple and then forgot he had taken them and just kept taking more until he fell asleep?"

"We thought of that, too." This time it was Roger who answered, "The coroner said it wasn't likely. He also said that even if there was a way to pinpoint exactly when each pill was taken, it still wouldn't change the cause of death."

There was silence for several moments before Jordan spoke first again. "Is it possible he thought he was taking something besides sleeping pills?"

The three Shapiros looked at each other wordlessly confirming that none of the others had considered that option. "It's possible, I suppose." Roger thought for a moment then continued, "Is there any type of medication that Dad would take that many of?" He looked to Daryl and Karen who were both wracking their brains and coming up empty.

"The only thing I ever saw Dad throw into his mouth by the handful was M&Ms." Daryl suddenly became excited as he thought back. "You know... he did mention that day that he had a bad case of indigestion. I've seen him dump a few antacids out of the bottle and toss them back. Those tablets are pretty big so I'll bet five or six of them would take up about the same space in your hand as 20 of those little sleeping pills." He sat forward in his chair. "Do you think that could have been what happened?"

Both Karen and Jordan were leaning forward on their seats already. They were nodding, but Rog remained cynical. "I don't know," he began. "First of all, you chew antacids and chocolate. Even if he didn't notice a difference in taste, he would certainly have noticed that the pills were a lot smaller than those tablets. Secondly, the bottle of antacids in their bathroom is huge and those sleeping pills are in a little prescription bottle. How in the world could he get those confused?"

"I don't know." Daryl was irritated at having his theory pooh-poohed by his older brother. "We know how upset he was about losing Mom. He could have been reaching for the antacids at the same time as he was thinking, 'I'm never going to get to sleep without my wife.' One thing led to another and he mixed up the bottles." Daryl paused for confirmation that never came.

"Think about it. Remember how flustered he seemed that night? It was like he had to think twice about every little movement he made. You and I even talked about it after he went up to bed. We talked about how we had never seen him scatter brained and how lost he was going to be without Mom. Don't you remember?"

Roger Shapiro, Jr. wasn't the type of individual to become openly enthusiastic, but Jordan could see from his face that the puzzle pieces were fitting in his mind, too.

"You're right, I do remember that. It doesn't seem likely that he would make a mistake like that, but the other things he was doing that night didn't seem like him either." He cupped his face in his hands as the carefully hidden emotions came out. "That had to be it."

The pieces all fit together for the Shapiro family, but Jordan knew there were still pieces missing. The doctor's death had not been an accident, and it wasn't suicide.

Karen consoled her husband, Daryl sat nodding his head, and the twins woke up in the other room.

Jordan excused herself to go check on her children and decided it would be a good opportunity to say her goodbyes. She did a couple of quick diaper changes then led the boys back to the other room.

Rog had composed himself and was talking about how things finally made sense again when Jordan came back into the room. Almost as quickly as they turned their heads and noticed her, Roger and Daryl stood. *Apparently*, she thought, *chivalry is not dead.*

"I think it's time we say our goodnights," Jordan said. "I've got a couple of pretty tired little boys here, and I want to get them home before they get their second winds."

Roger and Karen both gave her the nods of understanding that only other parents appreciate. "It was very nice getting to know you all, and I hope you stay in contact." Jordan wasn't sure that was how she really felt, but it seemed appropriate to say it.

Always the gentleman it seemed, Daryl crossed the room towards her. "Let me walk you out to your car."

Jordan tried to protest but knew immediately it wouldn't do any good. As Daryl slipped his shoes on, Rog and Karen came over to say goodbyes, too. Rog shook her hand, but Karen hugged her like she was saying goodbye to a life-long friend. A friend she wouldn't be seeing again for a long time.

"Thank you so very much for coming over here today. I can't tell you how much you've... helped." Karen wiped a tear from under her eye.

As Jordan stepped onto the porch, Daryl closed the door behind them. It was only about 30 feet to her car, but that seemed like miles to weary toddlers who wanted to go back to sleep. Hudson had his arms raised in the universal language that says, "Pick me up" while Hayden had pulled his hand out of hers and went to the bottom step of the porch to have a seat.

"I've got him," Daryl said as he stooped down and picked Hayden up off the step. "I don't know how in the world you can manage both of them by yourself. You must have the patience of a saint."

"No," Jordan answered as she bent down and lifted Hudson into her arms, "but I learned from one. Your mom helped me in so many ways."

She could see he hadn't thought of that and was feeling badly about her poor choice of words. Obviously his loss was far more significant than hers, but he did such a great job of coping it was easy to forget. She quickly tried to undo the damage. "It's a lot harder when they're tired. Normally they're not this difficult to deal with."

Daryl loaded Hayden into his car seat while Jordan buckled Hudson into his. She could see that he was struggling with the latch and walked around the car to assist. "I guess I'm not much help after all, huh?" he asked light-heartedly. She was glad that the momentary tension was gone.

"You were a huge help." Jordan clicked the seat belt into place and turned to face him. "Thank you very much." Suddenly she was aware of how close they were standing to each other and felt a little self-conscious. "I'll bet they'll be asleep before we even get home."

Maybe because he could sense her discomfort, or maybe because he was feeling some himself, he backed up a step and grabbed the edge of the car door. "Let me get this for you at least."

Jordan stepped out of the way and walked around him to the driver's door. As she reached for the door handle, his hand fell on top of hers. The schoolgirl feeling rushed back. "Let me get that," he said from a distance close enough to generate heat.

He pulled the door open as she backed out of its path, then he turned to face her. "We really do appreciate you coming over today. I'm sorry about my brother." Jordan shook her head signaling that no apology was necessary, but he continued anyway.

"When he gets fixated on something, particularly something that he sees as an injustice, he… well, he obsesses. The sad thing is, and I would never say this to him OR Karen, but even if we figured it out, I'm not really sure what difference it makes. Dad is still gone and the people who think he killed himself are going to continue to think it."

He reached up and brushed his hair back from his forehead with a sigh. "I'm sorry. Anyway, it really was a huge help for you to be here. If nothing else, hopefully Karen won't have to deal with my brother obsessing about this anymore." Suddenly Karen's goodbye made a little more sense to Jordan.

"It was no problem, really." Jordan agreed about the futility of the conversation but was glad that at least some good came out of it. "It was really nice to get to know all of you. Are you all heading back home now?" She wasn't really sure why she asked. She just wasn't quite ready to say goodbye yet.

"Well… Rog and his family are leaving the day after tomorrow. He needs to get back to his practice. I don't know if he even mentioned it, but he's an MD, too. I'm going to stick around for a while though. Someone needs to finalize all of Mom and Dad's affairs, so I'm going to take a semester off and get everything taken care of here." Jordan tried to pretend she wasn't just a little bit thrilled he would be staying.

"What are you studying?" Jordan hoped the rise in her spirits wasn't obvious.

"Psychiatry. I've only got about a year left before residency, but it feels like I've been in school forever. Maybe a few months off will help re-charge my batteries." Jordan smiled and nodded as if she understood exactly what he meant, even though she really didn't. She had always loved school. Everything was so cut and dried and rarely varied from its routine. There were no grey areas in school. Jordan liked that.

"Well... I'd better get going. Thanks again." She turned and climbed into the driver's seat.

"Could I give you a call and maybe get together for coffee or something?" He spoke confidently enough, but she had taken a few psychology classes herself. She noticed his fidgety foot and lack of eye contact. He was nervous.

Warning signs were flashing through her mind. So far everyone she became close to developed an incredibly short life expectancy. Wasn't it only a couple of days ago that she had decided to keep herself and the boys isolated? Common sense was telling her to decline his offer and focus on the boys until everything was... better. Unfortunately, emotions and common sense rarely cast the same vote.

As much as she hated to admit it, she liked Daryl and she wanted to see him again. She agreed to coffee and convinced herself that everything would be fine. She would be careful. Besides... if it didn't work she could always end it.

Chapter 39

Jordan woke the next morning feeling great. It wasn't because she missed the Shapiros any less than she had the day before, but for some reason she felt confident that today was a new day. She told herself it wasn't entirely due to Daryl. For the first time in over a week there were no feelings of impending doom. The calm felt good.

The boys were still sleeping, so she went downstairs to the kitchen and started a pot of coffee. It looked like it was going to be a beautiful day, a great day to take the boys to the park. Since there wasn't anything they had to do that day, they may as well take advantage of her mood and make it a day of fun.

The coffee had begun its slow drip through the coffee maker when she heard the first sleepy cry that indicated the boys were about to start their day.

By the time she reached their room, Hudson was standing in his crib rubbing the sleep from his eyes. As soon as he saw her in the doorway his arms went up in the air. His whimpering turned to wailing as he called out, "Momomomomom."

As Jordan scooped him out of his crib and kissed him good morning, he hugged her tightly around the neck and confirmed for her again that this was definitely going to be a great day.

She changed Hudson into play clothes for the park as he struggled to wiggle free and get back to the truck he spotted from the night before. "Ok, you're done, buddy," she exhaled deeply.

"Sheesh, it's getting harder and harder to wrestle clothes on you. Go ahead and play and I'll get your brother up." Hudson was already pushing the truck around the nursery when she gave him permission. "Do you want to go to the park today?"

Hudson stopped playing with the truck instantly and jumped to his feet. "Yeh! Yeh!" She immediately regretted making the offer before Hayden was ready to go because Hudson was already heading for the stairs. After a lot more wrestling and a little bit of crying, all three of them were ready to leave the house.

San Diego boasts the best weather in the country, and Jordan never doubted it was a fact. Days like that one were perfect examples. The morning fog had already burned off and there wasn't a cloud in the sky.

On the drive to the park, Jordan admired the foliage while the boys rattled off a continuous stream of gibberish. More and more she was noticing real words sprinkled in with their baby talk and realized how soon it would be before they were talking in complete sentences.

Pulling into the parking lot, Jordan was a little disappointed to find the park nearly abandoned. Off in the distance a young couple was having a picnic and there were the usual groups of walkers and runners, but the playground equipment was completely abandoned. At least the boys would have their pick of the best play areas.

She had brought a magazine along, so while Hudson made a dash for the swings and Hayden plopped down in the sand to do a little digging, she took a seat on the nearest bench. She had become quite adept at keeping her peripheral vision tuned into the boys, so she wasn't concerned as they played on their own.

She was as engrossed as a mother of young boys can be in a magazine article about a toddler who saved his entire family from a fire. A shift in the bench told Jordan she was no longer alone. The hair on the back of her neck stood up.

"It's quite a lovely day for an outing at the park." The familiar voice had the same effect on her heart as a defibrillator. She felt the world moving in slow motion as she turned her head to look at Tanas.

He sat with perfect posture as he stared straight ahead. "Oh, my dear, surely you knew you would see me again at some point in the future. I see my son has grown a great deal since our last meeting."

"Don't call him that!" Jordan snapped. "How did you know we would be here and which of my children do you keep referring to as 'your' son?"

He laughed that same, patronizing laugh she had grown to hate so quickly in their last meeting. "Oh, my dear, you know I cannot answer the question that is yours to resolve. As to how I knew your whereabouts, you are not really so naive as to need an answer to that, are you? Would it be difficult for you to sleep at night knowing I am aware of your every move?"

"Then how about this question: what do you want?" Jordan glanced in the boys' direction. She couldn't see them peripherally when she was looking at Tanas. She wondered if even that was a part of his manipulation. To her relief, they were both still playing happily; neither seemed to notice that their mother was no longer alone.

"I want our son, of course." He continued to look straight ahead with a smug confidence that was both irritating and alarming.

"Well, like I told you before, you can't have him." She was about to tell him to leave them alone when he turned his head. Turned wasn't really an accurate description. His head whipped sideways so quickly there had barely been a trace of its path. His body continued to face perfectly forward. The movement of his head seemed completely disconnected from the rest of him. Her eyes grew wide. As much as she didn't want to be, she was terrified at the small glimpse of how inhuman he truly was.

"My patience with you is growing thin, as is the time allotted for making your decision. I will speak clearly so there is no margin of misunderstanding." His irritation was obvious as he over-enunciated each word and his eyes narrowed. "It is apparent that you do not fully understand the parameters of your options here." He took a deep breath and his body seemed to morph back into a normal relationship with his neck.

The condescending smile returned, but by comparison, Jordan learned she preferred it. Once again, he had easily put her in her place by showing her how truly impotent she was.

"I believe you are under the impression that you will be able to raise two children to adulthood. I imagine you also believe that you are in control of their destinies. Both of these assumptions are incorrect." Jordan started to interrupt him and was silenced at the raise of his hand. "The choice before you is simply this: you can either be involved in the life of one child or lose both." He paused and her heart went into her throat.

After what seemed an eternity, he continued, "As you have already witnessed to a limited extent, your children cannot co-exist. They have been battling each other in various ways since the day they were born. Very soon the ultimate battle will occur, leaving one a victor and the other dead. While I do not know the outcome for certain, I am confident in my son's abilities." He pointed his nose to the sun and took a deep breath.

"I do not expect what I am telling you now to prompt your ultimate decision, but just to make things sporting, I'll tell you anyway. The first of their direct battles will be circumvented by your actions. The second will not only result in a child's death but also in your own. If my son IS the victor, I will then take him to one of my many dwellings where he will grow and learn under my guidance. If *His* son is the victor, I will leave him where he lies wounded, to suffer until he ultimately dies of injuries or starvation." A smile spread across his face. "It's really quite handy that you don't have any friends."

He turned toward the boys as Jordan's mind raced a thousand miles an hour.

"As I've told you previously, the ultimate choice is still yours. You can choose now or watch one of them die at the hand of the other as you yourself take your last breaths. As for myself, regardless of your choice, I will go on and I will continue to create offspring as I have done throughout the ages. Whether it is your child or another, I will produce an offspring to fulfill the final prophecy."

He turned again to Jordan. "My patience with you grows thin. This will be the last time I attempt to save your life. If any part of what I have told you is the least bit unclear, I suggest you take this opportunity to clarify it."

Jordan looked down at her lap to avoid his gaze and shook her head no. All the strength and confidence she felt was gone. She was left feeling like a little girl, frightened and alone.

"Then I will take my leave of you. Time grows short, Jordan. Do not allow yourself the luxury of believing in a fairy tale ending." Her eyes filled with tears. He had successfully removed any trace of hope she had been feeling at the start of the day. She hated him more than ever for that. She looked up with the intention of telling him as much but, of course, he was gone.

Jordan's soft tears turned to outright sobbing. Both boys stopped what they were doing and turned to stare at their mother. In unison they left what they were playing and walked to each side of her. Hayden put his hand on her leg and patted as he looked up with an empathetic smile. Hudson put his little arm around her and kissed her arm as he consoled her with, "It otay, Momma, it otay."

Jordan put an arm around each of the boys and pulled them close. In her arms they never minded being close to each other. It was as if the three of them together made one perfect whole. Everywhere else they repelled each other but never in her arms.

As she kissed each one on the head, she couldn't help but ask herself how in the world she was going to choose. She wanted to believe there could be a God who would protect her from all evil. But if so, where was he? How could He let them suffer this way?

Jordan turned her face to the sky and asked God herself. "God, help us, please. I don't know what to do. I know I haven't turned to you often enough but please, show me what to do to save my children." She hugged the boys closer and bowed her head.

She felt the heat of breath on the back of her neck before she heard the words.

"He didn't save Mary's child. Why would he save yours?" She turned her head quickly. There was no one there.

Chapter 40

The unexpected meeting took all of the joy out of the park and the day. The boys were getting sleepy and she wanted to be where she felt safe. Did that place exist anymore? She wanted nothing more than to curl up in bed with the boys and use the covers to keep the world out. She wanted to wake from the nightmare she hadn't chosen. The drive home was a blur as she wavered between semi composure and near hysteria.

She struggled to carry both sleeping boys at once and decided the bags could wait in the van until later. This would be one of the last times she could manage carrying both of them at the same time; they were just getting too big. Realizing that her thoughts about their growth paralleled Tanas's words made her feel even sadder. One way or another, her time with both of her children was coming to an end.

Tears once again streamed down her cheeks. It took all the strength she had to carry the boys up to her bedroom.

She took off their shoes but didn't bother to change their clothes. She crawled between them and propped pillows behind her before she sneaked an arm under each of their little heads.

She pulled them as close as she could and alternated kissing the tops of their heads. If only there were some way for the moment to last forever. For the millionth time she thought about her options.

Killing herself would be the easiest solution, but it would leave both boys alone in the world and wouldn't prevent the ultimate battle that Tanas described. The thought of killing all three of them probably made the most sense, but as she looked down at the tops of their heads, she knew that would be impossible.

Putting the boys up for adoption was a heart-wrenching thought that she immediately dismissed for basically the same reason. Besides, that wouldn't guarantee they would be kept apart. After rejecting every other potential solution, she was left with the same plan she'd always had: Wait and see.

She hugged the boys until they felt too crowded and pushed her away in their sleep. Whatever was going to happen, they would face it together.

Chapter 41

Jordan startled awake with the distinct feeling she was being watched. She sat up quickly and saw Hudson sitting alone at the foot of the bed. His feet hung over the side and she could see his back clearly but something was wrong. Though his body faced the French doors, his face... his eyes, were looking directly at her. Her initial reaction was fear that he had somehow broken his neck. She sat straighter and began to lean towards him, fear and maternal instinct battling.

He had been watching her with a cold, unfamiliar stare. When she reached for him, he began to smile.

No. Smile was the wrong word. Sneer was a little closer, but even that would barely scratch the surface. He pulled his lips back, revealing shark-like rows of jagged razor teeth that stretched wider than the rest of his face.

She tried to say his name thinking maybe it would draw him out of whatever type of trance he was in. She was unable to mutter a sound.

His eyes filled with blood, until there was nothing left behind but dark sockets. They seemed devoid of everything, yet eternally deep. The blood completely erased the angel eyes that were as familiar to her as her own.

Jordan noticed a glimmer when the object he was holding caught the light from the hallway. As her eyes focused, she realized he was holding one of the kitchen knives.

In a maneuver too fluid for the human body to make, his little body twisted around and realigned with his neck. In the same motion, he crouched into a crawling position.

Hudson's smile widened as he reared back. She realized he was coming for Hayden! This was the battle that Tanas had told her was coming!

Hudson flew forward, catapulted by some unseen force. Acting more out of instinct than thought, she caught him in midair by the arm holding the knife. She tried to grab hold of his other arm and steer him away from Hayden at the same time. As he flailed his free arm in an attempt to make contact with anything in his way, she focused her energy on freeing the knife from the little hand that was locked around it.

She straddled his body to keep his legs restrained. One by one she peeled his fingers away from the handle of the knife as his free hand slapped and punched the side of her head.

With a firm grip on the knife handle, she raised it with both hands. She brought it down before reasonable thought could creep in. Jordan felt his body soften even before she looked down to see the knife handle standing straight up from her little boy's chest.

Reality washed over her as she began to comprehend what had happened and what she had done. Her grip loosened around Hudson's arms and for the first time since the skirmish began, she looked into his eyes.

The red/black eyes of the monster she had seen when she first woke up were gone. She found herself looking into the soft blue eyes of the boy she had given birth to. He didn't cry but as his mouth opened and closed there were no razor sharp teeth. She only saw the beautiful baby teeth that he'd suffered through bravely as they came in one by one.

"Oh, Hudson, what have I done?" The words were filled with pain that was pulling her heart inside out. She released his arms completely and clamped her hands against her mouth as tears filled her eyes and shock filled her mind.

Hudson wiggled slightly against the blade of the knife that had him pinned to the floor but was only able to muster a whimper. His pain-filled eyes sought out the help of his mother. He lifted his arms and strained to reach her, but the knife held fast to the floor beneath.

Still paralyzed in horror, Jordan watched as her son turned his head slowly from side to side spilling huge tears down his temples and across the bridge of his little nose. His movements eventually slowed then finally stopped completely, while Jordan helplessly watched him die. Hudson lay motionless except for an occasional, stuttered attempt at a breath. His eyes continued to search his mother's face for answers that didn't exist. Was he searching for the relief she had always been able to provide before and wondering why she wasn't helping?

Jordan had seen him through immunizations and scraped knees, a tumble down the stairs and countless bumps on the head, but she had never seen his eyes filled with the fear she watched now. He tried to call to her but as he began to make the "M" sound, blood overflowed the side of his mouth. His eyes lost their focus and his head fell limply to one side.

Hudson was gone.

Jordan sat motionless over her son, studying his face. Disbelief was probably the only thing that kept her from going completely insane as she looked into the lifeless eyes of her little boy. Like water filling a pitcher, the pain began to fill her. It started in her heart but quickly took over every cell in her body.

This can't really be happening! This cannot be the way things end; she had to do something to change it. She reached down with both hands and pulled the knife free. She fought back the urge to vomit as her son's body rose with the knife before finally falling back, lifeless, on the floor.

"Noooooooooo!" she screamed as she picked Hudson up and cradled his limp body in her arms. "Momma will make it all better, sweetheart. We'll sing a song and read your favorite book and everything will be alright again." She rocked back and forth as she sang, "You are my sunshine, my only sunshine…" She could feel her tethered sanity stretching too far and wished it would just let go. Insanity would be a welcome relief.

The laughter started too softly to pull her attention away from rocking Hudson, but it soon became an almost booming sound she couldn't ignore, even in her madness. She turned slowly, dazed, and saw Hayden sitting on the edge of the bed with his head thrown back laughing. She stopped singing as he brought his head forward and she saw the jagged rows of teeth. His eyes started filling with blood. "I always knew you would make the right choice." His lips were moving, but the voice was not his own.

Jordan screamed.

Chapter 42

The sound of Jordan's scream combined, then turned into the sound of the telephone ringing. She made no move to get up and answer it. Her pillow was soaked with tears. The details of the dream were still fresh enough to feel real.

Jordan felt paralyzed. All she wanted to do was turn back time. Go back to the time when choices were left up to other people. Her head spun with the possibilities and inevitable outcomes for each of her limited options, but they all came up the same. She would lose.

She heard her name as clearly as if it had been spoken directly into her ear and knew the voice by heart. It was Charlotte.

"Be brave, my dear." The voice paused briefly while Jordan's heart and breath re-started. Charlotte's voice was as sweet and strong as it had ever been.

"Never forget, you are dealing with a liar. His confidence comes from instilling fear, not from any real power. He is a master at using your own senses against you. He can make you see what isn't there, hear what isn't said, feel what isn't real.

It's his loophole around free will. He has been the master manipulator of mankind since mankind came to be. He will make you believe whatever illusion becomes the means to his end. What you see, hear, taste, smell, and feel can be manipulated." Charlotte paused as the force of her words sank into Jordan's understanding.

"His reach falls far short of heaven; we are all safe here. But there is only one place on earth that he cannot reach you. There is only one fortress that his illusions can't penetrate. It's the one 'sense' he cannot manipulate because it came from and connects you to God. He cannot touch your love, Jordan."

The phone rang again, leaving too many questions unanswered but severing the connection to Charlotte.

Jordan whipped her head to each side and found both boys still sound asleep. The relief she felt was overwhelming as she bent to each child and kissed his forehead. She hugged them tightly under the security of her blankets. The phone finally stopped ringing.

The caller either gave up or the answering machine kicked in. Either way she didn't care. Her heart was pounding in her ears, and all she wanted to do was cry.

Charlotte had been so close. Why did she feel so far away again?

Jordan lay in bed holding the boys and thinking about love. She had never made a conscious choice to love the boys but as she looked at them, love was all she saw. She wanted to follow

Charlotte's advice. She wanted to look deeply enough to see love in the right boy. Regardless of the child she looked at, she saw nothing but love in them both. She reminisced over events from her children's short lives.

In the middle of a memory about playing with the boys at the park, Jordan had a flashback to the terrifying dream she wished she could forget. She saw Hudson's face transform into something grotesque and unrecognizable. It flashed like a still photo inserted into a movie. It threatened to transplant itself into her heart like a real memory of her son. It threatened to take root as fear right in the middle of the memories of Hudson's smiles and hugs.

"He lies, Jordan." Charlotte's voice was unmistakable. Instantly Jordan felt as if she were wrapped tight inside her mother's robe. She was safe, and more importantly, she wasn't alone.

The renewed sense of security sparked hope. Jordan thought about her life before the boys were born and how empty it seemed in retrospect.

She was sure there had been times when she laughed so hard tears ran down her face, but she couldn't remember any before the boys. She could remember hundreds of times she'd laughed that hard after they were born, though.

She thought about the first time that Hayden sat up by himself and the look of surprise and pride that filled his face. She thought about the time that Hudson broke into a spontaneous dance to the theme song of one of his favorite cartoons.

She remembered the time Hayden drew a mural in the hallway while she was chasing Hudson to get his marker away. She thought about them running in the yard and "ooing" at the sight of a butterfly. She remembered the feel of their little arms around her neck as they fell asleep or when they hugged her with all their might.

Every fond memory of one of the boys branched into an equally endearing thought of the other. But every so often the still shot of Hudson or the mental recording of Hayden speaking in a different voice popped into her memory. Unwanted pieces of evidence in the trial without any witnesses.

Jordan tried to remember what Charlotte had said in the dream. It was something about Tanas's ability to manipulate her perception of reality. Her thoughts immediately went to her parents.

"We simply do our best to influence free will." That was how Tanas had explained his involvement in her parents' deaths. And that was the moment she knew.

Tanas could make someone's loved one look like his enemy! How could she tell what was real and what was an illusion if he could manipulate her so easily? Her heart started racing as she realized there would be no way for her to tell!

Understanding what he could do didn't bring her closer to knowing how to stop him.

The boys simultaneously started to stir. With every ounce of strength available in her body, Jordan pulled it together enough to sound cheerful as she greeted her sons' waking faces.

"Hello there, Sunshines. Are you hungry?" Hayden rubbed the sleep from his eyes while Hudson nodded his head. She realized it had been several hours since they had eaten anything. At least for the time being, she needed to put aside the weight of the world and take care of her children.

As the boys munched on crackers in their high chairs, Jordan finished dishing up their macaroni and cheese. She placed the plates on their trays as the phone started ringing again. This time she answered it.

"Jordan, it's Daryl Shapiro. I called earlier but you must have been out. I don't know if you got my message, but I hope you don't mind that I called back." His cheery voice was a little like a slap in the face that finally brought her out of the dream world. She tried to hide her disorientation.

"No... not at all." Jordan was trying unsuccessfully to sound coherent. "How are you?"

"I'm good," Daryl answered. "This is probably going to seem a little forward, but I was wondering if you'd like to get together for dinner sometime this week." When she didn't answer after a couple of seconds he added, "You and the boys, of course."

Her mind raced as she tried to think of what to say, as she tried to think of what to do. A big part of her wanted very much to get to know him better. There was no question she was attracted to him and it certainly seemed that he felt the same way.

Until his invitation, she hadn't even realized how much she longed for adult companionship. How much she wished she didn't have to go through the cryptic puzzle by herself.

"Jordan? Are you there?"

"I'm sorry. Yes, I'm here. You'll have to excuse me. I just woke up from a nap with the boys. I guess I'm not thinking very clearly yet. Could I call you back later?"

She felt badly putting him off but what was she supposed to say? *I'm a little scatter brained because I'm trying to piece together the advice your deceased mother just gave me?* Not likely.

"Uh, sure." It seemed like he was ready to say goodbye but changed his mind. "Is everything alright?"

She tried to lighten the tone in her voice but only succeeded in sounding like an airhead. "Sure, everything is fine. I'm just not myself until I've had at least one cup of coffee. I'll call you later tonight, ok?"

As Jordan hung up the phone, sadness again washed over her. She remembered Charlotte's words but couldn't imagine how love would help in her fight against Tanas.

She remembered back to the days when she believed she had found religion. She went to church regularly and loved the sense of belonging that came from the other members. It was the first time she felt like she really fit in. For a while, she even thought she could feel God's love.

It was the first time in her life that she believed in something. It was the first time something magical wasn't explained away as Hollywood gimmicks. Then when her parents died, it seemed like she had been the victim of a cruel joke. The God she trusted hadn't been there for her at all.

She remembered how much she hated God back then. She remembered walking around the campus lost in a fog, mentally screaming profanities at the God she felt had betrayed her trust. All of the people in the church told her that God would give her strength and that He had a grand plan. It certainly didn't seem grand from where she stood.

When the boys were born, the anger melted away... dissolved, she supposed, by happiness. But how had she felt about God since? Apathetic.

That left the big question of how she felt now. "Scared" was the only thing that came to mind.

Jordan wanted to believe that God was strong enough to defeat Tanas. She wanted to believe that all she needed was faith, and God would swoop down to her rescue. But what about Mary, and Jesus, and all of the other people who suffered? How much did their lives improve after pledging themselves to God?

Jordan knew that the time for choosing was quickly closing in on her. She knew Tanas wasn't lying about that; she could feel it. But what about everything else? As the day wore on Jordan found her sense of urgency increasing. She also found herself waiting to hear from Charlotte again.

She went through the motions of the day with her mind lost in thought. She thought about God with Moses. He pledged his loyalty and God made him suffer for 40 years. She thought about God with Noah and the thousands or millions of people who must have died. And then she thought about one story in the Bible that had plagued her mind ever since she heard it.

It was during a Bible study that was focused on the book of Job. According to the scripture, Job was richly blessed and a devout follower of God. Then the devil said, "Sure, but he's only devout because he's blessed. Give him some hardships. He'll turn from you." And God listened?! Job lost everything and still remained committed to the Lord. The Lord who is all-loving made a bet with the devil? Had He really ruined a devout follower's life to prove a point to Satan? Did Job know something she didn't that made it all worthwhile?

Jordan put both palms against her forehead and was instantly filled with peace.

"God never promised heaven on earth." Charlotte was back. *"He simply promised that it would be worth it in the*

end." The relief settled over Jordan's heart immediately at the sound of Charlotte's voice.

"God doesn't lighten our loads. He gives us the strength to endure. He doesn't pardon us from our trials. He gives us the courage to see them through. Each lifetime is but a stitch in the fabric of eternity. Sometimes the threads cross peacefully but sometimes they culminate into a snarl of knots. God guides us through inspiration and conscience... even through guardian angels." The light in Charlotte's voice twinkled a little at the end and Jordan smiled.

"He tries to guide us from the tangle but people are stubborn. Faith requires the ability to follow even where it makes no sense to go. Faith requires the surrender of your own will. It means being willing to be a part of a picture you cannot see right now.

"Sometimes a thread runs the entire length of the fabric. It may be a beautiful thread that compliments every stitch it contacts. Other times a thread might simply be a place holder, biding time until later on in the tapestry. Sometimes a thread breaks and the weak, frayed line comes to an end.

"No one can see beyond the lifetime he is living. You cannot see what is set in motion any more than you can see what has been prevented. The path behind you may hold the flaws of your ancestors, but sometimes it's the tangles in the fabric that give a thread the strength to hold it together to the end. The path before you is your choice. It is the gift and curse

of free will. Your choices are not about others, Jordan. This is your test and the question you must answer is 'what will you do?'"

Just as he did with Josef Mengele, Tanas will put thoughts in your mind, but they are only effective if you believe them. His only power comes from the actions he can provoke in humans."

Again, there was no announcement or preparation for her departure. There was also no question that Charlotte was gone.

How does his power come from me... and how can I stop it? For the first time in her life there was no one around to make the decision for her. Tanas himself, who seemed to have a vested interest in her choice, wouldn't, or couldn't, tell her what to do. Anyone else she knew would have her committed if she told even a fraction of the story.

Jordan studied her sons' faces as they played on the floor of the nursery. For the life of her she couldn't imagine that one of them was truly evil. In her eyes they were both little angels. They didn't look as identical as they had when they were smaller but the differences weren't significant.

She thought back over things that had happened in their short lives and suddenly it came to her. Natalie!

It had been several months since the incident at the daycare and with everything that had been going on, Jordan completely forgot about Natalie. Perhaps she had come out of her trance. Maybe she could provide some insight into what happened that day. Maybe she could tell Jordan which twin had provoked... the incident.

As she looked up the number, she felt excitement for the first time since her meeting with Tanas. She may be alone in her decision, but she could certainly make sure she was as informed as possible.

As she entered the numbers, the excitement was replaced with a grip around her heart. What was she excited about? Finding out for sure which of her children she needed to kill? She realized that even if she knew the answer she was looking for, it wouldn't make her decision any easier. When the receptionist answered the phone, she asked for Natalie Michaels' room anyway.

"Seventh floor nurses' station. May I help you?"

"Yes, I was wondering if Natalie Michaels is still there and if I might be able to speak with her." Jordan hoped the nurse wouldn't ask too many questions.

"And what is your relationship to the patient?" The nurse asked the question in the same way she had probably asked it a thousand times before, but it was the last thing Jordan wanted to answer.

"I'm a friend." Jordan thought if she added a little more information the nurse might be more likely to tell her something. "I was in to visit a couple of times but it's been a while. She was still in that frozen state when I was there the last time. I thought I'd check to see how she was doing before I drove all the way down there for a visit."

"Unfortunately there's been no change, but I'm not at liberty to divulge any specifics about her condition to non-family members. Her mother is in with her now. Would you like to speak with her?"

Jordan thought for a moment and realized she had nothing to lose. If there were even a tiny piece of information that Natalie could contribute, well, maybe it could help in some way.

As the nurse transferred her to the appropriate room, Jordan tried to think of the perfect opening to the conversation. Before the first ring finished, a voice on the other end of the line was saying, "Hello."

"Hi, my name is Jordan Sullivan. I'm a friend of Natalie's; my children were in the daycare where she worked. Anyway, I called to see how she was doing. The nurse said there wasn't any real change but thought you might have some more information for me."

"I'm sorry. You said your name was Jordan Sullivan?" That was the moment when hell broke loose.

As Natalie's mother finished the word Sullivan, blood curdling screams resonated through the phone line. Mrs. Michaels must have dropped the receiver because Jordan could hear her screams for a nurse intermingled with what she could only assume was Natalie.

After yelling "Hello" into the phone a couple of times, she resigned herself to the role of eavesdropper. She listened as the horror on the other end of the phone line played out.

Jordan could hear staff members yelling back and forth to each other as they worked frantically to restrain Natalie. "Hold that arm down!" "Where's the sedative?" "Get Dr. Jacobs in here stat!" There were a few other phrases that she could make out but most of the chaos on the other end was just that... chaos.

For the most part, the screams from staff members weren't substantially different than anything you'd hear on a television show – lots of medical terms and loud orders. The other screams, the screams coming from Natalie, were different than anything Jordan had ever heard in her life.

As she imagined the events taking place in that hospital room, she could almost picture Natalie's face, drawn out in screams that were pure terror. Then, as quickly as they started, they stopped.

For a split second the only sound was a ringing in her ears. No, not a ringing, it was a monitor signaling a flat line.

"She's gone into cardiac arrest! I need a crash cart in here NOW and where the hell is Dr. Jacobs?" The sound of scurrying feet and medical terminology went on for what seemed like forever as the sound of furniture being pushed out of the way intermingled with the rhythmic counting of CPR.

Moments later Jordan heard a man's voice yell, "Clear," then, a sound like someone had jumped on the bed. After a few seconds of silence, they tried it again, then again. The silence lasted longer, then the man whom Jordan could only assume was the tardy Dr. Jacobs said, "She's gone. Would someone mark the time, please? I'm calling it." Jordan hung up the phone.

She sat down at the kitchen table a little harder than she intended but was only slightly phased by the impact. Was it really possible that the mere sound of her name had sent Natalie into hysterics so extreme it killed her? What in the hell had she seen that day at the daycare?

Jordan thought back to Dr. Shapiro's description of the boys' births and of the way Hudson transformed in her nightmare. Is that what Natalie saw? Is that what scared her to death? She turned from the phone and saw both boys watching her. With the heaviest heart and only a tiny glimmer of hope, she knew what she needed to do.

Chapter 43

Ever since she had called Daryl to invite him over for coffee, Jordan had been having second thoughts. She turned to Roger and Charlotte Shapiro for help when things were unspeakable. Was it really fair to turn to their son now when things were worse?

She thought back to the meeting where she had confided her deepest fears to Dr. Shapiro and Charlotte. She'd been afraid they would think she was insane. At the very least they would end any kind of relationship with her, but they didn't. She hadn't really thought before about how easily they accepted what most people would have considered the ravings of a lunatic.

Of course, they had their own connections to Tanas but would that be something Daryl would know about?

She doubted it. To top it all off, he was well on his way to becoming a psychiatrist. He was positively going to think she was insane. He would probably suggest she spend some time on the seventh floor herself. It didn't matter… time was short. She had no other choice.

The clock struck 9:00. He would be there any minute. The boys had been asleep for nearly an hour, so they should be able to talk without interruption. She was still running through possible openings to the conversation when the doorbell rang.

After showing Daryl into the sitting room, she poured cups of coffee for each of them. Jordan settled into the chair directly across from him. She became aware of how much their seating arrangement made it seem like an interrogation.

Focus she reminded herself.

She stared down at her cup without taking a sip and searched for the words that would make everything sound more believable. She hadn't noticed how long they sat in silence but it was Daryl who spoke first.

"Is everything alright?" he asked. The simplest question in the world really, but the answer was anything but. She looked up into his eyes and saw a compassion that so closely reminded her of Charlotte she nearly broke into tears. Mustering every bit of strength in her body, she took a deep breath and simply answered, "No."

"I asked you to come over here tonight because I need to talk to you about something. You're going to think I'm crazy but please, please keep an open mind." Jordan's eyes were pleading as they searched his face. She saw Daryl start to nod but interrupted his gesture.

"I mean open further than you've probably ever had to open it in your life. After I tell you what I have to tell you, you're going to think I'm insane, but I need your help."

She could feel the tears welling in her eyes and fought with all her strength to keep them from coming. A single tear made it through her defenses and rolled down her cheek. Jordan took a deep breath and braced herself for the story she dreaded telling. Before she could start, Daryl jumped in.

"I don't know if you're aware of this, Jordan, but before I decided to pursue a career in psychiatry I spent some time in the seminary." He laughed a little to lighten the moment. "It drives my brother nuts that I have no focus. Rog knew what he wanted to be since he was two years old. I didn't, but I knew there was something. I felt lost so many times as I tried to find it." He took a quick sip of his coffee and Jordan didn't try to get back to her subject. She was relieved at the pardon and hoped his story would lighten things enough for her to tell hers.

He continued, "Anyway… one of the things I learned in the seminary is that immaculate conceptions have happened throughout history for a variety of reasons." Jordan's casual interest in his story suddenly turned to a confused captivation. *What did he know?*

He continued.

"Most people have a hard time accepting that idea because they want to believe that Jesus was the only one. He was the only Messiah but not the only immaculate conception." Jordan wondered if Charlotte had told Daryl what had been happening. But surely she would have mentioned it. He continued.

"One of the best known immaculate conceptions would be Isaac. He was born to Abraham and Sarah long after Sarah had gone through menopause. So… having said all that, I should probably tell you my story." He took another sip from his cup while Jordan waited.

He couldn't possibly know. Where was he going with this story? The urgency she felt earlier in the day was to the point of combustion and growing. What if it had been Roger who told Daryl what had been happening? She forced herself to be patient.

Daryl continued, "You know that Rog is older than I am, but what you don't know is that there were a lot of complications. My mom almost died during childbirth and they had to remove most of her reproductive organs. She was devastated. Both she and Dad had wanted a large family. They were both grateful that they had a son and that Mom hadn't died, but Mom never really got over the idea that she would never have any other children.

"Mom was never one to cram religion down someone's throat, but she was a devout Catholic. She believed that all things are possible through God. She was right. I don't really know all of the specifics, but I know that Mom becoming pregnant with me was a physical impossibility. She and Dad knew it too. A woman doesn't just grow new reproductive organs.

"Anyway… when I was in the seminary, I talked to Mom a lot about feeling lost. I told her about feeling like I had a purpose, but I just couldn't find it. That's when she told me about my birth. I think the reason she told me was because she wanted me to know that I did have a purpose. And maybe also that it was worth finding." He took another sip of his coffee before continuing.

"Dad didn't really feel the same way. He didn't want to believe that my purpose could be a spiritual destiny. If you think about it, most of the people sent by God haven't exactly been treated… kindly. Dad knew that acknowledging my purpose would most certainly mean the sacrifice of my own life. Plus, he was just more of a realist.

"He wanted to believe there was some other reason Mom got pregnant. He held firm to his stance that we just couldn't explain it yet. But every so often, after a couple glasses of scotch at Christmas time, we could usually get him to admit there might be miracles. I think his denial of miraculous intervention was his way of protecting me.

"Mom, on the other hand, knew that protecting someone physically wasn't the most important thing. You see, Mom had visions while she was pregnant with me. Maybe they were just dreams, but she never thought so, and I guess I don't either.

The dreams were conversations with God about me and about why He was giving me to her.

"In one of the dreams, she was told that I was to be the guardian of the world's most precious gift since Jesus. He wasn't more specific than that and Mom never told me what she thought it meant. I suppose she thought that offering an opinion was imposing her own will and that wasn't Mom's style." Daryl smiled at the memory.

"Until she met you, that is. Mom didn't talk to you a lot about me, but she talked to me about you almost daily. She knew that you were the fulfillment of the prophecy." He struggled for a moment as he remembered his mother and her ultimate sacrifice at the end.

"Mom wanted, more than anything in the world, to help you save your sons from their destiny. Not only for the boys, I think she also thought it would mean saving me from my own destiny. Both of your boys have abilities beyond human comprehension. One of them has the ability to save the world and the other has the ability to destroy it." He paused only briefly. "Mom didn't want me to wind up in the middle of that if she could prevent it. It turned out she couldn't."

Jordan was afraid to find out if Daryl knew which of her sons could be capable of the horrors that had already occurred, and yet she needed to know. "So which..." Her throat became thick with the question she couldn't voice. He understood.

"I'm sorry. I don't know. I have no idea which one is the Savior. What I do know is that he is the only being on earth capable of stopping the other. I also know that his abilities will take longer to mature than his brother's."

Daryl noticed the look of confusion on Jordan's face and immediately clarified. "It isn't because his abilities aren't as strong or anything like that. But think about it, Jordan. Children are experts of mass destruction as soon as they can crawl but the more refined things, like fine motor skills, they take longer to master. Personally, I think that's why two and three year olds have temper tantrums. They're just boiling over from the effort it takes to hold back their little monster."

"Unfortunately, it's going to be the same way with these two. Whichever one is evil already knows that he has to eliminate the other before adulthood."

The thought hung in mid-air. Jordan knew that he was right, but she still had no idea what could be done to protect one without hurting the other. For the millionth time, she wished she didn't have to make the choice. There was no hiding her look of disappointment.

"Jordan, I want to help you. I was put on earth to help you and I believe I know what we have to do. It will be the most difficult thing you've ever had to do and I'm sorry for that, but I need you to trust me."

Her eyes darted to the stairway. The boys lay sleeping in their cribs one floor away from her. She thought back to

Roger's solution and how fortunate she was that the boys had been gone. She wasn't so fortunate that night.

"The only thing that can be done is to separate the boys." Daryl probably thought he was giving Jordan the worst possible news. He was wrong. He obviously didn't know the solution his father tried to carry out.

"I can't tell you it will be easy, but I give you my word that if you allow me to take one of the boys, I will protect him as my own. I don't know which one is evil, Jordan, but if it turns out it's the one I take, I will do everything possible to try to save his soul."

Jordan stared at him for what seemed like forever. Finally, she rose from her chair and moved quickly towards him. He didn't know what to expect but braced himself for the likely crack across the jaw that was coming. He flinched a little when she came in towards him and wrapped her arms around his neck.

Tears streamed down Jordan's face as Daryl held her without knowing what she was thinking. Several moments later Jordan leaned back and wiped her eyes. She stood without saying a word and crossed the room for a tissue.

Daryl watched as she moved, but there were no words left to say. He sat in silence waiting for her decision.

Jordan returned to her chair, blew her nose, and eventually composed herself enough to speak. "Thank you." She said the words quietly, but the understanding between the two of them was complete. There would be no visitation arrangements, there would be no long goodbyes, but there would be hope. Finally, there would be hope.

"When would you like to take one of them?" Tears rolled down her face and her heart broke in two. She didn't even know which son she was giving away, but it didn't matter. Losing either one would mean that half of her heart would be gone. It was the only way to protect them both... for a while.

Daryl didn't seem prepared for her question. He was prepared to convince her he was sane and he stuttered a bit.

"Well, there really isn't any reason I couldn't take one right now. It might be easiest not to dwell on it."

Jordan thought for a moment. "You're probably right, but I need to have one more night. I know it won't be any easier in the morning, but I guess I want to have a little time to say goodbye in my own way. I just want to hold them both for one more night. Plus, I'll put together clothes and toys and some things you'll need. Ok?"

If Daryl had known about his father's visit, if he had known Jordan had left town to run from his father, he may have insisted on taking one of the boys right then. As it was, he had no objection to giving her a chance to say her goodbyes.

The two of them talked for a few more minutes to arrange the time that Daryl would be over in the morning. There was no conversation about which child he would be taking. Jordan didn't want to know. There were no care instructions given; that would make it too real.

Jordan knew in her heart and her mind that they had reached the only possible solution. She would not allow herself to think about it any deeper than that.

She could live with the idea of Daryl taking one of the boys for a little while. He was so much like Charlotte. It had been easy to trust him from the very beginning. She knew he would care for her son as his own. She also let herself believe that the arrangement would just be temporary. It was only for a little while.

Jordan walked Daryl to his car and said goodnight. She was exhausted, but the last thing she wanted to do was sleep. She had one night left with both boys. She wouldn't be wasting a moment on sleep if she could help it. She wanted to rock with them and read to them and play with them and hold them.

She retrieved her cup of lukewarm coffee and finished it as she heard Daryl's car pull out of the driveway. She leaned forward to set the cup on the table, but it crashed to the floor when the screaming started upstairs.

Chapter 44

When Jordan heard Natalie's screams, she was sure there couldn't be anything worse. She was wrong again.

As she raced through the house and up the stairs two at a time, she heard hundreds of different people screaming in unison. The voices blended together in demonic harmony. Some of the screams were in octaves higher than she had ever heard, some were lower, and some of the tones were anything but human.

They all had two things in common. They were all screams of agony and they were all coming from the twins' room.

She had to grab the door frame to keep from sliding past as she rounded the corner into their room. Once inside, she stopped dead in her tracks.

The first thing she saw was the fire. A large ball of fire hovered several feet off the floor between the two cribs. It moved slowly closer to Hudson's crib then back the other way toward Hayden's. For a split second she thought the room was on fire but then realized it was a ball of fire suspended in mid-air. She looked at each of the boys. They were standing in their cribs with their arms outstretched. It looked like a pyrotechnic volleyball game that had been put on pause.

She realized the twins were controlling the ball of fire, trying to push it towards each other. She watched Hudson's face contort from the effort and was reminded of the earlier nightmare. The moment of choice was upon her and she was frozen.

She watched the twins struggle for several moments. Should she grab one of the boys? And then what about the other?

The boys' eyes remained fixed on the ball of fire. They seemed oblivious to their paralyzed mother. Her mind was spinning and the screaming seemed to be stemming from everywhere and yet nowhere, all at once. She couldn't think straight. The screaming was hurting her ears.

The ball seemed to be dipping lower and lower with each pass. It had just hovered less than a foot from Hudson's head and was starting to move back.

She was closer to Hayden's crib when she decided to act. She snatched him up and covered his head while she lifted him out and away from the crib. For a split second the screams became louder, and then the ball of fire exploded into the empty crib.

Jordan crouched down instinctively when she heard the explosion. When Hayden struggled in her arms it didn't take much for her to lose her balance.

She toppled over backwards and saw the flames from the crib beginning to lick the wall and climb their way to the ceiling.

Hayden, free from her arms, was running toward his brother's crib. She tried to get to her feet but was knocked backwards when the lamp from the corner hovered up from the table and crashed into the side of her head.

She pulled herself up to a sitting position and wiped away the blood that was dripping down her forehead. She wasn't sure if it was the blow to her head or the heat from the flames, but everything in the room was spinning and warping.

Furniture was flying up and slamming into walls. Toys were swirling around the bedroom like they were being carried by a tornado.

Meanwhile, the fire was encompassing the outside wall of the room. Hayden was attempting to scale the side of Hudson's crib, but his progress was slowed by the onslaught of flying objects.

Jordan watched as toys and fragments of broken furniture slammed into her son as he tried to climb his brother's crib. She looked at Hudson who stood with his arms outstretched. He didn't look much different than he did the countless times he had put his arms out to be picked up, but yet she knew this was indeed very different.

She saw the flames dance as he moved his arms like a maestro. He was orchestrating the chaos that was holding them all captive. She heard Tanas's words in the back of her mind, *"You can choose one of your sons now or watch one of them die at the hand of the other as you yourself take your last breaths."*

She tried to focus on Hayden but couldn't quite think straight.

Jordan looked down at her lap and saw the growing puddle of blood. She felt the tickle of it streaming down her face. It was getting so hard to see and even harder to think straight, but Tanas's words still rang in her mind.

As Jordan wrestled with consciousness, Hayden was trying to swing his leg over the top of the crib. She knew she needed to act quickly or Tanas's horrible prophecy was going to come true.

With the last of her strength, she pulled herself to her feet and made her way to Hudson's crib. She grabbed Hayden and, with nothing left to draw from but maternal instinct, she pulled him free of the crib and stumbled out of the room. When she reached the doorway, she turned to take one final look at Hudson. "I will always love you; God, please save his soul." And with that she took the son she had chosen and left the other to die in the fire.

Chapter 45

By the time they reached the bottom of the stairs, Jordan had nothing left. She saw herself in the mirror as they descended the stairs. She was covered in blood.

If she could get Hayden out the front door, he would be fine, even if the fire took the whole house.

She fell once at the bottom of the stairs and narrowly missed landing on Hayden. He rose to his feet first and reached out to take her hand. Hard as she tried, she couldn't seem to raise her arm. She was about to tell him to open the front door and walk outside when it opened on its own. There in the doorway stood Tanas.

"Tsk, tsk, tsk. It is a shame your inability to choose a path has again determined your destiny. I knew if you waited until the first battle that your human understanding wouldn't be able to tell the difference between causing havoc and holding it at bay. Holding it back, at least in the human form, requires a greater exertion. Had you chosen earlier, you may have been able to logically figure that out. You may have been able to watch your son grow up. As it is, you have only enough time to watch my reunion with mine."

With that, he knelt down and Hayden rushed into his arms. Jordan watched in disbelief as her son threw his arms around Tanas's neck. She watched him give her enemy a bear hug that had previously been reserved for only a select few. She tried to speak but between her injuries and the shock of what she was seeing, she couldn't.

When Hayden pulled his head away from his father's neck and turned to face her, she saw the face that Natalie and Dr. Shapiro had been unable to describe. As he snarled in her direction, his eyes began to fill with blood and the last remnants of the child she had known were gone.

Tanas continued, "Perhaps this way is best, and I really should not minimize your contribution. After all, it was always your choice. I must give credit where credit is due. You chose well." He rose with Hayden in his arms. Jordan's leg kicked against the floor, the pathetic outcome of her effort to climb to her feet.

"Please, don't get up on our account. As you listen to His son's final screams, remember you chose the stronger twin. And just imagine... before you know it, you can ask Him personally why He wasn't here."

Jordan tried to lift her arm. She wanted to reach for her son but the arm was too heavy. It was over. With the last of her strength, Jordan raised her eyes to where Tanas had been standing. They were gone and the front door stood open.

She tried to scream for help but couldn't even accomplish a volume high enough to reach the door, much less the street.

She needed to get to Hudson. Even if she couldn't save him, she needed to tell him she was sorry. She needed to comfort him. She needed to hold him while they died. She reached out an arm and dug her fingertips into the tile. She tried to pull herself forward but only succeeded in bending her fingernails back from the nail beds.

"Dear God," the words were barely more than a whisper, "please help us. Please help me save your son." She pulled her knee up as far as she could and pushed herself forward on the tile floor. She moved little more than an inch but it was something. She tried again and moved another inch. She fought hard to overcome the feeling of hopelessness as she looked up at the impossible staircase that was still over two feet away.

Try harder! She screamed the words in her head and fought back the question of how far the flames had already travelled. She pulled her knee up and reached her arm out again. She was able to move a few more inches. As she gasped for breath and tried to reach out again, she heard footsteps coming through the door.

"Jordan? Oh, my God, what happened here? Are you alright?" She turned as far as she could and was able to make out Daryl's face.

"Hudson... In his crib... Fire..." Jordan's words were soft but Daryl understood. He raced up the stairs and into the twins' bedroom as smoke billowed out of the doorway. She wasn't able to turn her head to see what was happening but she heard him call out to Hudson.

As she lay in a pool of her own blood, her prayers continued, "Please, God, let Daryl reach him in time." Her mind swirled and the room took on a gray hue that reminded her she didn't have much time. She closed her eyes. *"Just a moment of rest, that's all I need,"* she told herself.

She felt a hand on her shoulder and opened her eyes to see Daryl holding her abandoned son. Hudson's arms were clutched tightly around Daryl's neck. She tried to speak but couldn't.

"Shhhh," he said, "Hudson is going to be fine. Save your energy. I've called an ambulance and the fire department. They should be here any second. Is Hayden in the house?"

"No." Her voice was barely above a whisper and he had to lean forward to make out the words. "Tanas took him. Take Hudson. Take care of him and protect him."

"I will, Jordan. I promise I will, but try to hold on. The ambulance is on the way. You're going to be fine."

Daryl set Hudson on the floor next to his mother and pressed something against the pain on her forehead. The little boy wrapped his arms around his mother's neck.

Her strength was gone, but Daryl took her right arm and draped it over her son's back. She looked into Daryl's eyes and said, "Thank you." Her words were barely audible but it didn't matter. He understood.

The last sounds she heard were the sirens as they made their way down the block toward the house.

She knew there would come a day when the twins would have to face each other again, but for now at least, Hudson was safe. At least for now, Tanas believed he was dead.

A Note from The Author

Where do I begin to thank the many people who helped turn my twisted imaginings into a novel? I suppose at the beginning.

Thank you to my husband Tom and my son TJ, for allowing me to write about nightmares without having me committed. Thank you to the most amazing editor and friend in the world, Deborah Merkwan. Your patience and belief in me through re-write after re-write merits Sainthood.

Thank you to Yousif Admon for turning the vision in my head into a beautiful book cover, and Lori Stime for your creative input. Thank you to my beta readers, Dave, Russ, Dennis, Dee, Paige, Brooke, Carla, Glynis, Yvette and, of course, Laura. Without your questions, insights, and suggestions, *Choices: Arrival of the 4th Generation* wouldn't be the story it is today.

And thank YOU for reading the story. I hope you enjoyed it and I'd like to invite you to follow me on Facebook at "Coleen Liebsch Author" to be the first to receive news about the next book in this trilogy, *Decisions: The Age of Reason.*

With Love!
Coleen